DESIGNER BABIES

Volume One

The First Mothers

David Witt

Fat Chance Publishing

DESIGNER BABIES VOLUME ONE THE FIRST MOTHERS

ISBN 978-1-7342023-2-8

FIRST EDITION

Cover Design by Matt Witt

Attributions:

"Vecteezy.com"

"Designed by vectorstock (Image #25179632 at Vector-Stock.com)"

"Photo by ���� Janko Ferlič on Unsplash"

To Karen, my awesome and lovely wife without who's unending support this novel would not have been possible. From reading rough drafts to suggesting ways to publicize my work, she was an important part of bringing this book to market. She has been a constant source of encouragement throughout our life journey together, and I can't wait for our next adventure!

Special thanks to the Thursday writer's group who welcomed me with open arms and honest feedback. You offered me an education and a sense of community for which I am grateful. I am so glad we went online and continued in a virtual format in the face of the pandemic.

It is also important that I thank Morgan Williams for his perspective and editing. I admire his ability to take a good scene and point out ways that I can make it better.

Sincere thanks go to Matt Witt, my multitalented son, who created the cover for this book. Even as a child, he had an eye for color and design, and it was a special pleasure to see him take my input and create something far beyond what I imagined.

DESIGNER BABIES

Volume One

The First

Mothers

_____

CHAPTER ONE

Bree Battle sat quietly in the back of her Uber ride to the clinic, saving her strength for her appointment. Wafts from the vanilla scented air freshener hanging on the mirror temporarily soothed her mind as a catchy tune played on the radio. The musical hook of the hit Gwen Blaze song, *Why Me?*, soon had her humming along to the lyrics: *Why me? Why me? It's a question that I used to ask, used to ask, but not anymore, anymore. Why me, why you, why any of us? Watch me, watch you, watch us take control. Watch me, watch you, watch us rise from ashes and soar.* She mumbled to herself, "Yeah, right. I wish."

The car stopped and she thanked the driver as she exited on legs as shaky as a newborn colt, gaining some semblance of balance with her aluminum walking cane. The security guard at the door had seen her so many times over the past year that he greeted her by name. "Good morning, Ms. Battle."

A weak smile graced her reply. "Every morning on this side of the daisies is a good morning, Artie." It was the same reply that she had given every time she passed through these doors of both dread and hope.

In short order, she was called back into an exam room where Anita checked her blood pressure, temperature and weight. Bree winced, then joked as she saw the number on the scales. "I wanted to lose a few pounds, but this is ridiculous."

Anita smiled sympathetically, shared a few words of small talk, then quickly entered the readings into the system before excusing herself. Bree was alone in the sterile exam room with her thoughts, and the ever-present pamphlets on various aspects of living with cancer stuffed in a wall rack. She had read them all at least twice and tried most of the recommendations to give her the best chance for survival.

Waiting, her eyes closed in the unrelenting weariness of her condition and her mind wondered, landing on a familiar refrain. *I'm too young for this.* She startled when Dr. Cofferman abruptly entered the room.

"Hi Bree, how are you feeling today?"

With his clear and concise way of explaining the intricacies of her particular kind of brain cancer it was obvious to her that he was one of the smartest people she had ever met. She looked up with a squint, hoping to detect his mood. "That will completely depend on what kind of news you have. Did you find a new clinical trial for me?" She caught the ever so slight dip of his head and braced for his words.

He spoke calmly and tenderly. "I'm sorry, Bree. I don't have good news. We've been heading toward this day for a while, and now it's here. The cancer has advanced to the point that you're considered too sick to enroll in any more trials. It's time for us to talk about what comes next."

This was the news she feared and tears flowed as her frail body shook. "I was just hoping..."

He handed her a tissue box, one of which was present in every exam room in the facility for discussions just like this. "We've talked about getting your affairs in order. How's that going?"

After wiping both sunken cheeks, she vented in a matter-of-fact manner. "A year ago today, I finished my first triathlon. Now I'm exhausted when I walk to the mailbox. It's pathetic."

He offered the tissue box again. "This disease is brutal, that's for sure."

"Life's brutal, Dr. Cofferman. With Mom and Dad both passing in the last seven months, all I've done is get affairs in order... that, and cry. I'm twenty-nine years old but feel like I'm ninety-nine. And on top of that, I'm all alone. There's no husband… not even a boyfriend anymore."

"I hope you have some close friends to lean on."

Dabbing moist cheeks, her head bowed. "I've moved so many times that my closest friends are scattered around the globe. Besides, I would hate to burden them." Her shoulders sagged and emotion choked her words. "This sucks, big time." She looked at him pleadingly. "Is there anything else that you can think of? Anything at all? I'm begging."

Dr. Cofferman sat with hands clasped in his lap over his white coat, glancing away in the windowless room for several seconds. Turning back, his eyes met hers with a new look, one she hadn't seen from him before, and couldn't quite decipher. He sighed. "Give me a few minutes. I'll be right back."

As he was about to stand, she reached for his hand with new energy. "Thank you, Dr. Cofferman!"

"Don't thank me yet." With that he stood and quickly exited.

Adrenaline surged with even the hint of hope, then she caught a startling look at herself in the mirror. Her hair had fallen out and now grown back in short brown patches she wore as badges of honor, never donning a wig. She turned, fully facing her reflection head on, taking in the hollowed-out eyes with red rims. Thin pale skin hung over her angular cheek bones. But now she also saw a sparkle in her almost golden eyes, a gleam that had been missing for a long time. Hope softened her stare.

The doctor reentered the room, closing the door behind himself with purpose, then glancing around nervously. He stretched out his hand revealing a flash drive and two slips of paper. "Here, take these."

When Bree accepted them, Dr. Cofferman wrapped his hands around hers and lowered his voice. "You must swear that you will never tell anyone you got these from me. Do you promise?"

Confused but desperate, she locked eyes with him. "Yes, yes. I won't tell a soul."

He spoke just over a whisper. "One of these papers is the referral to hospice. That's all that we can offer you here, and it's the last official entry that I'll make in your medical record. Do you understand?"

"Yes." She swallowed hard, her throat scratchy from the radiation she had already absorbed, understanding the implication of that statement while anxiously awaiting his next words.

"On the other paper is contact information for a former colleague, Dr. Cielo Chavez. She's brilliant, but definitely marches to the beat of a different drummer. I ran into her at a medical conference last week and she told me about some of the experimental work that she's doing in her lab down in Peru." His eyes narrowed and his words had an edge. "What she's doing is way out in left field and would be illegal here in the States. Hell, I think it's illegal everywhere."

Gently squeezing her hand his voice softened, compassion coating his words. "What she's working on could theoretically save your life... but to be clear, it's more likely to kill you. It's never been tested in humans and I could lose my license to practice medicine if it were ever discovered that I referred you to her. Do you understand?"

Bree nodded enthusiastically, answering through her wide smile. "Yes! I understand. Thank you Dr. Cofferman!"

He released her hand. "The flash drive contains your labs, medical history and all MRI's from the past twelve months. She'll need those, should you choose to go that route."

Sobs wracked her body as she expressed her gratitude. "Thank you! Thank you so much. Your secret is safe with me, I swear on my life."

Her bony frame was wrapped in a gentle hug. "I wish you the best, Bree."

She buried her face in his embrace, dampening his coat. "You're the best, Dr. Cofferman."

Stepping back, he opened the door and watched her walk down the hall with her cane flicking purposely, her baggy pants flapping as her spindly legs took each determined step. When she walked out into the waiting room, he closed the exam room door, then pulled out his cellphone and touched a name on the screen. On the third ring he heard a familiar female voice with a Spanish accent.

"Hello, my friend."

He grinned conspiratorially. "She fell for it. Hook, line and sinker."

CHAPTER TWO

The flight to Lima landed just before midnight. By the time Bree maneuvered through the cramped airport and got to her nearby hotel it was nearly two in the morning. Entering her room, she collapsed onto the bed, not bothering to put on pajamas or even pull down the faded floral print bedspread. Sleep came quickly, and she startled when her phone alarm rang at seven. She awakened stiff, realizing she had not moved a muscle all night. But today represented hope, so she summoned inner strength from her dwindling reservoir and rose from the still made bed. Looking in the mirror, she addressed herself with a broad toothy smile, contrasting with her gaunt skin. "You look like shit, but at least you're still on this side of the daisies."

After splashing her face with water and brushing her teeth, she checked out of the hotel and in just a few minutes found herself back at the teeming, chaotic airport. She slowly advanced in the long line for a domestic flight to the city of Cusco, high in the Andes Mountains. Each step forward depleted her energy but she reminded herself that everything depended on reaching the mysterious doctor, so one foot continued in front of the other. Native Peruvians outnumbered a good size minority of tourists headed to the city that served as the gateway to the world treasure that is Machu Picchu. With her considerable language skills, she eavesdropped on businessmen talking about sales strategies and anxious tourists from every corner of the globe excitedly chatting about a trip they had dreamed of for years. The ever-present specter of her cancer triggered a macabre thought. *If this treatment kills me, maybe they can bury me atop one of the sacred mountains, like some Incan sacrifice.*

Once onboard, she drifted off to sleep before takeoff, waking only when the passenger next to her dropped his phone. Awakened, she looked out the window, seeing snow-capped mountains in a semi-arid environment. The few scrub trees eking out an existence reminded her of her own struggle, giving her a feeling of kinship with the place.

Upon landing terror struck as she realized she couldn't muster the strength to stand. *God, I'm even sicker than I thought.* Panic and embarrassment caused her cheeks to redden as she was forced to ask the flight attendants for help to exit the aircraft. Inside the small airport, food court smells of grilled meats and strong coffee assaulted her. She leaned heavily on her cane, willing herself to walk on her own to the baggage claim area where she was supposed to meet her contact. Spying a sign with her name, she waved feebly.

A man looking to be in his early thirties, and dressed in a Tree of Life Clinic polo shirt, approached quickly. He addressed her in his thick Spanish accent. "Welcome to Cusco, Ms. Battle. I'm Miguel Hernandez and I'm here to take you to the facility. I'll get your bag, then bring the van to the curb."

Struggling to get a full breath, she answered. "Thank you."

"Ah, the altitude. I have something for you. I'll be right back."

In just a few minutes she found herself seated in the front passenger seat of a spotlessly clean white minivan. Miguel handed her a thermos with a straw protruding from a hole in the lid. "Drink this."

Bree took a first cautious sip, not knowing what to expect. The warm, sweet liquid felt good going down her singed throat. "Mmm, delicious. What is it?"

Miguel answered as he expertly maneuvered the vehicle with the required nerve of a matador in the Peruvian traffic. "It's sweetened coca tea. We've used it for centuries to help ease the symptoms of altitude sickness. Dr. Chavez thought you might need it."

Taking another sip, she savored the warmth as much as the flavor while admiring the sights of the regional capital city. "Are we close to the clinic?"

He took his eyes off the road for a moment and his words matched his surprised expression. "I thought you knew. The facility is not here in the city, it's in the Sacred Valley, almost an hour away."

Turning her head toward the passenger side window, Bree played it off. "Yes. Of course it is. This altitude is really messing with me." In truth she knew nothing about the clinic or this physician other than they represented hope, and that was enough for now.

Soon they were out of the city traffic, now on a two-lane road climbing even higher than the 11,000 feet of Cusco before reaching the summit and beginning the twisting route down the other side to the green valley swaddling the snaking Urubamba river. The contrasting scenery of soaring dry mountains split by the beautiful flowing water was stunning. "This place is amazing."

Local pride seemed to drive his response. "You're right, even though I often take it for granted. The Inca believed that the path of this river was a perfect reflection of the Milky Way. It's a very hallowed place for my people."

Bree settled comfortably in her seat as the radio softly played the catchy song she'd heard a couple of days ago in Houston. She turned up the volume… *Why me? Why me? It's a question that I used to ask, used to ask, but not anymore, anymore. Why me, why you, why any of us? Watch me, watch you, watch us take control. Watch me, watch you, watch us rise from ashes and soar.* Today the words gave her hope, and the beat was as infectious as a smile.

The smile remained as they sped past a farmer using oxen to plow while just down the road another sat atop a small red tractor; the ancient side by side with the modern. She was surprised when Miguel flicked the blinker, indicating a right turn onto a side road in the middle of nowhere. "I thought we were going to the medical facility?"

A light laugh accompanied his answer. "Yes, we are. It's just that Dr. Chavez likes her privacy. Don't worry, we're almost there."

They turned off of the blacktop onto a well-tended gravel road that immediately began twisting back and forth up the sheer face of a steep mountain. Bree alternated between gasps of amazement at the views that opened up below as they ascended, and gasps of terror as Miguel wheeled the van on the narrow road clinging to the side of the mountain, without a guard rail in sight. Her voice trembled. "How much further?"

They rounded a turn and straight ahead was a modern two-story stucco and brick building. "We're here." He pulled under the covered driveway. "Would you like me to get a wheelchair?"

"I think I'm okay, but thanks for the offer."

He came around and opened the door for her. As she exited and tried to get her cane properly placed, her legs buckled. The cane flew as her arms flailed, trying to grab anything to stop her fall to the concrete. Miguel's reflexes flashed and his strong arms caught her, but not before her right knee impacted the hard driveway. A staff member inside witnessed the slip and quickly brought a wheelchair. Bree blushed as she pressed her hand over a skinned knee, now bleeding through her torn pantleg. "I guess I did need the wheelchair."

In a matter of minutes Bree was in a hospital gown having her injury tended to by a nurse, her bloodied jeans placed neatly beside her on the exam table. She spoke to the woman dressing the wound. "Not exactly the first impression I wanted to make. When do you think I'll meet with Dr. Chavez?"

As if on cue a middle-aged woman wearing black scrubs entered, walking at a fast clip. She extended her hand, then spoke very directly. "Ms. Battle, I'm Dr. Chavez. Glad to see you have arrived."

As they shook hands Bree was struck by the business-like attitude of the doctor, so different from Dr. Cofferman's friendly approach. "I'm so pleased to meet you. Thank you for accepting me as your patient."

A quick smile appeared on Dr. Chavez's face, then disappeared. "Hmm. Please, have a seat in the wheelchair and I'll give you a quick tour of our facility. You've now seen our emergency department where we serve the local population in acute situations, as well as run a free clinic twice a month. It's a needed service and builds good will with our neighbors."

Now settled into the chair, the nurse began pushing her while Dr. Chavez walked beside Bree as they moved on in the impromptu tour. Down the hall they stopped in front of a frosted glass wall. Dr. Chavez entered a code into a numbered panel beside the glass, causing the frosting to disappear. As they stared through the now clear huge window, they saw twenty or so men and women in lab coats with some looking through microscopes while others stared at large computer screens or seemed to be conducting experiments with pipettes and petri dishes. As she pointed, Bree noticed the doctor's black polished nails, matching her scrubs. "I've recruited some of the top minds in the world to leapfrog those procedure and protocol bound labs back in the states... well everywhere, actually. We get results here because we do things differently."

Bree was about to ask about the differences when Dr. Chavez strode away. The nurse pushed quickly, scrambling to catch up just as the doctor made her next stop, again keying in numbers almost magically turning another glazed glass wall crystal clear. Bree saw an immaculately tended area with assorted sized cages on the far wall containing different species of animals. "Here is where mammal testing is done. This state-of-the-art facility is led by the former head of the San Diego Zoo. The testing is vital to my work, and I insist that the animals are cared for in the most humane way possible. Nothing but the best here."

The doctor spun and resumed walking, but this time the nurse kept Bree at her side as she continued describing the facility as they moved on. "There are procedure and operating rooms down there as well as the latest imaging and computing equipment. Most of the second floor is devoted to residential quarters for staff and special guests. They are modeled on the suites at the Ritz Carlton in Montreal, one of my favorite places. As you saw on the drive, there aren't exactly bountiful luxury accommodations nearby, and a happy team is a productive team. Again, nothing but the best. There is a room reserved for you... if you agree to my terms. Let's go to my office and discuss your situation."

The doctor's words confused Bree, but the fast-paced physician walked away before she could form a question, leaving her and the nurse to again follow in her wake. Once in the office Bree was wheeled up to a massive mahogany desk facing a large carving dominating the wall behind the aggressive physician, it was the same tree logo as she had seen on Miguel's shirt. Dr. Chavez stared intently at a screen to the right of her desk, scrolling through pages. This gave Bree a chance to look at her closely for the first time. She wore her jet-black hair cropped close, and that seemed right for this no-nonsense woman. Her makeup was minimal with the exception of thick black eyeliner framing her honey brown eyes. She presented an imposing image.

Turning away from the computer screen and toward Bree, Dr. Chavez got down to business. "Brain cancer killed my mother, and the day she died I made it my mission to conquer this cruel disease. I'm very sorry you are dealing with the same thing."

This was the first breath of humanity that she had seen or heard from Dr. Chavez, and even these words were delivered in a business-like manner. Bree tried to match her demeanor by speaking plainly. "Yes, it's been a hard year."

Dr. Chavez glanced again at the computer screen, then back to Bree. "I've reviewed your charts, labs and images and it is my professional opinion that you will fall into a coma in two weeks, give or take a day or so, and be dead in less than a month."

While Bree knew her prognosis, hearing it laid out so bluntly shook her. She suddenly felt very vulnerable, alone in a foreign country, sitting in a wheelchair clothed only in a paper-thin hospital gown. Her body tensed and her hands pulled into fists in her lap. "That's why I caught the first flight I could. I'm out of options."

The intense woman stared at her hard, then leaned forward, her elbows now on the desk. "As soon as you agree to my terms, we will begin treatment."

"That won't be a problem. I can pay." Bree had expected this would be expensive and knew that insurance would not cover this kind of experimental therapy.

Dr. Chavez laughed dismissively. "Have you been paying attention? Look around, I have plenty of money. That is not the price that I demand."

The words and the attitude confused Bree, so she spoke slowly and tentatively. "I don't understand? What *do* you want?"

The doctor leaned forward again, even further, seeming to come halfway across the desk. "I am sure that I can rid your body of cancer." She paused and put her hands, together forming a steeple. "I'm now moving forward on my next breakthrough and I need help from you… or some woman like you. You see, I'm working on a project which could prevent anyone from having to face this kind of cancer… ever. I know that you are desperate to be healed, but would you also like to play a role in ridding mankind of this insidious disease?"

Bree again found her breathing labored and she replied in a

breathy whisper. "Of course. I wouldn't wish this on anyone. But what could you possibly need from me?"

Dr. Chavez elevated her chin, seeming to get the answer she wanted. "Good. Let's talk for a moment about your life, your life after you are cured. Okay?"

Bree's head spun, as much from her difficulty breathing at this altitude, as from the whiplash conversation. She answered cautiously. "Uh, sure."

With her elbows now on the arms of the padded leather executive chair, Dr. Chavez began. "There is no next of kin listed in your file. No immediate family?"

Unsure of where this conversation was heading, Bree answered while looking at the doctor's face, searching for a clue. "That's right, no living relatives. It's just me."

Bringing her hands together and again forming a steeple, she now tapped her two forefingers deliberately. "I see. And when you walk out of here as a healthy young woman, can you see yourself starting a family, having children?"

Bree softly bit her lower lip, hesitant and totally at a loss. "I'm not sure... maybe. I mean I would want to get back to my work... and then I would have to find the right guy."

Slowly, the doctor leaned toward her across the desk for a third time. "To be clear, we will be using therapies at very high doses that will make having children in the future a long shot. I'm glad you are at least somewhat open to the idea of children because I have a solution that benefits both of us. The next phase of my research involves human embryos. In exchange for saving your life I require that you consent to the harvest of ten of your eggs. In a couple of months, when you have regained your health, one of those fertilized eggs, the healthiest, will be implanted and you will be required to carry the baby to term. This way you don't even have to go through the process of finding, as you say, 'the right guy.' Do you agree to these conditions?"

Confusion and revulsion colored her immediate response. "You want to do experiments on human embryos and then have me carry one to term? That's sick… and it's illegal. You're sick."

A slow smile creased Dr. Chavez's face. "It's a brave new world, Ms. Battle. The first test tube baby was born in 1978 to much consternation and debate, and now there are more than four million IVF births each year in the US alone. Scientists first cloned a sheep in 1996. Today, there is an entire championship team of cloned polo ponies in Argentina, and anyone with a few thousand dollars to spare can get an exact genetic replica of their favorite pet. Labs around the world are experimenting with new techniques to cure diseases. In fact, there is already a genetic engineered cure for a specific kind of blindness. I've perfected that technique for your disease and I'm offering the cure to you. In exchange I'm simply asking you to join me in taking the first bold step in designing a perfectly healthy human, one who would never have to face these kinds of diseases in their lifetime. Can you image the suffering that we could end? And to allay your fears, if any abnormalities are observed in the fetus, we'll abort. These advances are coming, whether you help me or not. I'm not a monster, Bree. I'm only trying to save your life and give you a beautiful, perfect child. A child you probably could never conceive on your own after these treatments. I just want to make the world a better place."

Dr. Chavez leaned back in her chair as Bree sat in stunned silence. After an awkward pause the doctor continued. "I don't need your answer at this moment. Please, stay here this evening and think about my terms. If, in the morning you wish to leave, Miguel will drive you back to the airport so that you may go home to make your final arrangements… while you're still able. But, should you choose to accept my offer, you can begin planning the rest of your long life… for you and your baby."

CHAPTER THREE

Bree was wheeled into an elevator then shown to a luxury suite on the second floor of the isolated medical facility perched on the side of the mountain. Despite her weariness, her mind ricocheted from thought to thought like a pinball in some futuristically themed arcade game. *Who is this woman? Is she brilliant or insane? Can she really do what she claims?*

Inside the room she found that her clothes had been hung in the closet or folded and placed in the drawers of an exquisite dresser. Taking a closer look, she saw that her torn jeans had already been mended. Heading toward the bed covered in a snow-white duvet, she saw a tented card on the bedside stand and learned her dinner options were either walking to the dining room just down the hall or ordering room service. "What is this place?"

Her mind continued to bounce between the outrageous offer just made by Dr. Chavez and the absurdness of this extravagant facility. None of it made sense. After changing back into her own clothes, she decided to make her way to the dining room to investigate further. Upon entering her breath was again stolen, not by altitude sickness but by the stunning view. She stood staring at a wall of windows framing the panorama of the Sacred Valley below and the majestic mountains on the other side of the narrow river. A low puffy cloud floating between seemed almost close enough to touch. Hearing her name called broke the trance.

The male voice called again. "Ms. Battle, care to join me?"

Scanning the room, she spotted Miguel, her driver from the airport, seated at a table beside the huge windows. Spying no other open tables, she waved, acknowledging his offer and began a slow walk toward him catching wafts of cilantro and cinnamon along the way. "Do you live here?"

"No, at least not full time. I live in Cusco with my family, but I stay here often, especially when someone might need a ride to the airport the next day."

She blushed, knowing that he was talking about her, then glanced around the room at crowded tables before changing the subject, "Is it always like this, all these scientists so engaged in conversations?"

His earnest smile eased her anxiousness. "Almost. These researchers seem pretty intense. I understand they are doing groundbreaking work, and stuck out here there's no one else with whom to share their enthusiasm."

Seeing that he had already started his meal of trout and quinoa, she spotted a single page menu on the table, and was surprised to see a banana mango smoothie as one of the choices. A formally dressed waiter appeared and Bree ordered the only thing she could swallow in her condition. She glanced out the window again. "I can't get over this place. I've traveled the world and never seen anything like it."

He nodded. "I'm used to it, but everyone who comes here for the first time reacts the same."

Her shoulders eased, then she glimpsed a uniformed guard through the window. He carried an automatic weapon while patrolling the well-tended grounds below. Her voice raised in pitch. "Since when do guards at medical facilities need M27's?"

Miguel laughed. "I'm impressed. You know your weaponry."

"I think my dad wanted a boy. He loved guns and passed his passion to me." Thinking of the man she had idolized as a child triggered a wave of happiness. "He gave me an education on a lot of things mom never approved of."

"I see. Well, the guards are here for a couple of reasons. The first is what you've already observed, this is an opulent place in a third world country. It could easily become a target for robbery, or worse."

"I get that. And the other reason?"

Moving closer, Miguel spoke quietly. "You've met Dr. Chavez. Don't get me wrong, my life has changed dramatically for the better since I started working for her, but she is a powerful woman with many equally powerful visitors. Most patients that come here are like you, they're regular people." He leaned in. "But others are different, they come on private jets and bring their own small armies. I think maybe she feels she needs her own small army too, you know, just in case something goes sideways." Now sitting straight, he changed the subject. "So, how was your meeting with her?"

"Let's just say it was not what I expected. She says she can save my life, but she's asking a very steep price. I don't know what to think, or do."

"That must be stressful. Can you afford it?"

Bree turned to the window with a lingering gaze across the valley, instead of down at the guard. Looking back at Miguel she answered honestly but kept it vague, not wanting to share too much with this stranger. "Yes. It's a price I can pay, it's just that I'm not sure that it would be the right thing to do."

His eyes widened in surprise. "I don't understand. Do you wish to die?"

"Miguel, it's complicated. Sometimes things aren't that simple."

He took his napkin from his lap and wiped his mouth, before placing it on his plate. "Ms. Battle, I'm not a university educated man, like Dr. Chavez, or these scientists, but I do know many of the truths of this world. One of them is that when the decision is between living or dying, it's always simple."

CHAPTER FOUR

When Bree returned to her suite, she found a note had been slipped under the door informing her of an appointment with Dr. Chavez the next morning. She sighed. "Life or death. Maybe it is that simple."

Sleep came easily, but dreams interrupted several times. The next morning, she recalled two of them in exquisite detail. In one, the famous scene from the movie *Alien* was recast with her as the crew member from whom a monster bursts from their chest. Blood and guts splattered everywhere as a scary creature emerged. She chilled at the recollection.

The second was much different. She remembered an evening from her childhood when she was cast as Mary in her Catholic elementary Christmas play. Her only thought before it started was to get through the performance without forgetting her lines. After the standing ovation at the end, she remembered the relief she felt, but even more, she remembered how proud her parents were as she lovingly clutched the baby doll prop used in the performance. *Since when did my dreams get so literal?* She took the last swig of her breakfast smoothie, then breathed deeply before speaking into the dressing mirror. "Time to face the dragon lady."

The elevator delivered her right in front of Dr. Chavez's office and the secretary waved her through the stylish waiting room. *Nothing but the best, she says.* In just a few more steps she was again facing the stern woman. Wasting no time, the brusque doctor began as soon as Bree was seated. "I hope your accommodations were adequate. Have you reached your decision?"

"This is a really big deal for me, so I have a few questions."

Dr. Chavez's head cocked slowly. "Really? I thought the terms were very straight forward." She flicked her fingers dismissively. "Go ahead, I don't have a lot of time… and neither do you."

Bree's hands clinched involuntarily, but she maintained control of her voice. "What can you tell me about the sperm donor, the biological father of this child? Would they have any parental rights?"

The right side of Dr. Chavez's mouth turned up in a crooked smile. "You're thinking about the future. That's very good." Her energy warmed as she held her now outstretched hands open. "You will never know the identity of the donor, and the donor will never know of you. It will always remain this way. You will be the sole legal parent of this new life."

Bree's fists released a bit. *So far so good.* "And after the birth, what role would you expect to play?"

The doctor's face brightened. "Of course, I will want to make sure you are both healthy. My belief is that this child will be the healthiest person ever born, but I alone will be in a position to identify any potential problems. You will be required to remain here for an extended period as we monitor both you and the child."

"Wait a minute." Bree stiffened. "That sounds a lot like incarceration. I want to live, but not if it means becoming a prisoner. I'll not trade my death sentence for an open-ended jail term."

The doctor folded her arms. "You are a good attorney, Ms. Battle. We'll be doing cutting-edge science and some follow-up will be absolutely necessary. What would you suggest?"

Her eyes narrowed. "While that may be true, law school didn't exactly prepare me for this." A sudden sharp stab of pain in her head reminded Bree of the stakes. She resisted the urge to rub her pounding skull and took as deep a breath as she could in her deteriorating condition. *Let the bargaining begin.* "We both have something at stake here, and I do want to find a compromise... so here's what I propose. The child and I will leave soon after the birth, then return once a year for check-ups, until it's three years old. I would guess that any abnormalities would show up by then."

Dr. Chavez returned the stare. "Let's make it three times a year until age four. The child will need things like vaccinations and you can't exactly walk into a run of the mill pediatric practice and explain the child's unique history, now can you?"

Bree's head nodded slowly. "Okay. That makes sense." Thoughts continued to spontaneously form despite the now throbbing headache. "Tell me, why... why are you suggesting I raise a baby I don't know if I even want? I know adoption law, and we could negotiate an agreement where I turn the child over to you. A simple surrogate mother contract. I get the cure and you get the child to raise as you please."

The doctor placed her hands in her lap and spoke softly. "The nature versus nurture debate is one of the oldest issues in psychology. I'm striving to achieve the best of both for this child. My work is on the nature side. I'll attempt to produce a nearly perfect human from a genetic point of view. But let's be honest. Having that child grow up here, in this place, with me as a foster mother? No one would say that's an ideal nurture environment. Being raised by a healthy young woman who is also the biological mother will give this special child the best chance to reach its full potential. I assure you my intentions are pure."

Staring back blankly, Bree was not sure at all about that explanation, but accepted it for now. "Let's talk about what happens if something goes wrong during the pregnancy... I mean, what you're planning to do is illegal for a reason, and I can barely fathom how badly things could go. I don't want to be responsible for bringing an abnormal science experiment of a child into this world. I'm pro-life, but it just seems like it would be against all of God's rules to bring a child with three eyes or four arms into the world."

"I share your sentiment. I am extremely confident that this will be a healthy child. But, as I said yesterday, we will monitor this pregnancy every step of the way. If we see anything abnormal, we will terminate." She paused, then turned the tables. "But think of the other side of that coin. What if this child is extraordinary? What if this child changes the world? What would you think of that?"

Shaking her head in disbelief that she was actually having a conversation about agreeing to carry a genetically modified child to term, Bree laughed at the absurdity. She wanted to get up and leave, but knew doing so would be signing her own death warrant. The gaze of Dr. Chavez was unrelenting, so she looked away for a moment, considering her stark choices. She now returned the doctor's stare and her voice cracked as she spoke. "For the sake of argument, let's say I agree to this deal, what happens to me? Before I could carry your lab grown egg, I would have to undergo your experimental treatment... and I've already been through a lot."

The warmth that Dr. Chavez had displayed vanished immediately. "Ms. Battle, as bad as you feel now, what's coming will be worse. You're almost too far gone, so the doses we will need to use must be raised accordingly. You have a strong body... for the shape you're in. And you are young. Those two factors work in your favor. But to be crystal clear, what you have endured to this point will pale in comparison to what you will experience. This will be rough, very rough, but after an intense treatment period I believe you will survive, and then thrive. You will exit this experience battered, but whole. Ready to live a long and productive life."

Bree sat in silence for a few moments as she brought her hands together, interlocking her fingers over her stomach. She imagined two semi-trucks barreling toward each other, with her standing in between. She desperately wanted to live, yet at the same time considered the idea of carrying a genetically modified human experiment revolting. The imaginary trucks rushed closer and closer and she saw no escape, as jumping out of the way simply meant postponing death for a few weeks.

The doctor pushed. "Every second you delay worsens your chances of survival. Make a decision now, or the disease will make it for you."

Sitting stone faced, Bree recalled Miguel's words from last night. *When the decision is between living or dying, it's always simple.* For the first time, the image of her holding a swaddled child entered her mind, and to her surprise it didn't cause revulsion. Her eyes cast downward for a moment and the imagery of the trucks evaporated. She had made her decision and looked back up, locking eyes with the doctor. "Then I chose life... for me... and the child to come."

CHAPTER FIVE

The ink on the paperwork was barely dry and Bree was already on a table in a sterile white operating room. Dr. Chavez spoke to the sedated but awake patient. "We're using the same entry as your prior surgery to lessen the trauma. Our virtual reality operating robot allows us to use a minimally invasive technique as we get these first new samples for analysis. These will be sequenced in the fastest privately-owned supercomputer in the world, allowing us to be ready to introduce tailored genetically engineered fixes matching both your genome and the precise mutation of your glioma."

Her head was immobilized in a metal halo, but Bree felt no pain as metallic instruments plumbed the inside of her skull. "And the eggs, when will they be harvested?"

"You've already been given medication to stimulate your ovaries. Very soon you will be given a trigger injection which will cause final maturation. We'll retrieve them in a relatively simple procedure a few days from now. Things will be moving very fast by then, but don't worry, you have the best team on the planet working to save you, and then help you have a perfect baby."

Those words sent a shiver down her spine, but very soon Bree was recovering from the procedure, this time in a completely different style. Instead of a traditional hospital room, she was back in the suite on the second floor. She snuggled under the down comforter and whispered to herself. "So, this is how the one percent do it."

At regular intervals nurses or techs would interrupt her sleep to check vitals or administer medications through the IV's. When the door opened a little after six, she was surprised to see a familiar face. "Miguel, what are you doing here?"

"Are you in the mood for a guest?"

The smile was immediate. "Only if you don't have a syringe hidden behind your back. I've had enough of those kinds of visitors today."

He laughed lightly, then pulled the rolling chair from the desk to her bedside. "I see you made the choice to live. I'm glad."

"I'm going to fight as hard as I can, but it's still not a sure thing. This particular procedure has never been tried in humans."

"Then you're in the right place. In the past year I've driven many of Dr. Chavez's patients to and from the airport and I've seen firsthand some miraculous changes. People like you, on the edge of death one day, then a couple of months later looking completely different. Strong and full of life. I pray the same for you."

A tear formed. "Thank you, Miguel. It's been a while since I've had anyone offer that kind of encouragement. It's very kind."

Hesitantly, he reached for her hand. "Ms. Battle, you are not alone in the universe. You have this team… and my prayers."

Only now did she fully realize the toll that being alone in this crisis had taken on her psyche. Tears flowed easily. "Thank you. And please call me Bree instead of Ms. Battle. That's what friends do."

He smiled again. "In addition to my employment here, I'm also training to become a shaman. Dr. Chavez has invited me to perform an Incan blessing ceremony for the facility tomorrow. Would you like me to include this room specifically? Kind of a high dose blessing?"

She wiped her eyes. "Yes. This wayward Catholic will take all of the blessings that I can get."

He beamed. "Then you're doubly in luck. Next week the local bishop will be here to perform a Catholic blessing. Dr. Chavez believes in covering all of the bases."

CHAPTER SIX

Three weeks of powerful treatments had left Bree on the precipice between life and death. Now convulsions wracked her body as Dr. Chavez shouted commands over the alarms. "She's seizing! Four milligrams lorazepam, slow push. STAT!"

The room buzzed with activity as technicians and nurses obeyed Dr. Chavez's commands. The syringe plunger slowly dispensed the drug into the IV line in Bree's arm, causing her unconscious body to gradually calm. "Vitals!"

The lead nurse fired back. "BP sixty over forty, pulse one-eighty! She's crashing!"

Dr. Chavez shouted at Bree. "Come on, Bree Battle! Live up to your name and fight!"

"Pulse thready and light! We're losing her!" The screeching flatline monitor sound of a stopped heart filled the procedure room.

The doctor called her next order. "Paddles!"

A technician wheeled the cart beside the bed as the nurse cut away Bree's gown. Dr. Chavez shouted as she grabbed the paddles. "Charging! ...Clear!" Then came the jarring sound of the defibrillator sending electrical voltage through the skin covering Bree's skeletal body.

The nurse shouted. "Still no pulse!"

Dr. Chavez again yelled at her patient. "Come on, woman! Charging to three-hundred! ... Clear!" Electricity again discharged and Bree's frail body tensed while absorbing the shock.

The nurse called out a welcomed update. "We have a pulse, it's weak, but we have a pulse."

The stern doctor looked toward the ceiling. "Thank God. It would have been bad for all of us if we had lost her."

"BP up to seventy over forty-five. Pulse, one-fifty." Relief sounded from the nurse. "She's hanging in there."

One by one the electronic monitors went silent. Dr. Chavez now smiled behind her black surgical mask. "You are as tough as advertised, Ms. Battle. If you make it through the night, you will live. We've done our part, now it's up to you to do yours."

∞

Twenty hours later, Bree opened her eyes on the main floor of the facility. Blinking a few times, she tried to focus, then spotted a scrub attired staff member. Her voice was weak and hoarse. "Water."

Smiling, the nurse moved bedside, pushed the button that raised Bree's head, then poured some water into a disposable cup. "Let me help you."

The water soothed her throat and felt good passing her parched lips. "More?"

"Let's take it slow; you've had a rough few hours. How about some ice chips?"

"Yes."

As the nurse went to procure ice, Dr. Chavez strode into the room. "You gave us quite a scare yesterday, Ms. Battle. How do you feel?"

With a raspy voice, Bree answered. "What? What do you mean?"

"You nearly died." Dr. Chavez now stared at her coldly. "It would have been a shame to get through the final treatment session only to lose the patient. I would have had to start all over with another subject."

Bree answered frostily. "It would have been quite an inconvenience for me as well, you know." Her eyes lowered as she tried to remember anything of the near-death experience. "Everything's a blank."

"That's very good, no traumatic memories to deal with. You're awake, your vitals have stabilized and you are coherent." The doctor moved closer and took her bony hand. "Ms. Battle, please understand that no one in the world is working harder for your survival than me. We both have a lot at stake here."

She glanced at the doctor warily, but felt thankful to be alive with the prospect of a full recovery. "Speaking of surviving, was that really my last treatment?"

"Yes. The radiation and chemo did their job, setting the table for the genetic modifications we made to stop, and then kill your cancer. We are ready to begin the next phase. The staff nutritionist will tailor your diet, and tomorrow an exercise physiologist will arrive to initiate a strength training protocol. We have an aggressive schedule."

Bree moved a hand to her stomach. "I've thought about this a lot during the last few weeks and I'm still not sure I want a child."

Dr. Chavez glared. "We have a deal, Ms. Battle."

"I didn't say I wouldn't do it, just that I wasn't sure I wanted a child. Don't worry, I'll fulfill my end of the bargain."

The reply was curt. "Good, we'll begin as soon as you are physically able. We're on the clock."

This was new information and her eyebrows arched. "On the clock? What do you mean?"

Dr. Chavez moved closer. "The science done here is the most advanced in the world and has saved your life when everyone else left you to die. But, like all research, it requires funding. Our investors are generous, but they expect results on a timely basis.

Delays are not tolerated."

"I don't understand."

"It is not important for you to understand, only that you regain your strength quickly. Are we clear?"

Bree met her gaze with as much intensity as she could muster. "Yes, I understand. Speaking of regaining my strength, I'm starved. When can I have a smoothie or something?"

The crooked smile returned. "An appetite, another good sign. I'll have staff move you back upstairs soon. At dinner you can have whatever you can swallow, but starting tomorrow the nutritionist and physiologists take control of every bite you take, and every move you make."

CHAPTER SEVEN

Bree entered the dining room and spotted Miguel. She made her way confidently to his table. "Hi, Miguel. It's been weeks."

"Wow! You look great! You'll be out of here in no time." He pointed to the open chair. "Please, join me for dinner."

Her happy smile seemed as fixed as a mannequin as she stood beside the table, still in bright red yoga pants and crop top after a workout. "Thanks, it's amazing." She flexed her toned biceps. "I've been training non-stop and I feel so much stronger, better than one-hundred percent. What have you been up to?"

"I've been on vacation with my family, and maybe you haven't noticed, but we have new guests." His eyes darted toward the window. "When I returned, I was temporarily assigned to the clinic protection team. I'm on my dinner break."

Bree caught his gaze and looked out the window as she joined him, spying men in different colored uniforms mingling among the facility guards. "I hadn't noticed. Is it one of those visitors you told me about? The kind that travels with their own army?"

He lowered his voice. "I hear it's some big wig from Europe. Word is yesterday was an important day for the clinic."

A bitter taste flooded her mouth and her smile disappeared immediately as she glanced again at the assembled fire power just outside the window. *Just when I thought this place couldn't get creepier.* She took a gulp of water. "Yesterday? Are you sure that's what they said?"

"What's wrong, Bree."

"It's probably nothing."

He placed his hand gently on hers. "What's going on? You can trust me."

She mulled his words, hoping they were true, desperately wanting someone in whom she could confide. "I… I guess I can tell you." She eased her hand away from his, placing it on her lap. "Remember when I said that Dr. Chavez demanded a steep price to save my life?"

"Yes, I remember."

Her shoulders rolled back as she drew in a deep breath, nervous at the prospect of telling someone her secret. "Well, yesterday it was time to pay up, and now I'm wondering if that's why this visitor is here."

"I don't understand."

Her eyes lowered as she searched for the right words. "You'll know soon enough." Her right hand moved to her stomach. "This might sound weird." She paused. "No, this will definitely sound weird."

"I'm your friend, Bree." He spoke softly. "You can tell me anything."

She raised her hand to wipe her mouth, then returned it to her stomach, taking a moment to rationalize her decision. *I might as well tell him, it will be obvious very soon.* "I'm … I'm going to be a mother." Her head dropped. "The embryo was implanted yesterday. That was the price Dr. Chavez demanded."

Miguel reached across the table and rubbed her arm. "What? Wow… really? That's crazy."

Looking back up, she saw a comforting gaze. Relief spread through her body, glad to see compassion and not revulsion. "Thank you. I need a friend right now."

She could almost see the wheels spinning in his head as he spoke again. "So, you think that's why he's here?"

There was a ruffle of noise behind them as several people entered the dining room. Turning, Bree saw three large men wearing black suits, dark glasses and earpieces, seeming to scan and secure the space. A few seconds later a tall older man with wavy blond hair dressed in a gray suit followed, choosing a seat against the far wall. The waiter immediately brought a bottle of wine for his approval, then poured a glass of red.

Bree stared hard for a moment, then turned back. Her voice trembled. "That's the big shot?"

"Yes, that's him. What's wrong?"

She took another covert peek, then glanced at Miguel with eyes round as silver dollars. She whispered. "This might sound nuts, but I think I recognize him!"

Miguel shot a quick look toward the man, then back to Bree. He spoke in a lowered voice. "What do you mean, you recognize him?"

Her phone was in her hand and she immediately began flipping through photos, her mind racing. "First of all, I've always had this crazy good memory. On top of that, since my parents died last year I've been going through a lot of old photos, loading some of my favorites onto my phone. When I miss them most, I scroll through and remember the good times." She flicked the screen repeatedly, searching. "Here it is. Look at this."

Miguel viewed the screen. "Is that little girl you?"

"Yes, when I was eight or so. Forget about me, look at the man with the fishing pole beside me and my father."

He put his fingers on the screen, enlarging the image, his voice sounding doubtful. "I don't know, Bree. This picture is what, at least twenty years old? I mean, I see some resemblance, but I can't say for sure. What makes you so certain?"

Bree's eyes once again went to the man, then back to the phone image. Her shoulders relaxed and she sighed. "You're probably right. I mean, it is an old picture of me and dad visiting his friend in Prague... and what would Mr. Svoboda be doing here anyway?"

Miguel placed his hand over hers and stared at her hard as his whispered voice trembled. "What did you say... the name of the man... in your picture?"

Her shoulders stiffened again and her golden eyes bore into him. "His name is Mr. Svoboda, Kristoff Svoboda."

Miguel went pale, like he might faint, his quivering whisper now rose in pitch. "Bree, that's what his guards call him, Mr. Svoboda!"

The tension in her body spiked exponentially as she struggled to keep her excited words contained to only Miguel's ears. "Something's wrong, bad wrong. I can feel it in my bones! I'm a human guinea pig in some kind of bizarre science experiment, which is weird enough, and with his arrival it just got weirder."

"What do you mean?"

Shadows of very old memories and emotions seeped into her brain. "He's a dangerous man. I just know it. I always had fun when my family visited his estate all those years ago, but nobody needs the number of armed guards he had, even back then. That part of our visit always gave me the heebie-jeebies. If he and his private army are involved in my situation it can't be good."

Miguel cast a quick glance at the armed men stationed around the room. "You've got a point about the guards. He brought a bigger arsenal with him than any other visitor we've ever had, even bigger than the Mexican drug lord last year."

Feeling her stomach churn, she confided to her only friend in this isolated location. "This whole thing has felt off from the very beginning. My secret referral here, the strange bargain.

Even all this luxury in a hidden location screams something's wrong." Bree pulled herself together and a plan spontaneously formed in her mind. She gave orders. "Here's what you're going to do. You leave first and casually make your way to the parking lot. Find us a vehicle and be ready to leave as soon as I get downstairs. Got it?"

He nodded. "And what are you going to do?"

Ancient survival instincts were surging and she felt an overwhelming desire to be anywhere but here. "I don't know what's going on, but something's up and I'm not sticking around. I'm going to get my passport and then get the hell out of here as fast as I can. Will you help me?"

Again nodding, he took a short breath. "I'll meet you downstairs."

Bree watched him walk through the dining room, waited a couple of minutes and then strode through the room, carefully avoiding making eye contact with the stranger. Once out of sight, she quickly made her way to her room, retrieving her purse and passport. In less than five minutes she and Miguel were wheeling out of the gate of the clinic. "Take me to Cusco. I'm getting on the first flight to Lima, then back to the US."

"What will you do there?"

As they drove, Bree gazed into the starlit night, the smell of honeysuckle in the air. "First, I have some questions for a certain oncologist."

Back at the facility Dr. Chavez entered the dining room and joined the mysterious guest. "Did she see you?"

His brilliant white smile flashed. "Yes. It went exactly as we predicted."

She smiled back. "Miguel will get her to the airport safely and then we're on to the next step. I'm so glad that you are the Patriarch of the Council. We're entering a new phase for the society and need your stable leadership. As you said, it's better for all involved if she thinks she's in charge. But most importantly it's best for the child. He's our future."

Kristoff took a drink of wine. "I agree. Everything is going as planned, but we must beware those in the reformed arm of our movement. Their fierce embrace of the old ways rejects this breakthrough as dangerous. They can derail all we hope to achieve, or worse."

Dr. Chavez rubbed her thumb and forefinger nervously. "I understand all too well because none are more at risk than me, especially while she was here. We all know the lengths to which they will go."

He poured wine for her, then raised his glass to toast. "To a perfect child and a perfect future. Expect a little something extra in your next payment, for the risk you have taken to advance the cause. You have exceeded expectations."

CHAPTER EIGHT

Gwen Blaze snapped a selfie with her red lips in an exaggerated pout, dressed only in a tiny green bikini accentuating her snow-white skin, the top barely covering her nipples. In the background was a rack of outfits that she had worn during her recent *Why Me?* world tour. She strolled over to Ray, who stood shirtless in his favorite pair of trademark skinny black jeans, wagging the large-screen phone displaying the image. At this moment, she felt on top of the world. "I'm going to caption it, 'Wait until you see me next!"

He pulled her closer to his tall muscular body, wrapping her from behind as he gently stroked the most famous bare midriff in the music business. "You'll be showing soon. Your social media footprint will quadruple."

Snuggling against him, her long blonde tresses brushed his shredded abs. "This is going to be epic, and you're so right. My fan base will explode as we drip out the details. I'll make the pregnancy announcement next week, then a few days later drop the first clues about the modifications."

Hugging her just a bit tighter, he spoke hesitantly. "Are you sure you want to do this so publicly? Who knows what angle the traditional media will take, who might get caught in the crossfire? Our baby is going to be special. Do we really want to put the spotlight on her before she's even born?"

Hints of black currant rose incense filled the room as she kissed his tattooed bicep, then lithely ran her fingers up and down his arm, wrapping him around her finger. "You'll learn, Sweetie, this is a big part of how I make my living. And besides, I couldn't hide this even if I wanted." She giggled, pleased with herself. "And just to be clear, I don't want to hide any of it. I'm so proud of what you've done. You're a brainiac, and because of that, we're going to become beacons of hope for other couples like us, couples afraid to have children."

Ray pulled her down with him into an oversized leather chair in their Malibu mansion. "I think most people will support us in screening for our inheritable disease, but lots of others have done similar things through way more conventional methods." He hugged her tenderly. "It's the *other* choices we made that will ignite a firestorm."

Giggling again, she licked her index finger, then traced the script tattoo of her name on his bare chest. "I know! I can't wait to see what happens when we tell them that our daughter will have beautiful jade green eyes!"

Uncertainty colored his reply. "Yeah... that's what I'm talking about. Choosing the sex, the eye color... all of our other choices. This could go sideways."

She gave him a quick smooch. "You're a freaking genius. Our baby would be awesome even if you hadn't made a few tweaks." She sighed wistfully, then giggled more. "We did this so she would be disease free, but while you were tinkering with her genome, I'm glad we decided to make a couple more adjustments. Why not make sure she's even smarter than you and have bigger boobs than me?" Her head fell back in a burst of unrestrained laughter. "And we simply had to make sure she got my singing voice instead of yours, didn't we?"

Ray snorted. "You're right, my voice sounds like two tomcats fighting in an alley. Still..."

Petite hands stroked his stubbled cheeks. "What's the matter, Sweetie?"

"When I learned how to make these modifications, I never dreamed I would be using them on my own child. There's so much we don't know. What if I made a mistake and she turns out... wrong? Can we live with that?"

Putting her forefinger on his lips, she tried to soothe his nerves. "Shh. You've seen firsthand what this curse has done to both of our families and will someday do to us. I'm lucky enough to have married about the only person in the world who has the expertise to make sure that our baby doesn't inherit Huntington's Disease. She's going to be perfect, make that better than perfect." She poked his chest. "And you said you learned from the best."

"I did. But I always thought Dr. Chavez was way over confident in her abilities, especially since we had never tested her techniques on a human embryo. I'm so glad I met you and decided to stay here, instead of joining her in that new lab of hers."

Gwen's million-dollar smile seemed to warm him, just as it always did her legions of devoted fans, nicknamed The Blazers. "I believe in you, Ray. When the world sees what you've accomplished, you'll be almost as famous as me." Her smile blossomed and her toned arms spread wide. "When I was a girl growing up in our white-trash trailer park, all I wanted was for people to hear my music, and to be bigger than the Kardashians. Together, that's what we'll accomplish!"

He rubbed his eyes. "Great! I can see it now. Triple the paparazzi that already follow us. Is that really what you want."

Her smile transformed, becoming more sincere, and her arms wrapped around his shoulders. "I do want that, Ray... but that's not all. Why do you think I wrote, *Why Me?* And why do you think it's been such a hit around the world? Just because bad things happen doesn't mean we have to give up in despair. I didn't, and neither did you. I want to inspire women everywhere to take control of their bodies, their lives, in whatever ways they want."

A wavering voice answered. "It's a good thing that we did everything in our own special lab, with no one else involved. Otherwise, someone would be going to jail, and that someone would be me."

She cupped her hands on each side of his face, her bright blue eyes staring deep into his amber tinted hazels. "I know all this media stuff is still new to you, but embrace the fame and ignore the haters. You and I are going to have a perfect baby girl." She kissed him again. "And as a bonus we'll surf this wave of publicity to a Grammy for me, and a Nobel prize for you. What could go wrong?"

"Well..."

Gwen cut him off with an aggressive kiss stopping only to speak aloud to the house. "Alexa, play *Why Me?*"

The computer promptly responded to the command and the speakers belted out her song. *Why me? Why me? It's a question that I used to ask, used to ask, but not anymore, anymore. Why me, why you, why any of us? Watch me, watch you, watch us take control. Watch me, watch you, watch us rise from ashes and soar.*

CHAPTER NINE

A wall of thick summer humidity hit Bree as soon as she stepped outside of the Houston international airport. She tapped her phone a few times, quickly hailing an Uber ride into the city. When she arrived at the clinic today it was very different than her last visit. Strong now instead of feeble, she bound out of the car, walking so briskly that she had to pause, giving the automatic doors time to fully open. Artie spoke in surprise. "Ms. Battle! Wonderful to see you again!"

She waved as she breezed by the doorman whose jaw hung open. "Still on this side of the daisies."

The elevator took her to the tenth floor where she bypassed the check-in desk, heading straight for the door to the exam rooms hallway. Pushing through, she nearly caught Anita square in the face. "Sorry, but I need to see Dr. Cofferman, now."

"Bree... Bree Battle? Is that really you?"

She felt in mission mode and answered impatiently. "Yes, Anita it's me and I need to see Dr. Cofferman! Where is he?"

Anita answered stiffly as her index finger pointed toward the door Bree had just crashed through. "I'm afraid you'll have to leave, or I'll call security. You have to have an appointment to see one of our providers."

Barely able to walk the last time here, she now easily pushed the small framed nurse to the side. "Never mind, I'll find him myself." She opened the first exam room and startled a woman with a scarf covering her probably bald head. "Sorry."

Continuing down the hall, she called out at the top of her voice.

"Cofferman, we need to talk! Don't make me open every door!"

A surprised look met her as the third door down opened. "Bree?"

Anita trailed the determined former patient and interrupted before Bree could answer. "Dr. Cofferman, should I call security?"

His face flushed as he took in the sight of the enraged woman. "No, Anita. Everything is fine. Would you please show Ms. Battle to my office?"

Bree paused as Anita stepped between them. She snarled at the wide-eyed physician. "Don't make me wait."

Within a couple of minutes Dr. Cofferman entered his office, finding a pacing Bree Battle. His voice sounded half a key higher, as if stressed. "I'm so glad to see you... alive. I didn't believe it would work."

Seeking answers, Bree jabbed a finger toward him. "What's your part in all of this?"

He walked around his desk, seeming to want to put some distance and a solid object between him and an angry patient. "I'm not sure I know what you mean, Bree. You were out of options. I gave you contact info for someone who might be able to offer hope, and it looks like it was successful. In fact, I'm amazed."

She slammed her hand on his desk. "Why did you send me to her? I want the truth or I'm coming over!"

Rolling his chair back, he fell into it. "I'm so embarrassed, Bree." He closed his eyes and rubbed his forehead. "I... I never dreamed it would come to this."

Her golden eyes sparked like tongues of fire. "Cofferman! I'm not kidding!"

Confronted, his head dropped. "I have a gambling problem."

In confusion, her head tilted and arms opened. "What the hell does that have to do with me, with this scheme?"

Glancing up, he answered sheepishly. "I owed some really bad people a lot of money, and someone offered me a way out. They said they would clear my debt if I would do this thing for them, and it was a pretty easy decision to do what they asked. We had tried everything here, and... honestly, I thought you would be dead by now."

The news hit hard. She sat, shaking her head. "Really? I was ex-perimented on because you owed the mob money? That doesn't make sense?"

More words tumbled out. "I don't know the whole story, but from what I gathered, there are forces out there that can make even the mob do their bidding. And you weren't chosen at ran-dom. My contact asked me to send one person to Dr. Chavez, and it was you."

Bree's mind spun, trying to piece things together. "So that's what Chavez meant when she said delays aren't tolerated. It's all connected." Her eyes stared into nothingness. "And Mr. Svoboda must be involved too. How did my dad know him all those years ago?"

"I don't know anyone named Svoboda, but yes, your father was involved."

This revelation snapped Bree back into the moment. "What do you know about my father?"

"He was my contact and I met him even before I met you. He was very concerned about your well-being and somehow knew that you would be coming to see me. He said that if I let you die, he would kill me, and Bree, the way he said it I didn't think he was joking."

With both hands behind her head, her world began to spin. "God, what's going on! I came here for answers and now I'm more confused than when I walked in."

There was a knock on the door, then Anita stuck her head inside, glaring at Bree while she spoke. "Dr. Cofferman, I heard yelling, so I called security. They're on the way."

Bree stood as Anita retreated. "We're not done, Cofferman, not by a long shot."

Now he rose to his feet, hands signaling surrender. "I understand. But right now, I don't think either of us wants to answer questions from security." He went to the door and pointed the opposite way down the hall. "There's a back stairwell right around the corner. Get out of here, and I'll give you a call tonight."

As much as she wanted to know more now, she didn't want a confrontation with security, so she scooted out quickly and bounded down the steps three at a time, glad to feel like her old self. Pushing the green button at the bottom released the security door and she stepped into the physician parking garage. "That didn't go the way I expected."

Just then her stomach growled so loud that it startled her. "I just ate an hour ago. I guess I'm still in recovery mode." A movement from the sidewalk on the other side of the concrete barrier caught her eye and she did a double take, seeing a woman pushing a stroller in the Houston summer heat. A jarring thought occurred. "Or maybe I'm already in another kind of mode."

CHAPTER TEN

Bree set the to-go bags from her favorite Mexican restaurant on the coffee table. "God, I'm starved." She ripped open the grease-stained bag containing the double order of tortilla chips and scooped two dips of hot queso before heading to the fridge. She grabbed a cold beer, then put it back. "Maybe I'll stick to water... just in case."

Plopping down on her couch she flipped on the TV and opened the rest of her Mexican feast, ignoring the local news as she attacked her food. "Mmm, this never tasted so good." In no time the complete meal had disappeared and Bree was licking her fingers, savoring every spicy morsel. A news story on TV caught her eye as she relaxed on the sofa, running shoes propped on the coffee table. "Hey, that's the clinic."

A remote reporter stood in front of the physician parking structure with yellow police tape blocking off a section near the stairwell. Bree turned up the volume and sat up straight, feet now on the floor, as the camera zoomed in on the action with reporter Martina Suarez updating viewers. "What's known at this time is that a local physician was gunned down as he headed to his car. At this point the victim's identity is being withheld pending notification of next of kin. Police are still working the scene searching for clues as to the identity of the shooter. No suspects have been named, and police are asking anyone with information to please come forward to help solve this horrific crime. This is Martina Suarez reporting from the Houston Oncology Clinic."

Bree clicked off the TV, a pit forming in her stomach. "That's

Cofferman, I know it." Just to be sure, she picked up her phone, calling the clinic where she was forwarded to Anita. "Hi, Anita. It's me, Bree Battle."

The sobs on the other end gave confirmation to what she already knew. "They killed him. He's gone…"

Despite what she had just learned about the doctor's role in her medical mystery, her eyes moistened. "I'm so sorry. He was a great doctor." After a few words of consolation, she hung up, wondering what all this might mean. She startled when her phone rang, showing an unrecognized number at which she stared, through a second, then third ring. Her thoughts whirled, thinking of all that had transpired and the new people she had met in the past few weeks. She answered suspiciously. "Hello?"

An unfamiliar male voice on the other end addressed her. "Bree Battle?"

"Yes. Who is this?"

"You might remember me, I was a friend of your father. My name is Kristoff Svoboda."

Every nerve in her body seemed to fire simultaneously as her mind raced. Her words attacked. "I know who you are, and I saw you in Peru. I don't know what you're up to, but you had better stay away from me!"

"Good, you do remember me." His reply was calm. "What you may not know is that your father and I were business associates, and also friends. He asked me to keep an eye out for you… should anything ever happen to him."

Thoughts bounced like lottery balls as Bree tried to process his words. "I don't believe you. He would have told me about you."

"Yes, you are right. He was on his way to meet you for lunch when he was involved in the accident, right? We had spoken of this just minutes before it happened. I am so sorry for your tragic loss."

Her chest tightened as she questioned. "Why... why would he ask you to watch out for me?" New, scarier feelings bubbled. "Did you have anything to do with what happened to him, or to Dr. Cofferman?"

The question about his role in her father's death and news of Dr. Cofferman's demise had no effect on his even cadence. "No. I loved your father like a brother. And about the doctor, that was the work of our enemies. Dr. Cofferman was a very valuable asset who we would never want to harm. I can explain everything, but not over the phone. Could we meet somewhere, say tomorrow?"

Bree ran her fingers through her short, newly regrown tawny hair. The unease that she had when she first saw him in Peru returned and even if this new information was true, she was nowhere close to trusting him. "No, I can't do that. I need some time to think."

His voice never changed pitch. "I understand. A lot has happened to you in a very short time. However, I must tell you that your life may be in danger. May I offer you... how to say it? May I offer you resources, like the kind you saw in Peru, for your protection?"

Visions of armed men flashed in her mind and her true feelings found voice. "That's a kind offer, Mr. Svoboda, but to be frank, right now I don't know if I should trust you, or fear you."

"Fair enough. Just know that I will always be on your side, and if you *ever* need my kind of help, I am only a phone call away. In the meantime, may I offer some advice?"

"Uh, sure."

"Get out of Houston today. Disappear. Go somewhere you feel safe. The people who gunned down Dr. Cofferman are dangerous and unpredictable. There is no telling what they may do next."

The hairs on her arms stood at attention. "Thanks for the warning."

Bree ended the call, her head spinning. *Where can I go that's safe? Where?* After a minute or so of thinking, she looked at her phone screen and began scrolling through names, searching for inspiration. Her eyes landed on one, and she stared at the screen, uncertain of how a call from out of the blue might be received. She mumbled. "Not a lot of options, so here goes nothing."

She pressed the name on the screen and held the phone to her ear. A familiar voice answered brightly. "Hi Bree! How are you?"

Relief washed over her. *Thank God. He seems happy to hear from me.* "Hi Ansen. I'm good, really good. Say, any chance that spare bedroom is available?"

CHAPTER ELEVEN

Getting out of town fast was the priority, so Bree took the first flight she could to Miami. Once there she checked into a hotel, caught a few hours of sleep, then hopped an early morning flight to the Caribbean island of St. Kitts. Upon landing, she slung her travel backpack over her shoulder and took the ferry to the neighboring island of Nevis. Her nerves calming, she sat up front to get the best view of Mt. Nevis, the jungle-covered dormant volcano that created the island.

Stepping off the ferry she took a deep breath of salty air. "Ahh, I've missed this place." It was warm and humid, but with a steady ocean breeze it felt much more comfortable than Houston's stifling summers. The light lapping sound of water against the dock pilings invigorated her senses and gave her confidence in her decision to come here. *Don't stress over seeing Ansen again. He's a good guy.* She snagged a taxi and was soon in the driveway of Ansen's beachfront bungalow. As the taxi drove away, she stared at the side-yard gate. "Alright, let's see if Maverick has forgiven me."

Approaching slowly, Bree heard a familiar low growl. Her voice sweetened. "Hey pretty boy, it's me. I'm back." The growl stopped abruptly, then turned to excited yips. "You have forgiven me!" She opened the gate and the muscular Belgian Malinois began the ritual of greeting an old friend, jumping happily and giving wet kisses. She returned the affection with hugs, smoothing his black and tan fur. "Such a good boy! I've missed you too!"

While Maverick ran to fetch a tennis ball, Bree pivoted toward the house, to which she no longer had a key. "Let's see. Where has he hidden the spare?" Her eyes scanned until she spotted a slightly off-color rock. "Moved the location, but same old fake stone." Smiling, she retrieved the key and gained entry into the home she once shared. Wasting no time, she changed into a red bikini that complimented her olive complexion. She made the short walk across the well-tended back yard to the tree line, then onto the sandy beach, running the last few yards into the surf. Her strong stroke quickly propelled her past the break into open ocean. Looking back at the green island, it seemed to float on the crystal blue water. Feeling she was far enough out not to be heard, she let loose at the top of her lungs. "LIFE IS GOOD!"

After a long swim, she found her way back to Ansen's house, smelling flowers along the way in a bouquet of sweet tropical notes. Helping herself to the fridge she ate a humongous lunch, then played fetch with Maverick. Next came lazing around the pool, waiting for her former boyfriend to get home. Finally, she drifted to sleep on a shaded chaise lounge before jerking awake to an ice-cold shock.

Ansen laughed and pulled the cold beer bottle away as she came up swinging. "You ate almost all of the food in the house, but didn't touch the beer. Are you really Bree Battle, or some imposter?"

His laugh was contagious and she spoke between giggles as she regained her composure. "You son of a bitch. Is that any way to treat a guest?"

He reached for her hand to help her up. "Give me a hug. It's been way too long."

His embrace triggered forgotten sensations. Dormant neurons fired bolts of energy through her once again healthy body. She hugged him tight. "I've missed you. Thanks for letting me crash for a few days."

His arms released slowly as his deep blue eyes lit. "I'm so glad you called... that you're okay. Are you really okay?"

Their bodies separated but their hands remained clasped. She had been unsure of how she would be received, considering their breakup. Feeling his warmth, her smile would not stop. "I am." She fudged a bit. "I got into a new clinical trial at the last minute, and look, good as new."

"That's awesome. No one deserves it more, not after the year you've had."

Even the reminder of the loss and pain that she had experienced couldn't break the good vibes of the moment. "Counting my blessings and glad to be on this side of the daisies. How are things with you, it's been a while since we've talked."

Releasing her hands, his smile dimmed a bit. "It's been a good year for me, worked some things out." He paused and stared at her intently, then as if carefully considering his next step, his full smile returned. "I'm starved. Let's get dinner started and I'll tell you all about it."

They laughed as they worked together in the kitchen, as if nothing had changed in the intervening two years since their relationship ended. As Ansen placed two Red Snapper fillets on the grill, Bree brought him another beer and slid close beside him. "I love this place. Everything feels simple, somehow right."

Accepting the beer, he took her by the hand as they walked to a bench where he could keep an eye on the main course grilling over hot coals. He spoke wistfully. "If only that were true. But complexity has found its way to paradise, too. In fact, there's something I need to talk to you about."

Her muscles tensed, reflexes seeming on overdrive. "What do you mean?"

Looking down at the ground he continued. "I made Junior VP at the bank, so I'm privy to all kinds of information." He hesitated. "And your account came to my attention last week."

Voice hardening, she replied. "That can't be good, Not at a bank like yours. What happened?"

"Our cyber security is pretty damned good, you know, to protect our more colorful client's accounts."

"You mean the tax evaders, drug lords and arms dealers?"

A half grin told the story. "As we say in the business, 'colorful clients."

It was her turn to look down, knowing bad news was on the way. "Tell me what happened. It will just be one more crazy thing on top of all the other crazy things that have gone on in the past few months."

The reply seemed to catch him off guard. "Uh, sure. So, I was happy to have you become a client as you consolidated your parent's investments into one account after their passing. I liked having at least one customer who only needed our normal services... not our *special* services."

"Yeah, I get it. I'm a normal customer, but I was looking for something else." She hesitated for a moment recalling their short conversations and emails as she transferred all of her savings here, fearing she would soon be dead." I was looking for someone I could trust... in case things turned out badly. Now, tell me what happened."

Glancing at the grill, he walked over and turned the fillets. When he returned, he stood facing her. "Bree, are you involved in something bad, something you want to tell me about? You know you can tell me anything."

Reaching for his hands, she pulled him closer and gently poked her finger into his chest, not ready to tell him about her last few months. "I know I can trust you, just tell me what happened."

"A week ago, someone was very interested in your account." He paused, then his voice took on a more serious edge. "It was subjected to a cyber-attack the intensity of which we seldom see, even in our specialized brand of banking. This was a major league hacking attempt specifically directed at you. We were able to protect your money and your data, but our experts suspect it was either a sophisticated criminal organization or a government black-ops attack. Either way, this wasn't random."

The coals flamed gently and she changed the subject, still not yet sure how much she was ready to share. "You better check the grill or we'll be having peanut butter and jelly sandwiches for our main course."

He spun and expertly wielded the grill tools. "Thanks! They're perfect and dinner is ready. Care to join me under the stars?"

For the next thirty minutes they reminisced on only the happy times between them and the best events of the intervening two years since their separation. Intentional or not they avoided prickly subjects, like their breakup and his news about her account. After sharing the delicious island meal under a gradually darkening evening sky, he finally returned to unfinished business. "Any idea who is targeting you, or what they want?"

She slowly placed her fork on the plate. Full, and more relaxed in his company, her defenses lowered and she opened up a little more. "The short answer is no. I don't know what's going on or who is involved. I'm beginning to suspect that it might have something to do with my father, but I'm not even sure about that. I've got more questions than answers." She paused as another thought came to mind. "Say, didn't our dads have some kind of business dealings with each other when we were kids? I mean, growing up we tagged along with them to China, went to more shooting competitions around the world than I can remember, and even spent time together with them in Prague. That had to be about business, didn't it?" Saying the word Prague caused her to stop. "Speaking of Prague, do you remember Mr. Svoboda?"

Ansen's face scrunched. "Mr. Svoboda, what's any of this got to do with him?"

Averting her eyes, she immediately regretting bringing him up, unsure of how much to tell Ansen. "Probably nothing." She switched the subject back to their parents. "My father always told me he was in the energy exploration business, but that's about all I know. How about you, do you know anything more about their business dealings?"

"I really wish I could help, Bree, but my father took his secrets to the grave as well. Looks like one more thing we have in common. By the way, have I told you how good you look? It's like there's a glow about you."

She blushed, then her hand went to move her hair behind her ear. She blushed brighter when she realized that her hair was still too short to cover her ear. "Thanks. You always seem to bring out my best." The warm salty breeze carried wafts of sweet hibiscus scents that took her mind back to happy days together. "Care to join me for a walk on the beach?"

He was at her side in a flash. "That's a great idea."

They walked in moonlit silence as he put his arm around her waist. She leaned into the embrace that tonight felt both familiar and new. Since leaving Peru all her senses seemed to be supercharged, as if they had been resurrected by her near-death experience and were now determined to never take another moment for granted. The incoming tide roiled fine wet sand around their feet, triggering a giggle. He reached down and in one motion swept her off her feet, bringing them face to face. Their eyes met and neither resisted the invisible forces that pulled their lips together in a long kiss. He carried her out of the surf, sitting her down gently on soft sand that retained fading mid-day warmth.

Without saying a word, Bree began unbuttoning his shirt, sliding it off his buff torso. Her hands slid across his muscular bare chest, the touch firing pleasure neurons in her brain. *I had forgotten how good he feels.* He returned the gesture by pushing her bikini straps down her arms, then unhooking the clasp in back.

Their skin-to-skin embrace triggered surges of emotions and she ran her fingers aggressively through his hair, pulling him down on her.

The intensity of their kisses gradually increased until she rolled atop and astride his body. His hands gently gripped each side of her waist until she moved them toward her breasts. Tender squeezes evoked a whispered reply. "Ahh, life is so good." Her eyes closed in a hormone fueled ecstasy. "Let's live in the moment."

The rising and falling of bodies accompanied soft moans backed by the sound of gentle ocean waves, all mingled in a sensuous symphony of movement, sound and emotional release. Multiple crescendos followed until a final climax. Now, laying side by side looking up at the bright stars, he broke the silence. "I've missed you."

Sated, but still riding the surge of endorphins, Bree answered. "No talk of the past... of things lost."

Ansen leaned on his elbow, his free hand tracing invisible shapes on her bare skin. "So, how about a quick dip and then live another moment?"

A devilish laugh accompanied her reply. "Last one in the water is a rotten egg!"

CHAPTER TWELVE

They shook the sand out of their clothes as best they could and dressed, leaving the beach with smiles and pleasant new memories. Hand in hand they made their way back to his house, enjoying the afterglow and each other's company. As they approached the property Ansen stopped. "Something's wrong."

Bree scanned the shadow strewn backyard, then whispered. "Where's Maverick?"

"Exactly. You remember, he always waits right here." He squatted and she joined. "Look, by the grill. Do you see?"

Her eyes slowly focused in the dim lighting and her body tensed at the sight. "Yes. I see someone... and looks like they have a rifle."

He felt his pockets. "I left my cell phone at home. You?" He glanced at her bikini clad body with only a thin wrap covering. "I see you don't have yours either."

"Sorry. How about a Plan B?"

His hands fished deeper in his pockets. "I have my car keys, so let's get the hell out of here. We stay low and keep our eyes wide."

As they crept around the perimeter of the property she halted and grabbed his arm, then whispered. "Look, there's Maverick. That's him lying beside the gate." Her words choked. "Damn it, looks like he's dead!" The sight sickened her and she fought to keep from throwing up. Swallowing hard, she pushed the acidic stomach contents that made it to her mouth, back down. Rage burned as she spat the next words, her voice shaking. "Those assholes. He was the best dog ever."

Ansen caught sight of his presumably dead dog. His jaw clenched and voice trembled. "Sons of bitches. He was a great dog."

Her hand went to his shoulder in sympathy. "I'm so sorry, I know how much you loved him. Those bastards!"

Pointing, Ansen spoke in anger. "Look. Another one of them hiding behind the shack-shack tree." He punched the sandy ground. "I can't believe they killed Maverick... that's sick!"

They continued their slow creep, mumbling profanities until finally reaching his BMW. The electronic key fob caused the car to automatically unlock as they approached, lighting the interior dome light. "Shit. Forgot about that."

A voice shouted from behind. "It's them, they're trying to escape!"

They broke into a sprint as Ansen yelled. "Get behind the car!" She ran past the front while he ran toward the trunk. In seconds he had popped the rear lid and retrieved two weapons on his way to join her behind the cover. Bullets now sprayed the car as he hunched down behind the vehicle.

Bree's eyes opened wide. "What the hell are guns doing in your trunk?"

Even with the sound of metal being pierced and glass shattering, he managed a smile. "A gift from a colorful client. Took them to the range yesterday and forgot to put them back in the safe."

She felt her heart begin to race. "Really! Colorful clients? Seems like fancy words for killers to me."

A sideways glance returned as he opened the bigger case and handed her the rifle, speaking as he uncased and loaded the pistol. "I'll worry about that if we get out of this, but right now it looks like we're on to Plan C. Shoot our way out."

A hail of bullets raked the car, sounds of metal ripping and glass breaking filled the air. After a few bursts, Bree sensed a break in the fire. She peeked above the hood and lowered the rifle in one swift motion, all of the instincts from years of shooting resurfacing. *Boom, boom.* A shadowy figure fell. "Got one! Payback for Maverick, you son of a bitch!"

Ansen muttered under his breath. "You were *always* the better shot."

"I heard that." An unbidden memory flashed in her mind of standing atop the winner's podium at a teen shooting competition, with Ansen in second place. Her lips turned up slightly at the recollection. *You're right.*

Another barrage of fire was returned and Ansen pointed to one of the large chunks of volcanic rock that framed the entrance to his driveway. "I'll draw their fire. Should give you a better chance to pick off another one." He bolted and clumps of gravel jumped behind his steps as bullets chased him.

Seeing him secure behind the stone, Bree moved to a prone position, just under the front bumper of the now bullet riddled car, forcing her mind to ignore the sharp edges of the gravel stone digging into her bare skin. Another of the unknown assailants fired toward Ansen's position, momentarily lighting the attacker's silhouette with flashes in the darkened backyard. Without hesitating she pulled the trigger twice more. *Boom, boom.* Another body fell to the ground. "Serves you right, scumbag."

Holding the rifle in her hand reminded her of the weapons and tactical training she received from her father, and the grumbling from her mother about guns. *Guess dad really did know what he was doing.*

Ansen peeked around the corner of the large rock and fired three shots in the general direction of another shadowy figure, eliciting more return fire. He yelled. "See him?"

Two more booms dropped a third assassin. "Saw him."

Moments later, a car's engine roared to life down the street and soon the sound raced into the distance.

The acrid scent of spent gunpowder filled the air as silent seconds ticked by. Finally, Ansen rose to one knee. "I think they're gone. You okay?"

"Yeah. You?"

He looked to where Maverick lay, then turned to her with pain infused pleading. "What the hell just happened? Why were they here... trying to kill us? None of my clients are angry right now, at least none that I know about."

As her head lowered, she answered meekly. "We need to talk. There are things I need to tell you. This may not be about you and your colorful clients."

Stepping closer he put his arm around her shoulder and she detected a change as he spoke, now much more business-like. "And maybe there are some things I need to tell you as well, but not now, not here. The police will arrive any minute and I think it would be better if you weren't here. Give me the rifle. All of the kill shots were from this weapon, and I can justifiably claim that I was defending my home. No need to involve you."

She glanced toward the three bodies splayed across the lawn and slowly shook her head. Thoughts of Peru, and of Dr. Cofferman flashed in her mind. "I agree. The last thing I need are more complications."

"Our bank greases a lot of palms on this island, and with my position there, I can make this all go away, fast." He pointed to the shed beside the pool. "I still have the scooter. Take this pistol, just in case, and grab your things. Go to the Arista Hotel and let them know that you are a client of mine. They will put you in their guarded VIP wing. You'll be safe there."

"Got it. And you?"

A hand ran through his hair as he exhaled. "This is a mess, but I can handle it. I'll deal with the police tonight, then square things away at work in the morning. They need to know about this. I'll meet you for lunch at the Blue Lagoon."

Bree's chin trembled. "This is worse than I thought."

A firm gaze met her comment. "We'll talk at lunch. Now get out of here."

She wrapped her arms around his waist. "Thank you for everything." Now on tiptoes she kissed his cheek. "We make a good team, don't we?"

A wry smile seemed to almost form. "We used to. Maybe we can add that to the things we talk about over lunch. Now, get going."

She gave him another quick peck, grabbed her things from the bedroom, then headed for the shed. In just a few minutes she was gliding through the night with the wind in her face, the dark ocean to her right and the even darker dormant volcano to her left. A thought occurred as police cars sped past her toward Ansen's house. *I just killed three men, but the only things I can think about is how sad I am about Maverick and how things ended between Ansen and me. God, I was a big-time jerk to such a nice guy.*

Bree tried to shake those feelings as she checked into the hotel. As promised, she was escorted to the secure wing of the property. After throwing her backpack on the bed, she began searching for the room service menu. Finding it, she immediately placed an order. *How the hell can I be hungry again?* After devouring an entire pizza, a debilitating surge of tiredness swamped her body. *What the hell is wrong with me?* Rather than trying to answer the question, she succumbed. Almost as soon as her head hit the pillow, her dream began. A twisted, recast version of the classic movie, *The Fugitive* started playing. Endless chase scenes and shoot outs tortured her night.

CHARTER THIRTEEN

Bree's eyes finally opened and located the clock on the side table. "11:30? Shit!" She sprang out of bed and hit the shower, rinsing away sand and salt from the previous evening. Thoughts of the start of that night brought a satisfied smile as she toweled dry. Glancing at her phone she saw it was already well after noon. She sent a text to Ansen. *Be there in 10.* Hustling, she made her way from the hotel to the Blue Lagoon restaurant, spotting Ansen in his khakis paired with starched button-down, sleeves rolled to his elbows. The water side table looked straight out of a movie under its bright yellow canvas umbrella. "Sorry I'm late."

He rose as she seated herself. "I was starting to think you had ditched me."

Blushing, she recalled their last day as a couple. "Nothing like that… ever again. I promise. I'm surprised you've forgiven me." She paused. "Have you forgiven me?"

Ansen's words sounded flat, devoid of emotion. "It doesn't hurt much anymore, but the scars are still there." Now his usual sunny disposition began to emerge. "And after our walk on the beach last night, it stings a little less."

Her blush now bloomed rose red, complimenting her tangerine blouse. "I quite enjoyed the first part of our evening."

With that quip his cheeks matched hers. "Yes. A memorable night… from beginning to end."

The comment grounded her as she rationalized her lack of empathy for the dead men. *They killed Maverick and that's just wrong.*

It was them or me, and I deserve to live.

Ansen snapped his fingers. "Hey, space cadet. You okay?

"Yeah… sure." She redirected the conversation, not wanting to vocalize those thoughts. "How did it go with the police last night?"

He glanced, eyes tight and worried. "You sure you're alright?"

Temper flashing, she replied. "I said I'm fine!" That was far from the truth, but now was not the time to lose control. Her hands silently kneaded the napkin under the table as she regained her composure. "Really, I'm okay. How about you? The police?"

His gaze relaxed. "They had a lot of questions, and some suspicions about my story. But they bought it, or at least accepted it. Our investment in local law enforcement usually gets us the benefit of doubt."

Bree nodded knowingly. "Just another cost of doing business with colorful clients."

He chuckled. "And thanks to last night, now ALL of my clients are colorful." His bright mood didn't seem to last long. "I think we need to lay our cards on the table."

"Yes, but can we order first? I missed breakfast."

A waitress was waved over and orders were placed. Ansen picked up the conversation after the server was out of earshot. "What the hell is going on, Bree?"

"It's complicated." Last night she had killed three men and not a nerve frayed. *That was black and white. Kill them before they kill us. No hurtful past, questionable motives or cloudy mysteries.* Her palms began to sweat and she again kneaded the napkin. *As much as I don't want to, I have to tell him at least some of what's going on.* She steeled her nerves and began. "Like I said last night, I'm in the dark about what's really happening. What I do know now is that my father somehow knew that I was going to get sick and apparently set some kind of plan in motion before he died. That might sound crazy, but that's what seems to have happened."

She looked at him, but didn't see confusion. Instead, she saw a look on his face she had never seen. "Last night you told me that you had information. Do *you* know what's going on?"

His jaw clinched. "I told you that my father took his secrets to the grave." He paused, appearing to gather his courage. "But he didn't take them all."

Bree leaned in. "Ansen, what do you know?"

Glancing both ways, he spoke just above a whisper. "I shouldn't be telling you this, but those bullets last night change things. You deserve to know."

"Yes, I do. Tell me!"

"It seems your father and mine weren't only involved in business together, they were also involved in a secret organization. A very old secret organization. One that will go to great lengths to achieve its goals."

His words didn't make sense and on top of that, she sensed an inner turmoil in him she had never seen. "I have no idea what you're talking about, but it sounds kind of ominous. Whatever it is, you know you can trust me."

Leaning back, he rubbed his chin lightly, seeming to decide how to proceed. "Inside each of us is the desire to see our children have a better life than we do, right?"

Cocking her head slightly, she answered cautiously, not sure what he might know already about her situation... and not sure how much she wanted to share. "I... I guess so. What are you getting at?"

"This takes a minute, so just go with it." He glanced around a second time. "Well, a few centuries ago a select group of men and women decided to take matters into their own hands." He paused and reached for her hand. "They're called the Founders...

and those pioneers, those visionaries… they are our ancestors."

She pulled away and her mind spun. "What? What the hell are you talking about? I've never heard any of this."

Ansen reached out to her again. "You and I are descendants of those original members, a kind of weird royalty. I just learned the basics of it a couple of years ago. My dad knew he was dying and started my initiation process."

"Initiation?"

"Just listen. In medieval times life expectancy was about thirty years. Can you imagine?"

Pulling her hand away again, she ran it over her still short hair and spoke defensively. "Unfortunately, I can."

"I didn't mean it like that, but in a very concrete way, you understand better than me what a waste it is to see a productive life snuffed out so young. Our ancestors set in motion a plan to change those odds, at least for our families. You and I are part of that story."

The waitress approached the table bearing their lunch orders. His, a shrimp salad, hers a full seafood dinner platter. He laughed. "Missed breakfast, huh?"

Bree leaned over her food, sniffing fried goodness and butter-soaked bliss. She quickly snagged a fry. "Shut up. I can't help it. I'm hungry."

The waitress left and Ansen resumed. "You eat, I'll talk."

She mumbled agreement with a mouth full of sautéed shrimp.

"From what I've been told it started informally, with match-making between the healthiest young adults of the found-ing families. This naturally facilitated business links between extended relatives which became the backbone of financial support for succeeding generations. As you might guess these arrangements flourished and quietly the network eventually spread around the globe. Looking back, it's hard to say if better genetics or simply better financial success was responsible for improved life expectancies, but that didn't seem to matter as long as the result improved the chances of a healthy and prosperous life for their children. Is this making sense?"

She held up her index finger as she washed down a bite with water. "Yeah. I'm shocked that dad never told me about any of this, and it's super strange, but nothing crazier than a lot of cultures that have arranged marriages. Are you sure about all of this?"

His eyebrow arched, seeming to acknowledge the weirdness, and her acceptance of it all so easily. "Yeah, I'm totally sure. And I haven't even gotten to the really weird stuff yet."

Pausing her eating for a moment. "It gets weirder?" Her eyes blinked hard. "Are you sure you're talking about our strait-laced families?"

A shrug appeared to signal his understanding. "Just listen. As crazy as the matchmaking was, things began to evolve when Darwin published in 1859. Then there was a whole new set of scientific explanations for what the Tree of Life Society had been doing for all those years."

A bolt of recognition struck her like lightning on a clear day. She grabbed his arm. "That's the name? The Tree of Life Society?"

"Original, right? A lot of us have a tattoo like this to identify each other." He held out his left arm and on the inside of his wrist he revealed a 'Tree of Life' symbol.

A gasp nearly took her breath. "I've seen that design before."

"Really, where?"

Pursing her lips, she stalled, still uncomfortable sharing details of her ordeal. "I'll tell you in a minute. You were saying?"

Resuming the intricate family history lesson, he continued. "Yeah. Well, anyway, things began to get way more complicated."

She had almost wolfed down the entire platter of food, so she set the fork down. "How so? I mean, didn't that give them exactly the kind of science they needed to explain what they were trying to do?"

"From what I understand the answer was both yes and no. Yes, it validated the approach and gave them a new way to think about their goals, plus it opened entirely new scientific avenues to explore. But it also opened up a Pandora's box of challenges, the biggest of which was eugenics."

Bree gulped. "Please tell me our families weren't involved in things like the Holocaust?"

Shaking his head, he continued. "Fortunately, no. Our families stayed on the path of trying to improve our stock, so to speak, without downgrading others. Some members, however, broke away in a splinter group that did follow those dark ideas. They believed the best way to improve the entire human race was to eliminate groups considered inferior. They used methods like forced sterilizations of those deemed deficient, or as you mentioned, even more drastic measures. Many of the originators of those kinds of ideologies came from that branch, now called the Reformed Tree of Life Society. Scary, huh?"

Disgust sat like a pit in her stomach, temporarily pushing away all thoughts of food. "That totally creeps me out." She looked down, ashamed of the possibility of her family being even remotely linked to those atrocities. "Are you sure this is true? That you're talking about our families?"

"I'm one-hundred percent certain."

Her head tilted as her words still carried the air of doubt. "Okay, if you say so. Sounds strange, very strange." She paused and her forehead wrinkled as she considered his story. "Let's say for the sake of argument that I believe you, that we come from a long line of weirdos. What does that have to do with us getting shot at last night?"

Ansen glanced around yet again, making sure there were no prying eyes or listening ears. "As I understand it, eugenics went out of fashion after World War Two, but the people who held those views didn't cease to exist, they just melded into the background, and returned to the movement's roots in a hard-core way. But our faction didn't stop advancing the cause of human improvement. The leaders of our branch saw a new opportunity and got in on the ground floor of the gene editing movement."

The hairs on Bree's arms stood, and her stomach dropped. "I don't feel so good."

"What's wrong? Something you ate?"

It was her turn to look around for eavesdroppers before speaking. "Let me guess. My father, your father, our so-called faction was somehow involved in a super-advanced science project to create a perfect human."

Both of Ansen's eyebrows arched. "Wow. You made that leap without many clues. I'm still new in the society, so I only know the broadest of outlines, but that's what I hear."

Falling back in her chair, her hand went to her head. "Ansen, remember me mentioning that last minute miracle clinical trial that I found, the one that saved my life?"

"Yes."

"I knew nothing of a quote "society", but what I went through is definitely connected. As a matter of fact, the facility where it happened is called the Tree of Life Clinic. That's where I first saw that logo. This is worse than I imagined."

He reached for her hand. "What did they do to you?"

Her response was instantaneous, and a lie. She could barely accept the deal she had made and there was no way she was ready to tell anyone what she had done... even Ansen. "So far, all that's happened is that they have cured me, but now I owe them. I have no idea if they'll ever ask for some kind of pay back, but they didn't seem like the kind of people who do things out of the goodness of their heart." She stole a glance at him hoping that he didn't see through her deception, then added emphasis. "This is really bad."

Now he fell back. "That explains a lot. The biggest fear of those old eugenics believers is they would someday become the inferior humans, like they viewed the races that they formerly persecuted. The two branches have waged a low-level war for years, and they'll stop at nothing to halt our group's work."

Glad that he hadn't questioned her story, she was able once again to speak the truth. "That's why those men were at your house last night. They were sent to kill me."

Looking pale, Ansen seemed to weigh the evidence in silence, with only the sound of small waves lapping on the nearby beach. Finally, he spoke. "If you're somehow involved, then you're not safe here. And I don't mean just on the island, I mean you're not safe sitting at this table, out in the open. We've got to get you someplace more secure."

Her lips pressed together. "You're right, but before we go could we talk about us for a moment? What happened two years ago? Maybe over dessert? I'm still hungry."

His laugh was automatic. "You always know how to make me smile." He called the waitress over and Bree ordered the chocolate volcano... with two spoons. He snickered as the server walked away. "You didn't need to get a spoon for me, you know I'm not a big dessert guy."

A sly grin emerged. "I was hoping you would say that, but I didn't want her to think I was a pig."

"This is what I missed most." His hand reached toward hers again for a quick squeeze. "Things were always so easy between us, so natural. After you left, I came to fully understand how rare that is."

Her bottom lip quivered. "We had something special, that's for sure." She fought to hold the tears back, but succeeded only in delaying them for a few seconds. She wiped them with her napkin and continued. "But things weren't perfect, and I made them worse."

A light sigh and shift in his chair seemed to signal his discomfort. "Yeah. That day was rough, but I survived."

In this moment there was no thought of food, only in making amends and setting the record straight. Bree pulled herself together, not wanting to embarrass herself by falling apart in such a public venue. "Before I apologize and beg forgiveness for how I handled that day, let's take a step back. We came here together, hoping to balance both of our careers. That was a struggle on the mainland, and while this is an idyllic setting, it's also isolated. Great for ultra-private banking, but it sucked for me. Then the opportunity to become lead counsel for Third Rock Sustainability happened. Remember?"

"How could I forget." His voice now registered hurt. "There are a lot of ways to try and save the planet, why couldn't you choose one that you could do from here? You chose that job over me!"

Her head bowed as she fiddled with her napkin, knowing he was right. "You know how passionate I am about saving the environment. That was my dream job and there was no way to do it remotely. The logistics simply didn't work, no matter how much I wanted. I didn't realize it at the time, but I let the opportunity blind me to what a good thing we had.

With a downward stare, he slid his left loafer back and forth on a smooth deck plank. "And it didn't seem to go over very well when I mentioned wanting to start a family."

Bree's hand automatically went to her stomach and she looked away, fearing that if she made eye contact, she would blurt out her secret. Her bottom lip quivered, but she kept her composure, not wanting to add another layer of complexity to the already delicate conversation. Her words carried the weight of truth. "No... and that's still a touchy subject for me." Her shoulders fell. "They gave me a week to decide."

"A week of arguments as I recollect."

Her heart pounded as she recalled everything. "We had that big blow-up on Wednesday night, then you went to work super early the next morning. It seemed like you just wanted to be away from me."

Leaning in, he objected. "Wait a minute. I loved you. I just needed some time to cool off. I thought we would talk about it more after work." His next words hit as hard as a rock thrown through a windshield. "But that didn't happen, did it?"

Releasing a long slow breath, she continued, ready to bare her soul. "To say I was pissed at you and frustrated by the situation would be a huge understatement." She chuckled nervously. "I remember staring deeply in Maverick's eyes, asking if he had any ideas on how to solve the impasse. His answer was to run and get a ball to play fetch. That didn't help at all, but it did make me laugh, and in that moment the idea of just packing up and leaving flashed in my mind." She reached for his hand, then looked into his eyes, eyes full of hurt. "It was impulsive and cruel. I know I should have worked harder to find a solution... one that worked for the both of us. I could have demanded more time to make the decision. I could have passed on that opportunity, and who knows, maybe found something even better." Her grip on his hand tightened. "Most of all, I so wish I could change how I left. I was a bitch, and even if we were having problems, you didn't deserve that. Can you ever forgive me?"

The waitress arrived and seemed to sense the awkwardness of the moment. She set the giant dessert between them, then beat a hasty retreat. The corners of his mouth lifted just a tiny bit. "I said that day was rough, but I never said that I didn't forgive you. I was stubborn and bullheaded too. That added fuel to our already smoldering fire. Over time, I came to be as mad at myself as with you. I could have just as easily considered looking for an opportunity back on the mainland. I've replayed that night in my mind a thousand times, wishing I had defused the situation instead of exploding." He held her hand, then kissed it. "How about you give me one bite of that mound of chocolate calories and we call it even. Then we talk about getting you someplace safe. Deal?"

She smiled the biggest smile she could remember since she left the island last time. A weight lifted from her shoulders. "Deal."

CHAPTER FOURTEEN

Zadie Springer's first year of Reformed Tree of Life board meetings had mostly been routine and uneventful, but today she sat transfixed. The staid deliberations of those previous meetings were now replaced with an air of electricity. Reviewing the paperwork provided ahead of time, it was clear that something had gone very wrong. She knew that there were alliances and competitions between cliques, but as the youngest and newest member of the board, she had yet to align with, or even fully identify all of the subgroups. Her eyes lifted from the numbers on the pages as the meeting began.

Benjamin Brown, the chairman, called the session to order and brought up the first item. "Discussion is now open on payments to the families of the three slain martyrs killed in the Nevis shoot out. You should have the totals in the packet provided. Any questions or comments before we approve the expenditure?"

Jim Campbell cleared his throat, then addressed the much older Ben. "How could that team fail to kill one woman? I expressed my doubts about this mission, and look where we are now."

A wall mounted Tree of Life sculpture framed Ben as he stood, buttoning his gray suit jacket over his sizable girth. His easy smile blunted the sharp-edged response directed not at Jim, but toward Liza Howard. He leaned forward placing both hands on the massive oval table. "We had to move fast, and if you'll recall, since Ansen Clayborn was with her, I lobbied for a seven-man team. But *some* on our board argued for restraint."

Liza's eyes shot around the room, landing briefly on Zadie before continuing, seeming to gauge the moods of each member. "Not so many years ago the shoe was on the other foot. Our views were the ones seen as radical. The originals fought us by using the court of public opinion, and they won, humiliating our forefathers... but they never came after us with guns."

Standing to his full six-foot-four height, Ben waved his massive mitten of a hand dismissively. He looked toward Ezra Slaughter, who appeared to be his main ally on the board, his voice rising as he responded. "Liza, that's old news. It's true that our forebears followed eugenics down some dark trails. But this is different! Those radical originals have taken up exotic sciences and they're going to change humanity forever. Everyone not genetically enhanced at birth will be a second-class human. We have to terminate their project before they become our overlords, before it's too late!"

Head swiveling back toward Liza, Zadie watched as if at a tennis match. The senior woman on the board rose to confront him. Her slim figure was clothed in a red suit that seemed to match her mood. She aimed her thin porcelain index finger like a gun. "Let's be clear, Ben. What our sect did happened many years ago, but not so long ago that we can forget the damage we caused. The eugenic laws we promoted resulted in the forced sterilization of over 64,000 people here in the States. And overseas things were a lot worse. Remember? Six million Jews died at the hands of the Nazis. So, yes, what's happening now is a big deal, but it's still in its infancy. And just like they won by working behind the scenes to overwhelm us with public sentiment, we're winning the same way. We've already succeeded in making genetic editing of parental germ-lines illegal, or so denounced it's effectively stopped the research everywhere. Even China's onboard. They even sentenced two scientists to prison for experimenting on human embryos. So what if they produce one or two children? As long as public opinion is on our side we're winning. We don't have to get more blood on our hands."

The large man paced at the front of the room between two faux Roman columns placed at the corners, energy radiating like a lion ready to pounce. "When will you wake up, Liza? You are making my point for me. If you could go back in time and stop our sect from going down the eugenics road would you? Would you do it even if it meant having to kill a few of our most vocal former leaders? A little blood on our hands then would have saved so much blood later, and you know it."

"We can't go back in time, now can we? Besides, this is different, the world is on our side and we're winning without anyone dying."

Zadie stared as Ben's face turned blood red, his words punching back. "Why can't you see where science is taking us? Look, the World Wide Web was launched in 1990, and now you can get internet service anywhere on the planet. It only takes one or two concrete examples to start a tsunami that can inundate everything in its path. We can't allow this child, or any other like it to be born! The stakes are too high."

Chin rising, Liza responded forcefully. "I respectfully agree to disagree. Someday I would like to see our schism mended, to go back to one effective organization working together for the good of humanity. If we insist on killing their members, that will never happen. Besides, Ben, children are the future of our society, right? Think of the long view."

The comment on children hit close to home for Zadie, prompting her to speak up. "As the only board member currently in family building mode, I support Ms. Howard's views. Children, and renewed unity with our brethren are the overriding principles. When Kade and I soon have little ones, I want them to inherit a better future. That's always been the goal of our society."

Ben turned his broad back as he walked toward the head of the table where he spun and gave Zadie a sustained stare. "As Liza said so eloquently moments ago, I agree to disagree. I do hope that we can at least act in unity to approve compensation for the families of those who gave their lives for the cause." He finally broke eye contact. "All those in favor?" A chorus of yeas responded. "All those opposed?" No voices objected. "The payments will be made immediately."

Aside from her vote in favor of the payments, Zadie kept her mouth shut, not wanting to tip her hand. On the inside, she was screaming. *He knows! He knows the problems we're having! We need to conceive soon, or else!*

Ben sat down, flashing a look that chilled Zadie to the bone, before addressing the group again. "On to new business. We have reports that the woman, Ms. Battle, is traveling to China hoping to find refuge with Master Li. I propose we send a team to begin reconnaissance, should we decide to once again attempt to end this threat."

In reed thin words, Jim voiced concern. "Master Li has kept relations with both branches of our order. We need friends in this war, so I'll support an advance team, but that's all for now."

The chairman sneered. "Ms. Howard, Ms. Springer, can we at least agree on responsible surveillance?"

Liza clasped her hands together on the table, her massive diamond rings sparkling in the conference room lighting. She answered for both with words as hard as those diamonds. "Surveillance, yes. But not another step without full agreement from this board. We've all seen how high-minded ideas can lead us astray by taking that first step down a dark and slippery slope."

CHAPTER FIFTEEN

Zadie's phone dinged as a text came in from her husband. *Almost home.* She could picture Kade wheeling his Mercedes SUV into the driveway, waving to their neighbor, Molly. At this time of day, she would be herding her two elementary-aged children from the bus stop back to their neighboring patch of the upscale American dream. Molly was a good friend, but seeing her with her children always triggered envy in Zadie, and for that she hated herself. Now she heard Kade enter from the garage, through the mud room, into the elegant living area, listened as he stopped at the massive kitchen island, surely spying the home pregnancy test. She felt his stare from behind as she sat on the leather sofa in her fluffy pink robe. The Gwen Blaze song, *Why me?* was set to play on repeat. *Why me? Why me? It's a question that I used to ask, used to ask, but not anymore, anymore. Why me, why you, why any of us? Watch me, watch you, watch us take control. Watch me, watch you, watch us rise from ashes and soar.*

The sound of his steps changed as he left the terracotta tile of the kitchen, stepping onto the oak boards of the den. She waited, a box of tissues on one side and a bag of miniature chocolate bars on the other. This scene had played out too many times over the past few years, and it hurt afresh each month.

He rested his hands on her shoulders, her delicate body crumbling under his touch. "It's okay, Zadie. Nothing's changed, we still have each other." She now cried aloud as he walked around the sofa, wrapping her in his arms as he sat beside her. "I love you. Our time will come, you'll see."

Her splotchy face told the story even before words passed her lips. "This isn't fair, Kade. This isn't supposed to happen to people like us."

"I know. We deserve a baby. You deserve to be a mother and when it happens, you'll be the best mom ever."

She planted her face into his chest, sobs dampening his tailored shirt. "Why us? What did we do to deserve this shame?"

He stroked her silky black hair. "Shh. You're still a society board member. Don't let those other women's whispers hurt you."

"But they do, Kade, and they're right. We should already have two or three little ones by now. I dream of holding a baby in my arms, then I wake up, and the dream fades, like fog in the morning sun. My empty arms ache."

"We'll try something new." He hugged her tighter. "I promise."

Slender arms wrapped around his neck as if clinging to a life preserver in the open ocean. "I want to believe you, but we've already spent hundreds of thousands on invitro... and still no baby. And as much as I would like to adopt, it's out of the question. Society rules are clear, our children must be of our bloodline. I think those rules are as stupid and outdated as a VCR, but it would take an act of God to get them changed in our lifetime. Kade, I act tough, but I'm losing hope."

The staccato movements of each sob linked him physically to her body as he tried to reassure her. "There must be something we haven't tried."

Pulling back, Zadie's tears momentarily ebbed. "There is something... if we were willing to risk everything."

Kade stood and walked away, to the massive stone fireplace. He turned and faced her again, his firm manner returning as his voice rose. "You can't be serious. From what you've told me, this is the most divisive thing to hit the society in a hundred years. We would be directly violating core principles of our beliefs. We would have to keep it secret from our family, our friends...

from everyone. And if we were found out it... you've said it could very well cost us our lives. It's not worth the risk."

Rushing toward him, she hugged tightly. "But Kade, all I've ever really wanted was to be a mother, you know that. I told you on our second date."

His head leaned back releasing a single laugh. "That was a weird second date. I thought you told me that to scare me away."

Her tension eased and she stroked his dampened shirt. "But you stayed and I knew you were a good man, a kind man. Kade, I want a baby so bad it hurts. I'm always thinking about it, and every time I see a woman pushing a stroller, I'm filled with both massive happiness and supreme jealousy. I want this so bad I would do just about anything."

Cradling her, tears fell from his eyes as well. "Besides all of the other risks, it's dangerous, right? For both the mother and the baby. I don't think I could live without you. We can't do it."

Bloodshot eyes met his moist stare. "As I see it, we're already up against it. I'm thirty-six years old and I've lied to them for years. All that crap about putting my career first. We know that's a lie, and I think they're beginning to suspect the truth, especially Ben. How long do you think I'll be able to hold onto my board seat as a barren woman? Huh? I'm guessing not much longer."

Eyes lowering, he mumbled. "I don't think the situation's that dire."

"Really? That's what you think?" Frustration at the situation, and his attitude about it, boiled over. "If we don't have children, the best we can hope for is to become shadow members!"

Kade held her close. "We have plenty of other friends who know nothing about our hidden world, and their lives seem just as fulfilled as any society member. Maybe we do leave, renounce our membership and chart our own future with an adopted brood. We wouldn't be the first and I would rather do that than lose you."

With an ache in her heart, she pushed away to look him square in the eyes. "Our parents would be forced to disown us. Are you ready to never see them again? On top of that, we said vows Kade, or have you forgotten? We're both descendants of the founders, and at my initiation I swore that I would do everything in my power to continue the bloodline, the same as our parents before. You said the same words." Tears now flowed freely. "I'm not about to be the one who breaks that pledge and bring dishonor to my family, at least not until I have exhausted every chance to have children. Are you?"

A pained stare accompanied his answer. "Zadie, I love you. I want a family too, but the risks of doing this are so high we would be crazy."

Zadie summoned emotional resources that she wasn't sure she had, calming herself. "Listen, my biological clock is ticking, and we're running out of time. While we will have to keep this a secret and risk real danger, deep down you and I both know it's what we have to do. You need to face that truth."

Kade pulled her close. "This scares me to death." He kissed the top of her head. "It's risky as hell and I still think it's a bad idea."

She laid out the choices as she saw them. "There's not a good idea left in the playbook right now. It's either take the big risk for a big reward, be pushed to the shadows in a couple of years, or leave the society and our families forever. These options suck, but of the three of them only one even has a chance of giving us the lives we want. I don't want to go down without a fight."

He reached for her hand, wet from rubbing her cheeks. "I can't believe I'm saying this, but if you're willing to take the leap, we'll go hand in hand. We're a package deal, forever."

CHAPTER SIXTEEN

Ansen had been insistent about leaving. After finishing their lunch at the Blue Lagoon, Bree gathered her things and set out for the place they felt she could be safe. After an overnight flight to Shanghai, a short hop to Zhengzhou, then a taxi into the countryside, Bree finally arrived at a memorable location from her childhood. The green pagoda style roofline over the tree line was her first visual of the ancient Shaolin Temple. Turning a corner, she saw the pale red walls of the old main structure where atop the half flight of steps she spied her master.

Her teacher, Chojun Li, stood with a disciple on each side, ready to receive his former student. "Bree Battle. I live to see you again."

Respectfully, Bree bowed. "Sifu, your student has returned. Thank you for providing refuge."

"You have traveled far. Please, come inside and rest."

Tea was served as they sat on cushions around a low rosewood table with a mother of pearl inlaid base. Alone, the master spoke first. "Your father and his father before him were students at the temple. You were the third generation, and it appears that a fourth is soon to follow."

Bree blushed. "How did you know?"

"Have you not looked in the mirror?"

Reflexively, her hand went to her waist, her tone defensive. "I didn't think I would be showing so soon. I'm new at this."

"Hmm. I see. You once again walk these sacred grounds and as I understand, danger stalks you. As long as you and your unborn child are here, you will be protected."

She raised her cup, hoping a sip of tea might blunt the effects of jetlag. Hints of mint instantly triggered fond memories of her time spent here as a youth. "I am grateful, Sifu. I was also hopeful that you might be able to tell me more about the nature of those who mean me harm."

"In the proper time, Warrior. For now, rest from your travels and be ready to begin training in the morning."

Her reaction was automatic and swift. "But Sifu, it has been years since I practiced our discipline. I'm not prepared."

"No. This is exactly when you need training most. When both mind and body are strong, then we will discuss the answers you seek. A room has been made ready and student dinner is served at six-o'clock, just as it was when you were here as a youth."

Smiling, she bowed her head. "I understand. The old ways have not changed."

The master stood, signaling that their conversation was finished for now. "It is good to see you again, Bree." His eyebrows drew together. "But do not be fooled by the unchanging ways and customs visible to the naked eye. Much has changed here, as in the rest of the world. Your father sent you here for three teenage summers to perfect your form. In those days you were oblivious to the undercurrents of even those simpler days. Things are much more complicated now and even more obscured. Please, get some rest and I will see you in the morning."

As she was shown to her spartan quarters, the master's words rang in her ears. They were almost exactly the same as had been spoken by Ansen, in Nevis. Entering the small room, she saw a one-person version of similar accommodations from her youth. The mattress on the single bed was wafer thin, but wrapped in blindingly white sheets, a gray blanket folded neatly at the foot. Glued to the narrow closet door was a full-length mirror reflecting the ten-by-ten entirety of the space whose only other piece of furniture was a modest, well-worn dresser. She shrugged. "At least it's not like when I was fourteen and sharing with Josie, who always left her dirty socks on the floor."

Tiredness overtook her and she succumbed to a short nap, waking in time for the communal dinner. Walking in she saw a mix of students chattering over a meal at a half-dozen tables, same as in her years here. She joined the closest group. "Hi, I'm Bree. I came here for three summers when I was about your age."

An umber-skinned teen with a distinct accent answered. "I'm Sage Randall from Georgia and this is my third summer."

"I see. It's a wonderful place."

"Dad says I'll learn lessons that last a lifetime, just like he did."

The response caused a shiver. "Oh, so your father came here? Mine as well... something else we have in common."

"Yeah. Dieter and I have been here together for three summers in a row. His father and mother met here when they were young. Did you have a boyfriend when you were here?"

The chuckle was uncomfortable, but she answered honestly. "Kind of. And we're still good friends." Feeling cheeky she turned the tables. "Are you and Dieter more than just friends?"

Sage's brown cheeks flushed. "Not yet! I'm waiting on *someone* to make up their mind."

Listening to the conversation, Dieter Schulz chimed in confidently, with impeccable German-accented English. "We're figuring it out."

"I see. Then I hope you both find what you're looking for." Bree tried to access her memories of sixteen, wondering if she and Ansen were this gawky. Realizing that they were, she smiled and continued small talk. "My father was in the energy exploration business. What do your folks do?"

The young German answered first. "My father works at the Max Planck Institute for Molecular Genetics in Berlin, and my mother writes a crafting blog with over ten thousand followers."

The mention of molecular genetics made Bree queasy. "Oh. That's interesting." She glanced toward Sage. "And your parents?"

Sitting taller, she replied. "The IPO for their new DNA testing company just went public. It's called Tree of Life Genetics and they're going to make a lot of money."

The company name confirmed what she already knew in her heart. These were Tree of Life Society children, just like her and Ansen... and their parents before them. And knowing what she did now about the society, a thought came. *We're probably distant cousins.*

In the momentary lull of the conversation, Bree's stomach growled so loud even the awkward teens heard it and snickered. Sage teased. "Eating for two must be hard."

For the second time that day, Bree was caught off guard by this kind of comment. "It's really that obvious? I'm not that far along."

The girl shrugged. "My mom is expecting, and she's three months. You look at least that far."

Nervous fingers went to her lips as she considered those words. "I've enjoyed meeting you both, but I've had a long day. I think I'll take my food back to my room and call it an early night. See you tomorrow."

Closing the door, she placed her food on the dresser, then studied her body in the mirror. First head on, then in profile. "How can this be? It's only been a few days since I left Peru, not months. Damn." She turned to the other side, smoothing her clothes. "Something's wrong. I need to see a doctor soon, like tomorrow." Once again, her stomach roared. "Ugh! I heard you!"

CHAPTER SEVENTEEN

As had become Bree's habit, sleep came quickly, and so did the vivid dreams. The night's highlights played like a kung fu movie, with her cast as the heroine defending a child against some dark foe, whose face she couldn't quite make out. Sweat dampened pajamas clung to her body as her eyes opened in darkness. *Geez, this is getting ridiculous.*

At five in the morning, she found freshly pressed uniforms in the dresser, just like they were when she was here over a decade ago. She chose the orange set of robe and knee length pants over white knee-high stockings. To complete the outfit, she wrapped the stockinged lower leg in crisscrossing black ribbon. Sleek black kung fu slippers added the final touch. Pleased, she assumed the Cat stance and admired the warrior image looking back in the mirror. All of her weight rested on the back foot with her front toes barely touching the floor, ready to kick or transition to another move. Relaxing, she caught a glimpse of the mirror, again spying the baby bump that seemed even bigger than the night before. "That can't be possible, it's just my imagination."

While her stomach had not yet growled, she felt immense hunger and left the room with two missions. First, find and consume a hearty breakfast. Second, find her sifu and ask if he could arrange a discreet appointment with a local OB physician. While she wasn't ready to go back to see Dr. Chavez, she had to know more about what was going on with her body… and this baby.

After a quick but robust breakfast she found her way to the main pavilion, sliding into the back row as a monk led all students through their morning warm up in the open plaza. The smell of pine wafted in the mountain air as the leader began in his imperfect English. "We work on breath first. Breathe in." From the Ready position his arms tensed and slowly raised in unison over his head. The class followed along.

Her concentration was incomplete, but even still, she recognized the voice from her youth. She looked closely. *That's Chan. He's an instructor now.*

He calmly delivered the next instructions. "Breathe out." The previous move was reversed and fisted hands returned to the Ready position. "Breathe in and hold. Now down."

She followed along, breath held, slowly pushing open hands to the floor, bending only at the waist as she scanned for the master, but not yet finding him.

"Relax. Now breathe."

Bree was pleased with her flexibility and strength as both of her hands rested flat on the bamboo floor. *That exercise physiologist in Peru knew what she was doing.*

"Return to Ready."

As she stood, bringing her open hands back to fists alongside her waist, she finally spotted the master entering the large space. Away from the other students she approached him, bowing. "Sifu, a word?"

His serene look reassured her. "Of course. Please, join me for tea."

"Yes. Thank you."

They walked back to the same receiving room as yesterday and again sat beside the ancient low table. "Tell me, Warrior, what troubles you?"

She bit her bottom lip. "Sifu, as you observed, I am with child." While she was nervous saying these words aloud for the first time, his peaceful visage remained unchanged. She paused, trying to sound as calm as he looked, knowing how abnormal everything was for this pregnancy. "Things have been happening pretty quickly, and I think I'm at the point where I need to see a medical professional, just to make sure everything is alright. Will you help me find a doctor who can see me soon?"

Placing his cup gently on the saucer, he replied. "You are in luck. My favorite niece specializes in obstetrics and practices in Zhengzhou. I will call her and ask if she will see you later today. You are under my protection... as is your unborn child."

A wave of relief washed over Bree. "Thank you so much Sifu. Babies are born every day, but this is the first for me, and I'm pretty nervous."

He stood and extended his hand. "Every baby is special and a gift to the world. May your child find greatness in their destiny. Now, go back to the others. A good workout will calm your mind and body."

An unfocused stare accompanied her softly spoken reply. "Yes. Destiny..."

CHAPTER EIGHTEEN

Kade paced while Zadie sat on the sofa in an executive suite at the Novotel Tour Eiffel Hotel, her pink chiffon dress spread elegantly across the pastel fabric. A wall with a rectangular window framed her with a stunning evening view of Paris behind, providing a backdrop suitable for a Monet. His distracted mind finally noticed the magnificent composition of a beautiful woman in this romantic setting. "You look radiant, Zadie. Your happiness is worth every bit of risk that we're taking." The awaited knock interrupted. "She's here." He went to the door and welcomed the clandestine guest. "I'm Kade Springer. Thank you for meeting us, Dr. Chavez."

The woman walked in as if she owned the entire hotel. "I have a reception to attend momentarily. Frankly, I was surprised when I received your wife's invitation. The only contact I've had with the reformed movement has been threats to my life." Her neck turned ever so slightly, tilted haughtily upwards. The black pant suit, black rimmed glasses and matching fingernails and eyeliner lent a severe impression. "I'm intrigued."

Standing, she extended her hand. "I'm Zadie Springer, and I'm very pleased to meet you."

An eyebrow arched. "Really? Have you told your husband how you orchestrated the murder of my good friend, Dr. Michael Cofferman?"

Knowing glances shot between Zadie and her husband. "Based on what I know now, that was...unfortunate." She pointed to an armchair. "Please, have a seat. Would you like a glass of champagne?"

Seeing the doctor nod, Kade poured champagne into stemmed glasses. Once all were served, he downed his quickly as if trying to calm his nerves, then refilled it and took a seat, completing the triangle.

After a nervous breath, Zadie breached the topic of the meeting. "When I learned of your attendance at this meeting, I saw it as an opportunity to meet privately and advance a potential mutually beneficial arrangement."

The woman stared at Kade, seeming to make sure the champagne he had just consumed wasn't poisoned, then took a sip from her glass. "Mmm, a 2015. Best vintage since '47. Go ahead, I'm listening."

A feeling of relief flowed over Zadie, hearing she wasn't shot down before explaining her proposition. "You have a sophisticated palate, and an outstanding reputation in the field of genetics."

"That depends on who you ask. Some say 'outstanding' while others... like your organization, use the word 'notorious'. I don't play games, Mrs. Springer. Enough with the flattery. Tell me why we're here."

Zadie took in another anxious breath. "Do you believe that people can fundamentally change their world view?"

Setting her glass down, the doctor leaned forward, looking over her glasses in a stare as hard as granite. "I have seen it, but usually only in the most intense of circumstances. Have you had such an experience?"

Zadie's eyes cut toward Kade for the briefest of moments. "I would say that *we* have had such an experience. One that has opened our minds to new possibilities for our family. And if we are successful, could thaw the frozen schism between the two branches of the Tree of Life Society."

The doctor's stare narrowed as she glanced first at Zadie, whose hands fidgeted, and then at Kade, whose pupils seemed the size of dimes. Her mouth curled on each end. "This is going to be fun." She pointed at them, one at a time. "I would hazard a guess about your motives, but I would rather watch you two squirm." She picked up her glass, smiled, then took another sip. "Please proceed."

Clearing her throat, Zadie pitched the offer. "You know the goals of our society better than most. Healthy parents hoping to have even healthier babies. It's a story as old as mankind, yet sometimes things don't go as planned."

Dr. Chavez grinned as she watched the two of them dance up to the edge of the proposition. "Go on."

Again, Zadie shot a quick glance to Kade for support. "Here's the thing. Kade and I were both raised by parents who only support the traditional ways. They had good reason, after being on the wrong side of the eugenics debacle. It scarred them, and they vowed to oppose any straying from the vision of the founders."

"I know the history, Mrs. Springer. And just a few weeks ago your branch took up arms to reinforce that view. What's changed?"

She glanced at Kade a third time, steeling her resolve. "What I'm trying to say, rather delicately, is that we have tried every method possible to have children and haven't been successful. You know what that means for any Tree of Life couple. Just imagine the consequences for a board member. We need to have a child soon, or we'll no longer be part of the society. We're out of options and have heard that you can help."

Her face brightened, seeming to enjoy their discomfort. "And you're now willing to go against one of your most fundamental beliefs to achieve this goal? After all the lengths you've gone, the atrocities you've committed to attempt to stop this very procedure?"

"We were hoping that you could help us with a simple invitro process using your advanced techniques and skills. Not the same genetic editing of the fetus as *that woman* now hiding in China. In return, I vow to oppose any further action against you, forever."

Draining her glass, Dr. Chavez set it down hard. Words flew as sharp as shards of glass toward Zadie. "I've already risked my life and reputation just meeting you tonight. You are a fool, Mrs. Springer, if you think I would increase that risk so you and your frat boy husband can have just another baby." She stood. "Now, if you will excuse me, I have a reception to attend."

As the doctor started walking toward the door, Zadie sprang to her feet and grabbed her by the arm. "Please, we're desperate. We'll do whatever you ask, if you'll help us."

The iron-willed woman shook free of Zadie's grip. "Finally." Her index finger now pointed like a witch's wand. "The Battle woman, whom you seem to despise, was also desperate. But unlike you, she was brave enough, smart enough, and strong enough to take the risk. I can help you as well, but only if you are brave enough, smart enough and strong enough to do the same. You can have a child, a perfect child, but only if you are willing to risk as much as Ms. Battle and myself."

The couple looked at each other as Kade's eyes bulged. "Zadie, from what I know there would be huge risks to you with this procedure, not to mention what could happen to us if we're found out. I'm still not sure it's worth it, but this is ultimately your choice."

Zadie turned to Dr. Chavez, voice shaking. "Can you really do what you say?"

Her head cocked back. "I am the best in the world. If you put your trust in me you will be pregnant within a month. I have no patience for indecision. Make up your mind, now."

A final anxious glance was exchanged, knowing that there was no way back if they said yes. Zadie reached for her husband's hand. "We're in."

CHAPTER NINETEEN

Two monks joined Bree in the waiting room while a private contractor with a pistol under his jacket stood guard outside the door of the upscale OB office in the suburbs of the bustling city. Everything about the place, from the computerized check in process, to the staff in mint green scrubs would have looked perfectly normal in the US. What stood out was Bree and her entourage, and the fact that she was the only patient in the waiting room. Only a minute or so after sitting down, she was leaving her protectors behind as she followed a nurse, whose size and build vaguely reminded her of Anita, from Dr. Cofferman's office.

She found herself in a non-descript exam room, sitting on a floral print papered exam table, while the nurse recorded her pulse and temperature. Ugly memories flooded her mind of all the times she had gone through this routine before receiving cancer treatments just a few months ago. A cheerful, thin Asian woman with tortoise shell glasses entered, greeting her in English with a distinctly Boston accent. "Good afternoon, Ms. Battle. My uncle says that you are one of his all-time favorite students."

The voice caught Bree off guard. "You're not what I expected."

The woman chuckled. "I get that a lot. There are not a lot of mixed ethnicity people in this part of the world. My father is Chinese, but I was raised in the US by my Irish-American mother. After Harvard medical school I wanted to explore my paternal roots, so I moved here."

Bree took a more careful look at her newest health care provider, now picking up the subtle different eye and nose structures of the stylish doctor compared to other Chinese women she had met. "It's a pleasure to meet you, Dr. Li. Thanks for seeing me on such short notice."

The nurse exited, leaving Bree and the white jacketed physician alone. "It's my pleasure. In fact, I cleared my entire afternoon for you."

Bree gasped. "Why would you do that? I just want a simple pregnancy test and well check."

Dr. Li sat on a wheeled stool and rolled closer to Bree, her jet-black hair pulled back in a pony tail, glistening under the fluorescent lighting. She gently reached for her hands. "You may not fully comprehend this, Ms. Battle, but you are an important woman. Your unborn child could be the savior of mankind."

Bree yanked her hands away, and when she did the sleeve of Dr. Li's jacket slid back enough for her to see a tattoo identifying the doctor as a Tree of Life Society member. "You're one of them, like Kristoff and Ansen... and all the rest."

Smiling benevolently, Dr. Li replied as she stood and wheeled an ultrasound machine bedside. "Relax, Ms. Battle, we're all here to protect you and this child. That is our highest priority." She flipped switches to power the machine. "Would you like to hear your baby's heartbeat?"

Nerves on edge, but curious, she answered hesitantly. "You can hear it already?"

"It depends how far along you are. Lay back and expose your stomach."

The urge to leave was strong, but her desire to know for sure was stronger, so she slowly lay flat on the bed, unbuttoning her blouse. "Will this hurt?'

Dr. Li moved nearer, her lilting voice reassuring a nervous patient. "I'll apply some warm gel and you should only feel a little pressure as I move the wand. Let's listen."

Exhilaration rushed through Bree's body as a womp-womp sound reached her ear. "Is that it? Is that a heartbeat?"

Twinkling eyes looked down. "Yes, Ms. Battle. You are definitely pregnant and your unborn child has a very strong heartbeat."

Bree's eyes bulged. "Holy shit. It's really happening."

The physician used a paper towel to wipe the ultrasound gel from Bree's stomach. "Would you like to see the child?"

"You think I'm far enough along to see it?"

"Well, the machine recorded a rate of 140 beats per minute indicating a fetus large enough to see. Should we proceed?"

"Yes. Of course!"

Dr. Li switched machines and was soon positioning a different device over Bree's stomach while watching a monitor closely. "There. See it?"

A face stared straight at Bree from the screen. "Is that real? It's so clear."

"We have the best equipment in the world, Ms. Battle." The face shifted position and all was captured in 3D. "Everything looks normal. Your child appears healthy and active."

"Can you tell if it's a girl or boy?"

The doctor repositioned the scanning device. "Mmm. Not yet. Maybe in another month."

She cried as the realization of a real baby growing within her hit like an estrogen wave. "I can't believe it. It's all happening so quickly."

Dr. Li placed her hand on Bree's shoulder. "I'm sure it feels this way. The first three months can fly by."

Her rollercoaster ride of emotions whipped her around again. "What? It's been less than ten days! That can't be right."

A furrow creased Dr. Li's brow. "One-hundred-forty beats per minute puts the fetus solidly at three months. Let's take some measurements." Clicks on the computerized control panel resulted in lines appearing on the screen, measuring the length of the unborn child. "Ten centimeters. Clearly defined facial features." Her shoulders shrugged. "I don't know what to tell you, Ms. Battle, but these readings are consistent with a three-month-old fetus."

Bree's hands pushed the device off of her stomach and she sat up abruptly. "I don't care what your machines say. Three months ago, I was on death's door. This can't be right."

Dr. Li sat down. "Unless..."

"You know something!" Bree pointed her finger accusingly.

The physician rubbed her chin slowly, seeming momentarily lost in thought. "I don't know anything for certain, but I might have an explanation." She paused, then looked up at her patient. "I'm not fully read in on your situation, so this is only a guess... but it fits."

"Go on!"

"From what I know, this child has been designed to have genetic advantages. Early maturation is an advantage in nature. What if this early development is simply the first manifestation of the many advantages that this child will have?"

Bree's eyes blinked twice, trying to comprehend. "You mean it's like some kind of super human? Not one or two advantages, but every single advantage they could conceive?" Her shoulders sagged. "I don't know exactly what I was expecting, but it sure wasn't this." Bree's voice trailed away. "And it also explains why I'm always hungry."

Dr. Li gazed through her oversized glasses, her eyes wide. "And if true, it can change everything."

CHAPTER TWENTY

Returning to the temple after her prenatal exam, Bree changed into workout garments and joined in the afternoon training session. She was held out of full contact sparring, but still worked up a good sweat. As the lesson wrapped, she saw Master Li enter the outdoor courtyard. She bowed and he waved her over.

"Warrior, your form has returned. Your muscles have quickly recalled the memories from youth."

Her face lit, pleased by his praise. "I had a good teacher, Sifu." They walked together out of the courtyard onto a covered patio overlooking a lush green valley. "Thank you again for providing refuge, Master. My life was in danger, and I'm only beginning to learn why. I hope you can help me understand more."

The octogenarian stretched his arm toward the woodlands below. "This forest has existed for over a millennium. Saplings become trees, then fall at the hands of an ax or in a storm in their old age. By taking the seeds from only the finest trees and planting them, new and stronger saplings grow in their place. Today the forest is more productive than ever."

His words matched what she had come to know. "And that's exactly what the Tree of Life Society has been doing with humans, trying to improve the world's population with stronger, more productive people."

"Yes, it has been a winding path, but that has always been the ultimate goal."

Bree stared at the sea of green below. "And do you think their efforts have made a difference? Is humanity like the forest, stronger because of what they have done?"

The master slowly lowered his aging frame onto a comfortable chair beside a small table as Bree did the same. "Up until this point I can say with certainty that many families, including mine and yours, have seen measurable benefit. As for the wider world." He hesitated. "I do not believe that case can be made... yet."

She turned to him, eyes focused and chin set. "And that's where this baby comes in. Right? They are counting on this baby being... special. Almost super human."

Master Li kept his gaze over the forested valley. "That is what many believe. Imagine a new sapling planted in the center of the forest, one that grows stronger and taller than all those that came before. It would soon tower over all others in the valley. The ability to reproduce an entire forest of saplings from this mighty oak could change the nature of the entire forest. With today's scientific advances it could happen in a very few generations."

Bree's hand went to her womb, her forehead creased and her voice whispered. "I understand. But Sifu, why me?"

The old man sat quietly for a few moments, finally turning to face the anguished stare of his student. "The society has lofty goals, but is led by men and women with sometimes competing agendas. As I understand, you were the compromise choice. One on whom they could all agree."

She felt blindsided yet again. "Compromise... I don't understand?"

A young monk came toward them, whispering into the ear of Master Li. The old man addressed her politely. "Warrior, there is important work to which I must attend. We will continue our discussion soon."

A feeling of finally discovering hidden truths about her situation seemed within reach. Her voice pleaded. "But Master, I need to know more."

Rising, he gently touched her shoulder. "All will become clear in time. Meditate on everything you have learned today. It will serve you well."

He walked away with the younger man, leaving Bree alone overlooking the trees. "That sounds all well and good, but how can I meditate when all I can think about is food?"

CHAPTER
TWENTY-ONE

Zadie and Kade sat across the desk from Dr. Chavez in her Peruvian clinic. It had been a week since they first met and her attitude toward them seemed to have only sharpened. Sitting in her black swivel chair in her customary black scrubs, she peered over her glasses. "Two millennials ready to step across the line. If you go through with this you will have to lie to your friends, your family, and commit what some consider to be crimes against humanity. Can you live with the betrayal of your precious ethics?"

Zadie was better prepared for this encounter. "In Paris, you asked if we were brave enough and strong enough to take this risk, and here we are. This isn't some weekend lark for us. We know the stakes."

The corners of the doctor's mouth twitched as she returned the gaze. "Yes, it seems you do. And how are you explaining your absence to your friends on the board? They would be shocked if they knew you were here today."

Pressing her lips together for a moment before she answered, the large Tree of Life Society carving hanging behind the doctor reminded Zadie of their duplicity. "We're supposed to be in Costa Rica on a romantic getaway. It's a perfect cover, because if you can do what you say, then we'll be able to say truthfully that this was when the magic happened."

Dr. Chavez's forehead crinkled as a cross between a smile and a smirk overtook her face. "You think you have everything figured out, don't you? But you have no idea what's in store if you go through with this. What's your story going to be when you and your preppy hubby are in a hospital delivery room in nine weeks?"

"Nine weeks! A normal pregnancy is nine months!"

Leaning forward, Chavez whipped off her glasses. "And in 1800 it took two months to get from New York to San Francisco. Now, it's a five-hour flight. The distance didn't change, just the technology."

Stiffening, Zadie returned fire. "It's as they say. You really are playing God, aren't you?"

Dr. Chavez leaned back and put her glasses on. "Not even close. God started with nothing and created life. I'm simply taking your egg and his sperm to create an embryo, just as in the invitro procedures you've tried. The only thing I'm doing different is genetically enhancing that embryo. Controversial? Yes. Difficult? Very. But far easier than what God did."

It took a second to recompose, but her glistening dark eyes soon returned the doctor's stare. "Will we have *any* say in which enhancements you'll make to *our* child, or will you be making all the decisions?"

A smirk tinted the response. "My choices are based on what's best for the society. You will have a very smart, very strong girl with an even temperament and extraordinary social skills. Leadership will be second nature to her. I hope you can live with these choices." Her eyes narrowed aggressively, almost daring Zadie to get up and walk away. "You are welcome to choose the eye color."

Zadie gritted her teeth and breathed through her nose, containing her temper. "It still sounds a lot like God to me."

The doctor stood and glared at the pair. "I'm giving *you* a choice! This will only happen if *you* choose this path. God gave Mary no choice. He simply chose to impregnate an unwed teenage girl, then Jesus was born. Let's be clear. I'm a highly skilled technician, but *you'll* be the one deciding to have this child. *You'll* be the one playing God."

CHAPTER TWENTY-TWO

Bree went to the dining room as soon as it opened, finding a table in the corner to scarf down a plate of eggrolls and noodles. She was surprised to see Sage and Dieter walk in holding hands. She observed the two as they went through the line, making their choices and standing as near as possible to each other. As they entered the seating area, they made a bee line for her. She spoke as they approached. "Care to join me?"

They smiled and sat down across from her. The dimples on Sage's cheeks stood out as she seemed to radiate happiness. "We have a question for you."

"I see you didn't have to wait for summer's end to define the relationship."

Dieter blushed brightest. "It's been a wonderful training season, and that's why we wanted to speak with you. You mentioned you met someone special when you were first here, and as you did, we hope to get some advice on keeping our... our relationship going. The session ends soon and we will be going back to our homes."

Thoughts of her own youthful infatuation with Ansen flashed through her mind, now surprised at how that young love had survived and then thrived. "I see. How can I help?"

Sage leaned forward and spoke with the seriousness of a nuclear arms negotiator. "We'll Skype and all that, what we wanted to know was how you handled the parents. Did you tell them, or work around them to stay connected?"

Two eager faces stared at her in rapt attention, seeming to hang on her next words. Bree nodded solemnly, suppressing a giggle. "I can see that you two are very serious. Before I answer, tell me a little about your parents. What kind of advice have they given you about this sort of thing? You know, about dating."

As she had since they met, Sage confidently offered her opinion first. "Mom's got her hands full right now with starting a company and a new baby on the way, so we haven't talked about it lately. She did say that there were a lot of handsome boys here when they dropped me off last month. I guess that's a good sign, right?"

"I would say so. And you, Dieter? How have your parents talked to you about girls?"

His blush had subsided, but now returned in full. He looked down for a few seconds, then back up, speaking haltingly. "Well... we haven't talked about it much... they say I should always respect women."

Bree gently nudged, sensing he wanted to say more. "It's okay, Dieter. Parents can be weird. What else have they said?"

His breathing seemed tight as he continued. "Well..." He ran his hands through his wavy dark brown hair and his voice rose in pitch. "Well... they've told me that if things get serious, I should always use protection... for both of us. And we have."

Bree sat back and crossed her arms at the revelation that caught her *completely* off guard. "Seems things have moved fairly quickly since we last spoke."

Sage turned her large eyes squarely on Bree, speaking frankly with the seeming confidence of a forty-year-old woman. "We're sixteen. We're not asking advice on sex, just on how to best handle our parents."

Shaken, it took a moment to recompose. Bree tried to quickly remember how she and Ansen had stayed in touch and a realization occurred. "I'm not sure I'm the one to be giving advice on this subject."

"We get it, you're not one of our parents." Sage's lips pinched. "That's *why* we've come to you. We could really use your help dealing with them. Please."

Their young faces begged and Bree relented. "Okay, I'll tell you how it went for me and my boyfriend." She shrugged her shoulders. "The truth is that we didn't have to try too hard. I told mom that Ansen and I liked each other, and after that it seemed that somehow our paths kept crossing. It's like we would meet at a shooting competition and then a few months later we would see each other at some social event that our parents were attending. It just kept going that way until we ended up at the same college. I think that means they approved or there's no way that would have happened."

A slow smile crept across Sage's face. "We tell them how we feel, then see what happens? Is that your advice?"

Bree nodded, thinking of her own experience with Ansen in this new light. Things had moved so fast since learning of the society's existence that she hadn't really stopped to think about her own life. Now it was right in her face, and it wasn't quantum physics, it was simple math. One plus one equaled two. Voila, the next generation of society parents. This place certainly taught high level martial arts, but it was also an unofficial matchmaking service. All that had seemed organic in her relationship with Ansen those many years ago was really just the way the Tree of Life Society worked.

Sage interrupted Bree's mental drift. "Are you okay, Ms. Battle?"

"Yeah... I'm okay. Yes. Just tell your parents you like each other and see how it goes. I'm guessing it might surprise you how supportive loving parents can be."

Dieter stood. "Good. Thanks for listening. I think we'll take our meal outside for a picnic, if you don't mind."

They excused themselves, leaving her alone with her thoughts and an empty plate. *I have to rethink everything I thought I knew about my life, everything. My relationship with mom and dad, with Ansen... everything.*

With her elbows on the table, she rested her head in her hands and spoke softly to herself. "I've been a puppet my whole life and didn't know it. I have to take control." Her stomach growled again, even after finishing the first plate of food. "Errrr... and now something else seems to be trying to take command!"

CHAPTER TWENTY-THREE

A week had passed since Bree's first prenatal exam with Dr. Li and she was anxious entering the clinic. Her nerves were on higher alert today, as Master Li had sent four fully trained Shaolin martial arts monks as well as two private security guards with weapons. In the waiting room she leaned toward the holy man she had first met as a teen in training. "I remember you from when I was here as a girl. You've become a good instructor."

Chan's face remained serene. "I remember you well. You were an excellent student."

"Thank you, Chan. Can you tell me why there are so many warriors today?"

"These are Sifu's instructions. My mission is to fulfill his wishes, not to question."

She prepared to ask another question but was called quickly from the empty waiting room to the same exam room as last time. As soon as vital signs were recorded, Dr. Li entered the room with twinkling eyes and a bubbly voice. "I'm so happy to see you again, Ms. Battle. How are you feeling?"

Bree didn't return her smile. "It's been a tough week. I'm trying to train per Master Li's instruction, but it's getting difficult. I'm always hungry, regularly experience heartburn and nausea and more often than not, I find myself exhausted. Is this normal?"

The doctor gently reached for her hand. "Each pregnancy is a little different, even in normal circumstances. Your case is many things, but normal, no. Let's take a look at how you are progressing, then talk about what you might expect from here. Lay back on the table and expose your stomach, okay?"

Bree dutifully responded as Dr. Li brought the monitoring equipment bedside. "You definitely have a well-formed baby bump. A good first impression. Now, let's take a closer look." She moved the transducer over Bree's exposed mid-section. "Look how your baby has grown!"

Bree stared at the monitor and saw a face with closed eyes and a smile. "Wow. It's so clear... so real. It still feels like this can't be happening, but there it is, smiling at me."

Dr. Li began digitally measuring the growing fetus and amazement infused her words. "No wonder you are so hungry! Your baby is five inches long, the size of a four-month fetus. You've advanced a typical month's worth of fetal growth in just a week. I've never seen anything like this."

Bree abruptly turned her body away and the image on the screen disappeared, a touch of panic in her voice. "What the hell did I agree to?"

The reassuring hand of the physician eased her to her back again. "I saw nothing abnormal, only rapid growth. Let's take another look, and be sure. Can we do that?"

Her shoulders lowered a bit as she forced herself to relax. "Yes. That's what we need to do. I have a deal with Dr. Chavez. The sooner we determine that, the better I'll feel."

Dr. Li patted her arm and again placed the transducer on her exposed skin. "Look, your baby is putting a thumb in its mouth!"

Bree again stared at the moving image. "That's normal, right?"

"Absolutely. Let's take a few more measurements, then get some blood from you. We can screen for a few genetic birth defects even at this stage. But based on this initial assessment, I would say that your baby is developing normally, with the obvious exception that everything is happening exponentially rapidly. You'll be a mother before you know it."

A chill ran through Bree's entire body and her voice trembled. "I'm not ready for this, not at all. I need more time. It's going to be hard enough being a single mother, but this is way beyond that. I don't know how I'm going to handle it." Her words choked. "I'm in way over my head, and I feel like I'm drowning."

The doctor spoke sympathetically, holding her hand. "Expectant mothers often feel that way, and none have ever had a pregnancy like yours. I'm sure it's a lot to absorb." She squeezed Bree's hand. "But what I see when I look at you is a strong, smart woman. Look at what you've already overcome. You can do this."

The pep talk helped and she caught a second wind. "Thank you for listening. You're very kind."

"I mean it, you are stronger than you think. You will be a great mother."

Bree wasn't at all sure about that, but the compliment calmed her. She sat up and began buttoning her shirt, her mind clearer. Feeling more like herself, new questions formed. "So, what's next? Should I continue the workouts? Am I going to feel any better, or just get worse?"

Dr. Li sat on the rolling stool beside the exam table. "One thing at a time. First, continue any workout that doesn't involve contact and doesn't cause discomfort. Exercise is very good for both the mother and unborn child, and it should help you recover more quickly after the birth."

"That sounds good. How about all these symptoms I'm having?"

"Your pregnancy timeline is not normal, but looking at fetal growth, you should begin experiencing what would be the second trimester for most expectant mothers. This is usually a time where nausea and fatigue are reduced. That's the good news. But since your baby is growing so fast, I'm guessing that your ravenous appetite and occasional heartburn will continue."

Bree exhaled loudly. "Don't get me wrong, I love food. It's just hard to think about anything else when my mind is constantly focused on the next meal. I have a lot of decisions to make, soon, with no one helping me." Her mind skipped to a new subject. "Could you tell if it's a boy or girl?"

"I expect we'll know very soon based on the pace of this pregnancy. How about returning the same time next week?"

Bree's brain raced. "Yes, next week. The way things are going, who knows what we'll see?"

CHAPTER TWENTY-FOUR

Kristoff Svoboda entered the conference room of the Security Trust Bank of Nevis, where Ansen waited. For an older man, he still moved with the grace and ease of a former athlete. He stretched his hand toward the much younger Ansen. "It has been too long."

Smiling, Ansen gripped the extended hand firmly. "Mr. Svoboda, it's great to see you as well. To what do I owe this privilege?"

Kristoff pulled out one of the high-backed chairs and made himself at home. "Have a seat and let us catch up. I understand that you are now an executive."

Ansen suppressed a low laugh, then unbuttoned the suit jacket he had worn especially for the patriarch's visit. "If Junior VP counts as an executive, then yes. I guess you can say that."

Kristoff continued in all seriousness. "We all took our first step on the ladder to success somewhere. You should be proud that people are recognizing your potential."

His reply came with a hint of questioning as he tried to get a feel for the direction of this conversation. "I was very happy to earn the promotion, but I'm surprised it warranted even a blip on the radar for a person as important as you."

Now it was Kristoff's turn for a low laugh. "Normally that would be the case, but I have had my eye on you for a long time, since you were a young boy. And with the recent good instincts you showed when Ms. Battle visited, let us say you have jumped up more than a few rungs."

Ansen's eyes widened at the mention of Bree's name. Still unsure what this meeting was about, he played it straight. "Someone tried to kill her. I just did what I thought was right for her, myself and our society. I'm sure anyone else would have done the same."

"Maybe, maybe not. The important thing is that you did not hesitate, and all of your choices were spot on. You got her out of your house and to safety before the police arrived. Then you handled the local investigators with tact and diplomacy while keeping your superiors informed. And most importantly you got Ms. Battle out of here when you realized her life might still be in danger. You have shown promise your entire life and all of that potential manifested itself brilliantly for the good of the society. Great things are in store for you, Mr. Clayborn."

Ansen felt warm, sure that his face must be turning red. "I don't know what to say Mr. Svoboda. I just try to do what's right."

Kristoff leaned forward and rested his left elbow on the arm of the chair. "Ansen, what do you know of the council of our society?"

He shifted in his seat. "To tell you the truth, not much. I guess it's composed of some of the wisest members who advise you on matters of importance. Kind of like the Board of Directors here at the bank."

"You are right, but there are a couple of other aspects that are not publicized. One of those is that it is very easy to end up with a disproportionate number of elderly members. That has always been a problem as we continually adapt to a changing world, but even more so today, as technology advances so rapidly. To deal with that reality, we have created additional board seats to be occupied by rising stars, and one of those seats is empty."

Ansen was as still as a statue as he responded stiffly. "I see."

Kristoff continued. "Another aspect of our council is that we always keep at least fifty percent of our seats filled by descendants of the founders, men and women like us. Over the centuries we have found that the balance between diversity and purity of the gene line has served us best. And as fate would have it, we have dipped just below that fifty percent ideal composition."

Frozen in place, Ansen's mind spun like a well-oiled machine, guessing where the conversation was heading. "Really."

Kristoff leaned back and pulled a large cigar from his suit jacket pocket. He took his time using a cutter to trim the end, then lighting the smoke with a torch lighter that emitted a brilliant blue butane flame. The end glowed bright red as he took a long draw. After releasing a cloud of cherry-scented tobacco fog, he resumed. "You see, Ansen. I have not started a search to fill the open seat on the council because, in my opinion, there is only one logical choice. I need someone who is young and has exhibited tremendous potential. Someone who is a descendant of a founder and who I have watched for a long time. Someone who has shown terrific instincts under pressure." He took another draw from the stogie. "I am here for one reason. That reason is to invite you to become the newest member of the Council of the Tree of Life."

Ansen's shoulders stiffened as he voiced disbelief. "You're kidding, right? I mean, really? Me?"

The older man's face brightened. "I know it is unexpected. But the fact is, you have been groomed for this role since the day you were born. This opportunity has presented itself a little earlier than for most others, but this has always been your destiny."

"I don't know what to say, Mr. Svoboda. This is all so unexpected. My father never mentioned anything like this to me. Are you sure I'm ready?"

Kristoff gave a small nod. "Oh, I forgot to mention one important detail. This appointment would come with a special assignment. We have received credible information that Ms. Battle's life remains at risk. Should you choose to accept this appointment, you would be placed in charge of the operation to keep her safe. You have already demonstrated that you would risk your life to save hers. So yes, I know you are ready. What do you say, Ansen? Are you prepared to accept the honors and responsibilities that come with this offer?"

Ansen's heart raced as he processed another threat to Bree. "When you put it like that the choice is easy. I would be proud to serve, Mr. Svoboda."

A satisfied smile creased his face. "Please, call me Kristoff. The council operates on a first name basis."

CHAPTER TWENTY-FIVE

As usual, Chan started the morning session with a series of exercises to warm up the muscles of the students. As had become her custom, Bree staked out a spot on the back row, and this morning she was joined there by Sage and Dieter. Chan shouted in his basic English. "Jumping jacks, begin." He set a fast pace. "One, two, three ..." all the way to twenty. Next came what had become Bree's least favorite warm-up as her baby bump continued to expand. Chan instructed loudly. "We work core! Everyone down on ground. Push up! One, two, three..."

By the time he instructed them to roll on their backs to begin a series of crunches, Bree had already started to sweat. She whispered to her young friends. "This was a lot easier when I was your age."

Sage snickered. "And before you were all prego."

Dieter laughed too loud, earning the ire of Chan. "What's so funny on the back row?"

Before Bree could cover for her young friends, gunfire rang out, startling everyone. Chan yelled at his students. "Run! Tunnels!"

Sage grabbed one of Bree's hands and Dieter took the other, helping her to her feet. "Come with us!"

This can't be happening again! She almost lost her balance as she glanced over her shoulder. A full firefight was underway. *No! Not here with these children!!!* She gripped their hands tight. "I have to get you two to safety"

Three monks lay bleeding on the ground and armed soldiers mounted a counter attack. Chan shouted directions over the chaos. "Protect the children at any cost!"

More shots sounded as the forty or so students scrambled through a corner door of the plaza. A cacophony of shouts sounded behind them and a bullet barely missed the trio, ricocheting off the door frame as they passed through. They charged down a set of stairs leading into a warren of underground passageways. At the bottom, Sage tugged and led them left. "This way." Fear pushed them as they continued to move quickly through the cool, damp air in ancient rough-hewn tunnels, dim lighting spaced tens of meters apart. Only four others had taken this path and when they reached the next fork those four went left while Sage, Bree and Dieter went right. After a few meters further they stopped, breathing hard. Sage held Bree's hand tightly. "What's going on?"

Far in the distance, additional bursts of gunfire were heard as Bree took over. "We'll figure that out later. Right now, let's get to safety. Where does this tunnel lead?"

Dieter's adolescent voice cracked as fear oozed through. "It ends near the highway. We use it sometimes when we're bored and want to sneak into town."

Despite the stress of the moment, distant, happy memories invaded Bree's mind, recalling when she and Ansen used to do the same thing as teens. She tried to lower the tension. "Is the pepperoni still the best at Corner Pizza Paradise?"

It worked. Even in the hazy light she could see the grins on their faces as Dieter answered. "Yeah. The Hawaiian is pretty good too."

Bree clasped both of their hands and a protective instinct kicked in. "Let's put some more space between us and those guns."

A few more minutes of running brought them to a metal door

that opened from the inside but locked when anyone left the grounds. Bree remembered. "Is there still a rock outside that we can use to prop the door open so we can get back inside if we want?"

Sage beat Dieter to the answer. "We use an old chunk of wood now, but same trick."

As they swung the door open, the bright sun temporarily limited their vision, but not their hearing. In the distance she heard sirens, then up-close, tires screeched and a horn blasted from the road. Fear shot through her until she heard a familiar voice. "Bree! Is that you?"

"Ansen?" She paused, still unsure if that was the identity of the man she heard. She asked anxiously. "What the hell are you doing here?"

He jumped from the passenger seat of a Range Rover and ran to embrace her. "Hop in and let's get you to safety!"

Bree tugged at her teen friends as they all quickly piled into the vehicle. As soon as their doors closed, the driver hit the accelerator and they sped away. Ansen turned around as best he could from the front passenger seat. "God, I'm glad you're okay. I thought we were too late."

From the middle seat Bree strapped the seatbelt around her waist. "Ansen, answer me, what the hell are you doing here?"

"It's a long story, I'll explain..." His voice trailed off as his eyes locked onto her protruding stomach that now rode above her lap belt. "Bree? Wow..."

Sage, Dieter and Ansen all stared as she felt her cheeks redden. She had kept her unusual pregnancy secret from Ansen back on Nevis, wanting to avoid a complex conversation, but that was now impossible. The best she could do was to delay it, at least for a little bit, giving herself some time to arrange her thoughts. Once again, she felt cornered. "I have a long story too. Let's get somewhere safe, then we can bring each other up to speed." No one said a word as the SUV continued through the lush green Chinese countryside. While she had postponed her talk with Ansen, there was now a growing force in her life she couldn't control. "Could we order some pizza when we get there? I'm starved."

CHAPTER TWENTY-SIX

Hugs and congratulatory wishes for Zadie were shared before the start of what was sure to be a contentious meeting. Hearing the kind words about her long wished for pregnancy gave her momentary joy balanced against the unease of her deception. Ben spoke as the Reformed Tree of Life emergency board meeting commenced. "We rejoice in Zadie and Kade's announcement that they are expecting. A reaffirmation of our mission."

Zadie blushed as she told her first public lie of what she knew would be many. "Thanks, everyone. After all we've been through, we waited a long time to announce. I'm already four months along and the doctors feel like everything is going smoothly this time." In truth, they had left Dr. Chavez's facility a mere ten days ago, but with the rapid fetal development that had been promised, they knew that they would need to start fudging the numbers now to look as much like a normal pregnancy as possible. The lies bothered her, but she rationalized the situation. *I'll only have to cover the timeline for a little while, then we'll have a beautiful baby.* Despite the lie, her smile was genuine. "We're very excited."

Ben stood as all eyes were now directed toward him. "As you now know, the team doing reconnaissance in China saw an opportunity to end the threat posed by the Battle woman and her unborn child, and an assault was launched. It is with regret that I announce that all four members of our team have been killed." The only sound in the room was the soft shush of airconditioned air flowing through the ceiling vents. He continued. "It is also with regret that I announce that Master Li was one of the seven monks and security personnel killed in the shootout."

Liza slammed her hand hard. "The board was crystal clear that this was to be recon only. How the hell did this happen? Who gave the order to escalate?"

Looking down, Ben appeared to feel the anger transmitted through their unblinking gazes. "A series of mistakes and bad decisions led to this unfortunate outcome. Moshe Mizrahi was lead on the team and with his Mossad background, he saw an opportunity to put a quick end to this threat." Ben sighed heavily. "He acted without full authorization."

"And why did he assume he had the authority to make that call? What, exactly, were his orders?"

His cheeks reddened under the interrogation. "I might have been a bit vague on how much latitude he had. This woman and her baby are a threat to humanity itself, making this no time to be timid."

Zadie watched the two senior board members clash as Liza pressed her cross-examination. "You are the chairman of this board, not a dictator. And in the last few weeks you've repeatedly stepped beyond your authorization. This time you've gone too far! In my opinion, your recklessness can no longer be tolerated. I'm making a formal motion for a vote of no confidence in your continued leadership."

Grumbles and whispers around the oblong table signaled that her request had hit a nerve. Ezra Slaughter entered the fray. "That's a serious motion, Liza. Ben has been chairman for ten years and our society has prospered under his leadership. Can't we pause for a moment before doing something rash?"

Ben fired back. "I've given my life to the society, Ezra, I don't need your protection. I'm perfectly capable of presenting my own defense." One by one he looked into the eyes of the other twelve members before continuing. "Wake up, all of you! Svoboda and that Dr. Frankenstein of his are on the brink of changing what it means to be human. When this goes mainstream who knows what we'll see next? An army of invincible soldiers willing to follow any order without thinking? Children born with gills, able to breath underwater? Imagine if they get it wrong and accidentally create a person with the morals of Hitler and the intelligence of Einstein? Or worse, what if someone creates that combination on purpose?" He sighed, then sat back down. "I've taken some big risks, risks that haven't turned out well. That's a fact. But everything I've done has been for all the right reasons."

A shiver ran down Zadie's spine as she listened to all the things that could go wrong... with the Battle woman's baby... and therefore with her soon-to-be born child. She rubbed her protruding stomach. *What have I done?*

Her momentary mental drift was re-centered when Liza spoke in heartfelt tones. "Ben, no one is questioning your dedication to our society, or to mankind as a whole. What I am questioning is your decision making. You rammed through the order to assassinate that oncologist in Houston to keep him quiet, which I argued was a mistake. Then you sent a team to Nevis to kill the Battle woman, which was a catastrophe. Now you've allowed a travesty to happen in China, despite this board's clear warnings. The result was the death of everyone on our team as well as Master Li, who also happened to be one of the few links between the two branches of our society. I think you need to step away and gain some perspective before you destroy all that you hold dear."

The air-conditioning system wasn't the only thing that brought a chill to the room. Liza now stood and addressed the assembled body. "I move that Benjamin Brown remain on the board, but be replaced as chairman." Her eyes darted left, then right, hoping to hear a second.

Looks of surprise zoomed toward Zadie, as the youngest and least senior among them spoke. "I second the motion."

As chairman, it fell to Ben to call for the vote on his own potential ouster, and beads of sweat formed on his forehead as he pleaded. "Before we vote, I beg of you, don't do this. I've gone a bit overboard in my zeal, but you know I'm right. This is the only designer baby in the world and we can stop this once and for all. Once the genie is out of the bottle it can never be put back. We can stop this if we act decisively, before it's too late." He glanced around the table, seeming unable to judge if his pleas had worked or fallen on deaf ears. His hand flicked dismissively. "Alright then, we vote." His eyes ran a quick circle. "All in favor of my removal, raise your hand."

Liza raised her hand first, then looked toward Zadie, who felt ghostly pale. Catching Liza's gaze, she slowly joined with a raised right hand. Nervous glances were exchanged until Jim Campbell raised his hand as well. His vote opened the floodgates and all others, except Ezra Slaughter, quickly followed.

Jim voiced sympathy as he spoke. "Ben, you're my friend, but your actions have left us little choice. We need your spirit and wisdom, but it's time to take a step back."

Standing, Ben's face reddened, making him appear as if he were going to have a heart attack. He exploded. "You fools! History will judge you as cowards for failing to stop mankind's demise! Mark my words, you'll regret this decision. I wash my hands of all of you." With those words he stormed out, slamming the door as he left.

The hum of air-conditioning was again the only sound in the room, until Jim stood. "No one said leadership was easy, but someone must take his place as chairman. We need someone strong enough to speak the hard truths and make the tough decisions. We've just witnessed that from one of our own. Therefore, it is my honor to make a motion to nominate Liza Howard as the next Chairwoman of the Board."

"I second the motion." No one seemed surprised when Zadie spoke this time.

Jim looked around the table. "Any motions for other candidates?" He waited a few seconds with no other names put forward. "Alright then, all those in favor, raise your hand."

The vote was swift and unanimous. Jim turned, smiling. "Liza, we need your leadership in this uncertain time. Would you like to say a few words?"

Glancing at faces with narrowed eyes and tense jaws, she buttoned her blood red jacket as she stood. "The Tree of Life Society has existed for hundreds of years with the goal of improving the human race for the betterment of all. Every one of us at this table, as well as thousands around the world, represent the latest, and hopefully, best generation. While we have made some errors along the way, I know that on balance we have been a force for good. When we stay true to our historical goals, adjusting only when we're sure it is for the better, we have thrived. You have my word that will be the North Star guiding principle that will drive my decisions as your leader." She paused for a moment and glanced at Zadie. "And while we've not seen times like these before, I know that we will again overcome the challenges of the day, leaving the world a better place for the next generation."

Liza surveyed the room, now seeing more relieved faces. "It's been a stressful morning. Let's take a break and resume in fifteen minutes." As the board members stood one by one, she moved closer to Zadie, touching her arm and pulling her aside. "Thank you for your support. That was very brave."

Zadie's shoulders remained rigid, muscles tensed, as the residual effects of adrenaline coursed through her body, her mind still processing the role she played in the overthrow of the former chairman. "I just did what I thought was right."

"I'm going to shake things up, rely more on people like you.

People who know right from wrong and act decisively for the good of the society."

Blushing partly from the praise but mostly from the fact that her vote was entirely rooted in self-interest, Zadie lied again. "Thank you for those kind words. I'm only here to advance the goals of the society."

Liza patted her arm a couple of times. "Your generation will see challenges like no other, like this Battle woman and her unborn child. With your expertise in PR, I'm going to appoint you as project leader to come up with our strategy to deal with her and the abomination she carries. They need to be seen as the monsters they are. We'll win this battle on the field of public relations, not by assassination."

Zadie felt her stomach churn as she spoke her third lie of the morning, saying what she knew Liza wanted to hear, and hating herself for it. "We must make an example of women like that, of children like that. You can count on me."

Liza beamed. "I know I can. And congratulations again on the good news. Children, like the one you are carrying, are the future of our way of life and what it means to be human."

Zadie felt weak in the knees, as if she might vomit. Her eyes flared and she spoke in panic. "Sorry... morning sickness!" She put her hand to her mouth and bolted, barely making it to the restroom in time. After emptying her stomach contents into the toilet, she rinsed her face with cold water, now staring at her image in the mirror. Her single-minded drive to have a baby had led her to cross black and white boundaries, boundaries she held sacred. Finally, she recognized her arrogance at thinking she could get away with the deception. The chalky complexion and worried eyes in the mirror gave rise to a terrified thought she had buried deep in denial. *I'm a liar and a traitor...and this board will kill me and my baby if they find out.*

CHAPTER TWENTY-SEVEN

Ray massaged Gwen's shoulders as she sat at her dressing table wearing a black lace kimono, the waves of the Pacific Ocean ebbing and flowing below their Malibu home. She scanned updated social media comments, her laptop nestled in a jumble of makeups and lipsticks. Giggling, she pointed to the screen. "Our Twitter numbers are off the chart. We just passed Rihanna for fourth place on number of followers and all we've done is announce that we're expecting and choosing to have a girl."

His fingers gently rubbed his petite wife's knotted muscles. "How are the comments breaking? Do they love that we selected the sex, or are they slamming us for playing God?"

Irritated by his comment, she pushed his hands away. "You know I don't give a damn about what they say." She did give a damn, but would never admit it even to her husband, seeing it as a sign of weakness. "We did this to have a healthy child, and that's all that matters."

Ray's only reaction was to tenderly stroke her recently tinted hair. "You look good as a red head. Matches the fierce way you live."

"I like it, too" Her shoulders relaxed again. "Thanks, Sweetie. You always know what to say." Her gaze returned to the screen. "To answer your question, looks like we're running about eighty percent supportive."

A relieved sigh signaled his reaction. "Good. That's better than I expected."

"Here's a post I really like. *So happy for you guys! Can't wait until she's old enough for you two to sing a duet!*"

A cross between a laugh and a snort passed Ray's lips. "They sure are going to be surprised at how fast that happens. If all goes as planned, by the time she's four years old, she'll have the physical and mental maturity of a twenty-year old."

Reaching back, Gwen caught his hand. "The only thing that matters is she'll know us. She'll know how much we wanted her, how much we love her."

Ray bent and kissed her head. "I'm working as fast as I can on the cure for us, like so many other labs around the world. It's just so much easier to make the genetic change in an embryo than in a fully grown human. Change that one fertilized egg and the child that's born will never have to worry about Huntington's Disease, or passing it on to her children. Adults have billions of cells, so it's much more complicated. I hope we live to see the cure."

"God, what a gift you have given us... and the world." She set her fingers on the keyboard. "It's time to pull back the curtain on our secret, just a little more. I'm going to let everyone know that our daughter will be born free of this awful disease." She giggled as she composed the post. "And I think it's time that we let everyone know she'll have beautiful jade green eyes."

Gwen caught Ray's reflection in the mirror, his black eyes looking sad. "What's wrong, Sweetie. We've talked about doing this for a long time. I'm so proud of you and want to let the world know what we've accomplished."

His hands fell away as their gaze met through the glass. "Are you sure, really sure we want to do this? These last few weeks have been so nice. Having you off the road and all to myself, getting ready for our daughter's arrival... living what passes as a normal life. All that changes when you post. Can't we just have one more week of bliss?"

Eyes narrowing, deep seated feelings surfaced. "I've been very clear on how this would go down... from the beginning. Our wedding vows even included that line about 'a commitment to live transparent lives'. Remember? I grew up ashamed of my family's poverty, the drug addiction of my parents, even the specter of Huntington's. I left that life behind and swore to always live in the open, never again in the shadows. You've known that from almost the day we met."

Moving around the chair, he faced her head-on. "Yes, but everything was so theoretical back then. There is going to be some serious blowback for me and you, and who can guess the collateral damage. This is going to be heavy."

Her chin rose and her eyes locked on him like an eagle closing on its prey, talons ready to strike. "Both of us watching our parents die horrible deaths wasn't theoretical. The two-point five million I spent building that high-tech lab for you wasn't theoretical. And implanting a genetically modified embryo into your wife wasn't theoretical, at least it wasn't to me. Listen, we've been packing our parachutes since we met, and now the plane is in the air." Her shoulders squared as she took in a deep breath. "I'm jumping into the wild blue yonder. You can hold my hand as we soar, or you can leave, but you can't live life halfway. Well, maybe you can... but not with me. So, make up your mind. What's it going to be?"

Turning away, Ray looked toward the vast ocean, his voice quivering, twisting his wedding ring as he spoke. "It was so exciting when we found each other. Hours spent talking about how we would change the world. Dreaming of having our own children who could live their lives without the cloud of death under which we grew up. But we always talked about the possibilities... the happy possibilities. And those happy thoughts still warm me."

He turned back to face her, his eyes full. "But now, as we're about to tell the world, I'm afraid. Afraid of what the world will think of us. I worry about our safety. I think about what will happen to others, like the scientists I worked with in Chavez's lab. I even fear for her, though I'm pretty sure she can take care of herself." He sighed. "But most of all, I worry about our daughter. It's one thing to grow up as the child of a celebrity, that's hard enough. But what's it going to be like growing up famous, or infamous, for something she had no voice in deciding. Don't get me wrong, I'm proud of what we've done and what it will mean for our family, to the world. But do we have to do this so publicly, right now?"

Reaching for his hand, Gwen pulled him closer, wanting to soothe his jangled nerves. "I hear what you're saying. But you're looking at this all wrong. You ask if we *have* to do this right now. And the answer is, no, we don't *have* to. But you know as well as I this *will* come out, and soon. The things you worry about might, or might not happen. You have to trust me when I say it's always better to manage the narrative, control the spin when you can. If we wait, others will paint this any way *they* want. You and I can't control what others might think, say, or do. What we can dictate is how it gets spun in the beginning. This is the last point in this long journey where we have complete control, and I simply will not give that up."

Ray knelt beside her. "You're right. It's just the world will never be the same after today."

She beamed and her spirit soared. "I know! It's such an exciting time to be alive! I've lived a thrilling life, and as it turns out, what's happened so far has only been the warm up act. You're brilliant, Ray, but you've got to learn to let go, live life on the edge. Are you with me?"

He kissed her softly, then wiped his damp eyes. "I can't image life without you, and I swore on our wedding day that our souls are joined. I go where you go."

CHAPTER TWENTY-EIGHT

The Gulfstream G IV private jet took off from the Zhengzhou airport on its way to an as yet undisclosed destination as Bree surveyed the scene. Mid cabin, three empty pizza boxes lay spread on the table where Sage and Dieter held hands, deep in teen talk. The security team bunched together near the bar in the rear. She and Ansen sat up front in facing swivel chairs with a modicum of privacy and she felt her body relax as they reached cruising altitude. "I'm so thankful we were able to get in touch with Sage and Dieter's parents. I can't imagine how worried they would have been if they heard about the violence at Master Li's somewhere else first. I still can't believe what happened."

A flinty stare met her words. "Reports are that Master Li was among the casualties. Those reformers have gone too far... again. I'm just glad you got out of there. Don't worry, they'll pay for this."

"They deserve it." Bree sat quietly for a moment thinking of how much Master Li had meant to her. "The world lost a very wise man." After a few minutes of looking out the window in silent contemplation, her mind turned to more immediate questions. "Now that we're safe, tell me why you're here in China. It can't be a coincidence."

"Where to start?" Glancing toward the ceiling and back, Ansen met her expectant gaze. "It all started after you left the island a few weeks ago. That's as good of a place as any to begin." He looked at her mid-section. "And when I finish, maybe you can bring me up to speed?"

Her free hand moved reflexively to her stomach. "Deal. You go first. What the hell is going on?"

His gaze sharpened and back straightened, his words taking on an all-business tone. "After you left, the police wrapped up their investigation of the shootout at my place fairly quickly. The Tree of Life investigation, on the other hand, was only beginning. I knew that my bank had dealings with the society, but I didn't fully appreciate how entangled they are until then. A secret team was dispatched to find out the identities of the men who attacked us. A separate digital forensic team was tasked with trying to determine if we could uncover their next steps before something worse happened. I had no idea you were so important to the society, but seeing you today, I'm beginning to guess why."

Bree looked down on the world from 35,000 feet, wishing she could be removed from this awkward situation. "Yeah... about that. I'll explain when it's my turn. You go ahead. Sounds like the teams came up with answers."

"They did. Turns out the men who were shooting at us were freelance hitmen. Once their identities were determined, the digital team took over trying to find exactly who paid them."

Bree's eyes darted. "We were sure it was that reformed group."

"Yes. But learning the specific details of how they were paid, and were any other similar payments being made was also important. Finding that information is what brought me to China. At least that's what Kristoff Svoboda told me."

"Svoboda!" Her head snapped at the mention of the name. "He's been part of everything that's happened to me!"

"He's also the one that sent me." Ansen looked around the plane. "He's the one who's paying for all of this. The security team, the jet... everything. Without him, you and those two kids would have been on your own with a hit squad closing in. He's not your enemy, he's trying to protect you."

Glancing back at Sage and Dieter intently staring into their phones, Bree let out a relieved sigh. "I'm glad they're safe, but I'm still not sure about Svoboda. I know he was close with our fathers, and we met him when we were kids, but are you really sure we can trust him?"

He shrugged his shoulders. "You can judge for yourself when we land in Prague."

"We're headed to Prague?" The more she learned about this flight, the less she liked it.

Tilting his head back, Ansen released a heavy breath. "Come on, Bree. You've had two attempts on your life that I know of, and he has a private estate with armed guards. If you know of somewhere safer, I'm all ears."

Falling back in her seat, she felt both alarmed and out of options... again. "I'm tired of being in the dark. It's about time I got some answers."

"Then we're going to the right place. He's the patriarch of the society and has answers to questions I don't even know to ask. And speaking of answers, I think it's time for you to give me some."

The rush of adrenaline from escaping the gunfire at Master Li's had ebbed, and her mind swirled with new information. Numbness leaked from her core, extending to every part of her body. Her arms spread wide in exhausted exasperation, exposing her bulging mid-section. Raw words tumbled out. "Just look at me. What do you think's going on?"

Ansen's cheeks reddened. "To tell you the truth, when I first saw you, my mind went to the beach that night." His tone turned shy and inquisitive. "Is it mine?"

A blush flashed. "Relax. I don't know who the father is, but I know it's not you."

"Well, just so you know, I've been wondering since we picked you up on the side of the road… and I would have been thrilled if you said it was mine."

She closed her eyes and rubbed them. "If only… I'm not saying I want to be pregnant, because I don't, but that would have been so much simpler. At least then, no one would have been gunning for me."

Leaning forward, Ansen retook her hand. "It's okay, Bree. You know you can tell me anything. What happened to you?"

Her tired eyes met his. "The long and short of it is that some plan my father set in motion ended with me meeting a Tree of Life doctor. She's a cross between a magician and Dr. Frankenstein, and she offered to cure my incurable cancer… on one condition."

It seemed his gaze was drawn magnetically to her stomach again and he spoke incredulously. "That's the condition?"

Nodding, she continued. "She saved me because I was the one chosen to carry the first designer baby of the Tree of Life Society. Master Li said I was the compromise choice, but I have no idea what that means." She looked down and rubbed the baby bump. "What I do know is that this pregnancy isn't normal. You saw me just a few weeks ago and I had abs like a washboard. And now?" Her words choked. "Look at me."

Again, he offered comforting words. "It'll be all right. I'm sure."

She yanked her hand away. The tiredness tugged as if she were tranquilized and being pulled down in invisible quicksand, feeling powerless to fight against it. She wiped her damp eyes. "Would you get me a blanket? I have to get some sleep before we land. Kristoff Svoboda owes me some answers and I need to be ready when we arrive."

Retrieving one from an overhead bin, Ansen caringly draped it over her as she hit the button that fully reclined the seat. She closed her eyes, expecting to immediately drop off to sleep, but that didn't happen this time. Instead, she felt his gaze land on her.

Ansen whispered. "No matter what happens, I'll be here for you."

Those words soothed her as she began to drift, completely submerged under the soft blanket. It was all she could do to stay still when he whispered again, almost imperceptibly. "I love you, Bree Battle. I always have."

CHAPTER TWENTY-NINE

Bree looked out the window of the Gulf Stream jet as it slowly taxied to a grouping of black SUV's. "A private airstrip. Wow. We flew commercial when we came here as kids."

A nod from Ansen confirmed her appraisal of the situation. "Like I told you, the Tree of Life Society has been benefiting families for hundreds of years. I guess this is what the very top of the organization looks like."

The jet came to a complete stop and Bree stood. "You're right, and this is the place to get answers." The door opened and a set of stairs were rolled up. "Time to go see the wizard."

An easy laugh followed. "He's the patriarch, not a wizard, and he usually likes to go by first names anyway."

"Oh, so now you and the big shot are on a first name basis?" The expected rejoinder did not come. She turned and saw a serious countenance. "What are you not telling me?"

"I guess this is as good a time as any." He reached for her hands. "I've been promoted since you left the island."

"At the bank? What does that have to do with anything?"

He held her hands gently. "Not the bank... the society. I'm now a council member, and my first assignment was to lead the team that secured your safety. The society wants you safe, and so do I. Kristoff said I was the right man for the job."

Her mind spun again. "What?" Uncertainty tinted her voice.

"Your *job* is my protection?"

"We're the last ones on the plane. Let's get out of here and talk about this later."

The scent of roses met them at the top of the stairs and Bree caught sight of a large bed of the flowers lining a portion of the runway. *First class all the way. Wonder what's next?*

They loaded into the last SUV for a drive through the country-side. At first, she assumed they were on a highway, but after a few minutes realized she hadn't seen any oncoming vehicles. It was clear, the airstrip wasn't just private, it was located *on* the grounds. "I had forgotten how large this place is."

Ansen pointed. "That's his castle up ahead. Seems bigger than I remember."

The vehicle pulled into the semi-circle drive and stopped in front of a broad imposing gray granite stairway. The door was opened for them by a valet and two uniformed house attend-ants stepped forward. The taller woman spoke. "Ms. Battle, my name is Frida and I will be at your call for the duration of your stay." She glanced next at Ansen. "Mr. Clayborn, this is Helga. She will attend to your needs. Please follow us to your suites."

"But..." Bree stuttered. "But I need to speak to Mr. Svoboda."

Frida's reply was automatic. "Perhaps you would like to freshen up after your long journey. Lunch will be served in an hour and Mr. Svoboda would like to meet you then."

Bree's stomach growl caught everyone's attention. "That sounds like a good plan, but maybe a snack for me now?"

Frida gave a knowing glance toward Bree's mid-section. "Of course, madam. I'll make sure you are comfortable. Follow us, please."

Although they each had separate assigned attendants, their suites were side by side. Frida opened the door for Bree, who spoke to Ansen before entering. "Knock when you're ready to go to lunch. We'll walk together."

"Sure thing."

The room was as impressive as everything else about the place. A four-poster canopy bed dominated the wall shared with Ansen's room, while a sitting area and the door to an ensuite bathroom lined the opposite side. A massive window, with curtains pulled back, looked outside. She walked toward the streaming sunshine and saw a garden full of blooming plants in yellows, reds and purples. Hummingbirds floated magically between open blooms.

Frida cleared her throat. "Madam?"

"Yes?"

"Since you did not bring luggage, a wardrobe has been prepared with an assortment of clothes in your size. Is there anything more you need before I find a suitable snack?"

"No. It's almost more than I could imagine."

As if she had heard that comment before, the corners of Frida's lips turned up. "Should you think of anything you need, simply pick up the phone and your call will be directed to me, day or night."

An almost celestial pull seemed to draw her toward the bathroom where an elegant Victorian style clawfoot tub stood as a centerpiece. "Hello, my lovely. After that long flight you are the prettiest thing I've seen yet."

She soaked in rose scented bubbles as Frida brought her a veggie and cheese charcuterie board before lunch. *Maybe Mr. Svoboda isn't such a bad guy after all.* After a long soak she towel dried and wrapped in the thick robe hanging near the tub. *Let's see his taste in women's clothing.* Opening the door of the built-in wardrobe revealed a store-sized inventory of new designer clothes. Her eyes lit, pleased by what she saw. *He even accounted for my pregnant size.*

As she finished dressing, she heard a knock on the door. Opening it, she saw Ansen, dressed in gray slacks with crisp white shirt, top button open. Her mind said, *God, you're handsome,* while her mouth said. "You look nice."

"You look stunning!"

She did a spin in the hallway for Ansen, Frida and Helga. Her words teased. "This little old gray A-Line, with sheer black lace overlay? Just a little something I found in the back of my closet."

Frida allowed a small grin, seeming proud that Bree liked the clothes. "Please, follow me. Mr. Svoboda is expecting you."

They walked down multiple hallways lined with portraits of prior patriarchs, going back hundreds of years. The pair finally reached a large outdoor patio overlooking a vineyard. Both the floor and small wall encircling three quarters of the space were constructed of large gray stones that looked as if they had been in place for eternity. The only thing out of place were the guards dressed in black suits and mirrored glasses. Just as in her childhood, they gave her chills, but after all that had happened lately, also a level of comfort.

Kristoff stood as they approach. "It is so good to see you both safe and sound."

Handshakes were exchanged as Bree took a closer look at the mystery man. As she remembered from Peru, he was tall with wavy blond hair. Up close, she saw it trending toward silver and she also noticed that even wearing a blazer over his pinstriped shirt, he seemed muscular for his age, which she guessed to be around seventy. "Mr. Svoboda, thank you for sending Ansen to China. I hate to think what might have happened to me and my young friends if you hadn't."

The trio took their seats as Svoboda answered. "Please, call me Kristoff." Bree shot Ansen a knowing glance as he continued. "The Randall's and Shultz's will be here for dinner. They wish to thank you both for your role in shielding their children from danger. After all, children are our greatest blessing."

Bree's hand automatically went to her waist, and both men seemed to notice. Her shoulders set as she took in a controlled breath. "Children... I think that would be a great place to start our lunch conversation. Would you both agree?"

Staff in black tie uniforms approached, seemingly awaiting Kristoff's orders. "I have taken the liberty of selecting sustainably raised trout paired with a garden salad and sautéed potatoes, all grown on the estate. If you would prefer something else, my excellent staff will have it prepared immediately."

Sustainably raised. Farm to table? Maybe I've misjudged this man. Her mouth watered. "That sounds delicious."

With his wave, the staff served. "We are aware of your interest in climate change and agree with your sustainability goals."

Rather than comment immediately, she took her first bites. "My compliments to your chef. This is delicious." While the cheese and veggies had taken the edge off of her appetite, she was still hungry. Her urge to eat took temporary control of the situation so only comments about the food and the beautiful setting interrupted lunch. Finally, she savored the last bite. "Thank you for a truly magnificent meal. One of the best I've ever tasted,"

Kristoff seemed amused as he glanced at her empty plate. "And you have certainly made it easy for the dish washer."

Ansen giggled softly as Bree blushed, acknowledging the observation. She took the good-natured ribbing in stride. "My appetite's been like this for a few weeks." The humor was a good segue as she turned the conversation back to the subject at hand. "Between my chats with Dr. Chavez, Master Li and Ansen, I've learned a lot about how I ended up here in this... condition." She now consciously rubbed her belly, emphasizing her situation. "But there is still so much I don't know. I'm told that you are the one with answers."

The older man's face softened. "You have been through so much. What would you like to know?"

With an expectant breath, Bree began her interrogation. "Let's start with my father. It seems he knew in advance that I was going to be stricken with an almost always fatal brain cancer. How could that be?"

The patriarch slid his chair back a few inches from the table, appearing to get comfortable for what might be an intense conversation. "That is a good place to start. See, the society has invested heavily in the field of genetics for many years in anticipation of this day... for the baby that you are carrying." He paused, perhaps to gauge her reaction to that statement. She sat with no reaction and after a few seconds, he continued. "As you might recall your family gave each other what were purported to be commercial DNA heredity tests a couple of years ago. Do you remember that Christmas?"

A wave of realization swept through her mind. "But it was much more, wasn't it?"

He spoke evenly, but bluntly. "That is correct. The samples for your entire family went to our most advanced lab, capable of tests not yet available anywhere else. We replicated this procedure for all society families. Imagine the burden your father carried as he learned that his beloved wife would develop pancreatic cancer and die in only a few months, and his cherished daughter would develop a fatal glioma shortly after. He was heartbroken."

Sadness pressed on her like dead weight. "I was busy traveling the world and living my life, but when I did see him, I remember a solemnness I couldn't explain. Now I understand." A thought came to mind. "But aren't society families supposed to live longer? Isn't that the whole deal?"

"That is the goal. Overall, society members live fifteen percent longer lives than the general population of the countries where they reside, but statistics paint only the big picture. We are all still human and susceptible to the same illnesses and diseases as everyone." He nodded and his finger tipped toward Bree. "And that's where you come in, and why your child is so important."

Hearing those words, her voice raised a half step. "I know my father wanted to save my life... and Master Li mentioned something about me being the compromise candidate. Even knowing that, I still don't understand. Why me?"

As soon as she said those last two words, the Gwen Blaze song of the same name started playing in her head. *Why me? Why me? It's a question that I used to ask, used to ask...* She tried to snuff it out as Kristoff began to speak, but the best she could do was muffle it, so she focused on his words with the determination of a salmon swimming up a waterfall.

"The society has funded Dr. Chavez's work for years to help us reach our centuries old dream of improving the health and lifespan of our offspring. When she told us she had reached the point of being able to achieve that goal, we needed to select our first mother. How do you think that process went?"

"Hmm. I would guess many would consider it risky, but surely someone would step forward to be the first, right?"

His nod was instant. "I see we think alike, but that is not what happened. There was a consensus that the first woman should be a descendant of an original society member, and that is where the problem arose. Only a small percentage of women in our membership are pure-blood descendants, so we began to consider other women among our number who would volunteer. That is when your father stepped forward with a proposal."

The brokered deal took form in Bree's brain. "I would be the descendant of an original who would go first if my life could be saved."

"Your father had already made arrangements for you to go to Dr. Cofferman for your initial care and eventual referral to Dr.

Chavez. I was on the phone with him right before his car accident and he was so happy and proud. Happy to be able to save your life, and proud that his family would be the first to step into this brave new world."

She looked down and grimaced. "He never got the opportunity to tell me there was a chance to survive what was coming. His crash left me alone to face the terror of dying young. He was a great man and I miss him so much."

Kristoff's face appeared more angry than sad. "Even worse, it was not an accident. The reformed branch learned of our plan and struck him down, believing it would derail our efforts... and it almost did. Only at Grant Clayborn's insistence did we formulate a revised plan to continue with you as the first mother."

Hearing his family name, Ansen joined the conversation. "What? My father was involved in all of this? Why didn't he tell me?"

The patriarch gave a brief shrug. "I do not have that answer. Perhaps since you and Bree had parted ways, he did not think you needed to know? Whatever the reason, it would not have mattered. Once we agreed, it was full speed ahead, and now here we are."

Bree's mind bounced from thought to thought like balls in a dodgeball game. "That's a lot to absorb, but it fills in a lot of blanks." She bit her lower lip as another topic came to mind. "And the rapid growth of this fetus? What's that all about?"

"Hmph. The good doctor surprised us with that, it was not at our request. She is a real piece of work. Brilliant, driven and always one to do things her way."

"Yeah, I noticed." Bree shook her head. "What crazy reason did she give for putting me through this pregnancy in overdrive?"

The left corner of Kristoff's mouth lifted. "I said she is brilliant and driven, not crazy. Her goal is to prove to the society that she can safely deliver what she promises. A one hundred percent healthy next generation Tree of Life child. A perfect child who could change the trajectory of mankind. A child who is immune to diseases, diseases like you suffered, and virtually all others. To prove her concept sooner rather than later, she sped up the timeline for the pregnancy."

As Bree leaned back contemplating what she had just been told, Ansen rejoined the conversation. "This ultra-short pregnancy is just a tool for the Chavez woman to get her pitch to market faster?"

A head nod accompanied Kristoff's reply. "Mostly, but she also had a secondary reason. She views the shorter gestation period as another advantage to entice other Tree of Life women to choose this path for their next pregnancy. Why be pregnant for nine months if you have the option to accomplish it in nine weeks?"

Rocking forward, Bree reengaged, her voice rising. "I get the argument for guaranteeing health for the children, and I can at least understand the benefits of a shorter pregnancy, but the other enhancements? Intelligence... strength... who knows what other tweaks she made. I'm carrying some kind of lab-grown freak."

Putting his hands up, Kristoff responded. "Slow down, Bree. It is true that the wonderful child you carry is special, but rest assured, it is one hundred percent your baby. Dr. Chavez genetically ensured an exceptional child, but these are your genes. Think of it like a family with many children. Some would be smarter than others, some would be stronger, but they would have all come from the same genetic parents." He folded his hands. "Of course, she did tweak *some* of those genes to produce the outcomes we wanted, but please realize that this is your baby, just as much as if you had conceived the traditional way."

"It's those tweaks that concern me. Just what are they and why is it so important to the Tree of Life Society to have genetically enhanced children?"

There was no immediate answer and Bree realized she had stumbled upon an important question. Her eyes bore into Kristoff as she waited in silence. He met her stare with equal intensity. "For centuries society members have risen to prominent positions in businesses and governments around the world." He paused and turned to Ansen. "Let's consider this bright young society member. With his education, aptitude and a couple of breaks aided by fellow members, I could see his career blossoming. Imagine him as the president of a major bank, or perhaps someday as Secretary of the Treasury? Think how much good he could do for humanity if he could increase investment in minority businesses, or developing micro-banking in the third world. Then think how much more he could accomplish if he were even smarter, more driven?"

Pieces were falling into place and she saw the entire picture in her mind. "I'm carrying the test case for a race of super humans! You want to build the next generation to take over the world, don't you!?"

Both hands went up again. "Whoa, Bree. Take a moment. Our society has worked behind the scenes for centuries, and we do not want that to change. We do not want presidents, we want Department of Environment heads, labor leaders, bank board members, elite scientists and doctors. Our goal is to make this world a better place for everyone, and for all succeeding generations." He took a breath and spoke calmly. "Imagine the progress we will make when the next generation are better leaders and predisposed to serve humanity. That is our goal."

Standing, Bree felt her anger build, her words carrying an edge. "Thank you for the answers, Mr. Svoboda, but I'm not sure that's all that's going on." She crossed her arms. "I need some time to think."

Ansen stood, seeming to be ready to join her.

Her emotions surged and she spat her words. "If you'll both excuse me, I'm going back to my room." She added cold emphasis. "Alone."

She took two steps away from them and the surge became a tidal wave, there was more she wanted to get off her chest. Turning back, her eyes stared wildly and nostrils flared. Her hand stroked her stomach, which felt another size larger than this morning. Her voice quaked as she vented. "This isn't a normal pregnancy in any way. I feel like a blackmailed rent-a-womb in your twisted plot. I don't even know the father of this genetic experiment, and before today, I wasn't even sure when it would be born." Her arm raised as her finger jabbed. "So, don't either of you try to pretend it's normal, because it's not." She was angry and it felt good to let loose. Then, as quickly as the surge started, it began to abate, her voice lowering. "I don't know what this child might become, but I made a deal to see this through… so even if I have doubts, I will. And most importantly, I'm taking control of my life from now on." Spinning on her heel she began walking away, until she heard Kristoff speak.

"Would you like to know the sex of the baby? Your baby?"

She froze in her tracks, then turned slowly, eyes narrowing. "You know the sex? How? Even Dr. Li didn't know yet."

Kristoff's hand gently patted the table. "When I was in Peru, Dr. Chavez shared that detail about your much-anticipated child. Would you like to know, or would you prefer to be surprised?"

Anger wrestled with confusion as her emotional rollercoaster ride resumed. "That's fucking perfect. She tells her investors before she tells the subject." Bree shifted side to side. "Well… I mean, since it's not exactly a secret." She chewed her lower lip, trying her best not to cry. "Well…" Moisture pressed her eyes as she fought hard against another emotional wave. "Uh… sure. Since *you* already know, I guess *I* should as well." She positioned her hand in a protective stance over her mid-section, her glistening eyes filled to the rim.

A wide grin spread across Kristoff's face. "You are carrying the hopes and dreams of our history. I am sure you will be a wonderful mother to your beautiful baby boy."

She felt the warmth of a blush spread rapidly as a trail of tears rolled down her smiling cheeks. "A boy? Are you sure?"

"Chavez is unpredictable, but I trust her word."

Bree turned away slowly as she restarted her walk back to her room. Her smile broadened when a flutter startled her. She swallowed hard. "Oh... wow." Patting her baby bump as she continued on her way, she spoke in a whisper. "Hey there. That's something new... little man."

CHAPTER THIRTY

After Bree left, Kristoff stood, joining Ansen. "I like to walk after lunch. Please, join me."

Ansen understood the offer more as a command than a suggestion. "Uh, sure. Some exercise sounds good."

They strolled the immaculately tended grounds trading memories of when Ansen and Bree came to the estate as youths, heading past the skeet shooting range toward the stables. Inside the barn, Kristoff scooped up a handful of feed, offering it to a dappled grey horse standing in a stall nicer than most people's homes. The muscular animal whinnied and gently accepted the treat. "Beautiful, are they not?"

Patting the sculpted neck of the horse just below the black mane, Ansen replied simply. "Magnificent."

Kristoff brushed his hands together, rubbing off a few lingering flakes of oat. "The shooting range, the horses, they are all reminders of the armed past of our order. Not so many years ago we were regularly forced to defend our people from external threats. It was how we secured their safety and loyalty. Today, we still maintain armed capabilities to protect our own. That is why the attacks we have seen in Nevis and on Master Li's academy must no longer be ignored, and as a new council member, it is time you learn more about our range of options."

Ansen suppressed his shock at the mention of options and answered with a slight tremble. "You mean like sending our own hit squad to kill them?"

Sunlight streamed through the open doors of the stable, creating a clear boundary on the floor between warm light and cool shadow. "That will certainly be on the menu of choices." Kristoff paused for a moment as he again rubbed the stallion. "As you have learned, our order has become much more modern and sophisticated, and unlike the reformed branch we have chosen to expand our methods. Perhaps we threaten one of them with financial ruin, or prevent one of their sons or daughters from getting into a prestigious school. Maybe we provide financial backing to a political foe or let them know of embarrassing photos that we will release anonymously to the media. There are many ways to pressure an opponent, and as an evolving modern enterprise we often employ these new methods to achieve our goals."

"And who makes these choices?"

"The council, of course. It will be the primary topic of the first meeting that you join."

"Oh? When will that be?"

"This afternoon. We have been patient with the reformed branch long enough. It is time for a response."

Ansen nodded. "I agree. I've seen the carnage up close. When will the members be arriving?"

Kristoff chuckled. "We rarely meet live these days. Our council members are spread around the world and virtual meetings are how we conduct important business. Since you are here, we will be together in my office for today's video conference. I will send a team to get you set up back home. Technology really does make the world a better place."

CHAPTER THIRTY-ONE

Zadie left work early to meet Liza at her home, as requested. While the summons from the chairwoman was cryptic, she had seen the Reddit trending story about popstar Gwen Blaze's announcement of her pregnancy. The singer hadn't used the term 'Designer Baby' in her twitter post, but it was the phrase that both those who supported her and those who flamed her were using. Having never been to Liza's house, she was surprised when she arrived at a gated mansion. She lowered the window in her Lexus while approaching the guard house. "I'm Zadie Springer, here to see Liza Howard. She's expecting me."

Zadie noted that the guard's uniform hung loosely on his painfully thin frame as he checked a hand-held tablet computer, then spoke with a voice that exaggerated his sense of self-importance. "Yes, I see your name." He pointed ahead. "Just follow the road around to the left."

She drove at least a quarter of a mile through well-tended grounds until reaching the circular driveway, the full size of the home now becoming apparent. Exiting the car, she spoke under her breath while walking to the massive set of double front doors. "And I thought my family was wealthy. Impressive."

After ringing the doorbell, Zadie was again surprised as a physically imposing man in a form-fitting black and gray private security uniform, complete with side arm in a shoulder holster, opened the door. He spoke with a southern drawl. "You must be Mrs. Zadie Springer."

"Yes, that's right."

Dimples appeared on both cheeks, softening his imposing impression. "Follow me, please."

It took a while to eventually reach a gazebo near a pool, complete with Romanesque statues and waterfall. She walked the final steps toward the chairwoman alone. "Liza, you have a lovely home."

Liza, dressed in comfortable white cotton shorts and top, remained seated, returning the warm greeting. "Thank you. It's been in the family for five generations. Please, join me."

As Zadie took her seat, a maid silently approached. "Would you like a refreshment, ma'am?"

"Water with lemon would be nice. Thank you."

As the woman turned on her heel and headed back into the house, the host's face brightened. "Speaking of generations, I'm so excited for you and Kade. Motherhood isn't always easy, but it's so rewarding."

Blushing, she told the truth, but not the whole truth. "Kade and I feel very lucky. It seems like the right time with both of our careers advancing. We couldn't be happier."

After a minute or so of chatting about morning sickness and cravings, the maid reappeared with Zadie's water. With her retreat to the house again, Liza switched from small talk to business. "Have you seen the stories about that singer, Gwen Blaze?"

Her comment was exactly as Zadie expected. "Yes, and I'm both surprised and confused. Everyone says she's talking as if she's carrying a designer baby. From the files you gave me on the Battle woman's case, I was under the impression that this is both an extremely difficult technical feat and also illegal in the US."

The tapping of Liza's fingers on the ornate wooden table signaled frustration. "You're absolutely correct... but there are ways to get around both."

Zadie's mind rushed, wondering how this information might impact her situation, however her voice remained as cool as the glass of water in her hand. "Ways? I don't understand."

"Our digital team has uncovered new evidence. Looking into past social media posts and hacking employment records, we've discovered that her husband once worked for the one and only, Dr. Cielo Chavez."

Just the sound of her name ran a chill up Zadie's spine. She quickly set the glass down so Liza wouldn't see it tremble. Genuine surprise masked her discomfort. "Interesting. So, more than one person can do this procedure?"

"It appears so, and that's going to complicate our PR campaign."

Professional training took over as Zadie suddenly felt comfortably in her element. "Maybe, but maybe not." Her voice brightened. "This could be an opportunity. One of the challenges of targeting the Battle woman was that no one knew her. We were going to be the ones to expose her to the world and rev up the outrage. With Gwen Blaze's huge public presence, she's already done most of the work for us. All we have to do is shine the light on her illegal and immoral act."

Liza cocked her head. "If only it were that simple. Remember, I mentioned there are ways around this. Word is that her husband did this all on his own, with no outside help. The law is very fuzzy on what you can and can't do to your own body. Her egg and his sperm belong to them, so it's not a black and white question."

"But you can't just tinker with the human genome. The court of world opinion is pretty united on that, and we can win that public relations fight with one hand tied behind our back." Zadie's brain felt fractured as she had just argued against her own unborn child.

"One would think." Liza shook her head. "The Battle woman will be a black and white fight. The fact that both Gwen Blaze and her husband carry the gene for Huntington's Disease, which would have surely been passed to this child, makes them a sympathetic case. The fact that she's a skilled social media influencer with a huge fan base will add to this challenge."

With her head swimming in a sea of divergent thought, unchecked words fell out. "Why does life have to be so damned hard?"

Liza's hand reached her in a second, seemingly unaware of what really triggered Zadie's outburst. "Don't worry. We've got allies. We can do this and ensure that those two designer babies will be the last ones. No one else will want to suffer through what we're going to do to those women."

Zadie's stomach turned and she lowered her head as she considered what would happen to her if the true nature of her pregnancy were revealed. She again told the truth, but not the whole truth. "I know, and I'll lead the charge. It's just that my hormones have swung like a pendulum these last few days."

Patting her hand, Liza spoke softly. "I remember those days. And you said your morning sickness was pretty bad as well."

Smiling, she replied, happy her subterfuge was working. "I'm told it often eases. How was it for you?"

Sitting tall, Liza seemed to revel in her motherhood story, oblivious to what was really happening right in front of her. "I was as sick as a dog for a big part of all four of my pregnancies, but I wouldn't trade my children for the world. Don't worry, dear. We'll handle Gwen Blaze, and you'll be blessed with a baby even more perfect than the one she carries."

Zadie nodded. *If you only knew.*

CHAPTER THIRTY-TWO

One by one, faces filled individual squares on the large monitor in Kristoff's office with their name and global location displayed below each of the other fourteen council members as they came online. To Ansen, the different ethnicities reminded him of a miniature United Nations, and the diversity reassured him the society really was a forward-thinking organization... at least that's what he desperately wanted.

With all present, Kristoff called the meeting to order. "We assemble today with mixed emotions. First, it is with profound sadness that we must mark the death of one of our own, Master Chojun Li."

Murmurings broadcast from multiple sites were punctuated with a declaration from Imka Nkosi, of South Africa. "Those reformers have gone too far. They must be brought into line and pay for what they've done."

Kristoff's voice cut like a sword through the chorus of jumbled online comments. "On that we all agree. Before we put the matter on the table for discussion, we have happy news as well. I wish to introduce the two new members joining us today." The feed from Zhengzhou China was enlarged, featuring a young face. "While we mourn the loss of Master Li, we are fortunate to have another able society member ready to step in and continue his legacy of strength and wisdom. Most of you already know Chan Fong, who studied under Master Li. Upon his elevation to this council, he will now be addressed as Master Fong.

Welcome Master Fong, we value the energy and insight that you bring to our body."

Chan bowed, then stared with tranquil dark brown eyes into the camera. "While the wish for revenge is natural and gnaws at me, I also know that were Master Li still among us he would counsel that eventual reunion with the reform movement is of paramount importance."

Nodding, Kristoff continued. "Well said, Master Fong." He now turned to Ansen. "It is also my pleasure to introduce Ansen Clayborn as a new member of our council. He is a direct descendent of George and Clarissa Clayborn, two of the founders of our society. It is of note that both he and Master Fong have been responsible for protecting Bree Battle's life in separate attacks from the reformers. Ansen, we value the bravery and understanding that you bring to our assembly."

Ansen noted the serenity Chan displayed and tried to match the solemnity. "I will do everything in my power to advance the goals of our society, and this council."

Smiling, Kristoff seemed pleased with both new member introductions. "We have two primary agenda items today, our response to the attempts on Bree Battle's life and the corresponding death of Master Li. We all understand these types of attacks can no longer be tolerated and action must be taken. The question is, how should we respond?"

Imka's words made her anger clear. "Master Li was one of the most beloved members of our society and I know that I speak for many who want a strong statement delivered to those terrorists. They have crossed a line and need to know that we mean business. I propose taking out one of their board members. That would get their attention."

From Sydney Australia, Charlotte Beckett joined the conversation. "That's certainly what they deserve, but to Master Fong's point, all of us still hold out hope that one day we can bring the two sides of our warring organization back together." Her short silver hair glistened on the screen as she continued. "If we eliminate one of them now, that day will be more distant than ever."

Ansen sat stone cold in shock, reigning in his outward expression as he watched these pillars of the society casually discuss the pros and cons of assassination.

With the range of responses beginning to form, Kristoff added new data. "At this time, I must inform you I have received new information that is so sensitive I cannot share it today, even on this secure line."

A bald man from Seattle, identified as Sameer Raj, laughed like a prankster. "Kristoff, you have more surprises than an episode of *Game of Thrones*. The last time you teased something like this, one of our members was selected to join the Board of the Federal Reserve."

The wisecrack loosened the mood of the virtual conference, causing Kristoff to chuckle. "I am glad you remember, Sameer. That proved very profitable to all of us, if you recall. And like then, I shared what I could until it was safe to reveal everything. I ask your same trust now."

Imka's hard gaze softened and curiosity seemed to replace the anger in her voice. "You are a man of mystery, Kristoff. What can you tell us without spilling the beans?"

Ansen had no idea what was going on as he watched the older man lean back and fold his hands, cocking his head jauntily as he spoke. "We have learned of a secret about a member of their board so destructive, that if made known could very well break their trust in each other." He paused, then grinned like a sly fox. "It is so damaging, that if leaked, might cause the entire structure of the reformed branch to implode."

Charlotte gleefully chimed in. "Finally, we have them by the short hairs. I'm tempted to recommend releasing the information and blow them up once and for all. In fact, why don't we do that?"

Mumbling from five continents seemed to agree with that response and Kristoff appeared to enjoy the momentary cacophony, until finally putting it to an end. "I share your desire to rid us of this civil war, but if we play this right, we can pull most of the reformers back into the fold. Often the threat of destruction can be just as effective as actually doing the deed, and a lot less bloody. Agreed?" He appeared to have made his point. "With your consent I propose to threaten them with their very destruction if they make a single move against Ms. Battle. Will you trust me and support this plan?"

Looking at the faces on the monitor, Ansen judged Kristoff had made his case. Casting his first ever council vote in favor, his guess was confirmed with unanimous support by the others.

Kristoff acknowledged the favorable vote. "Thank you for your faith in my decision, and I believe we will be rewarded for our patience. If not, then we pull the pin on our information grenade and witness the explosion that destroys them."

After the vote Charlotte asked a question Ansen didn't expect. "We have a lot invested in Bree Battle. Are you sure we can trust her? She's obviously got the lineage, but she's not a Tree of Life Society member and she already knows more than enough to cause a lot of trouble for us, if she wished."

Ansen listened carefully, not sure what to expect, but hoping it would be good for Bree.

Kristoff tilted his head. "It is a valid concern, but at this point I see no reason to worry. There has been a recruitment plan in place for some time and there is hope she may yet follow the path her parents wished. I will keep everyone informed, should events on the ground change."

The meeting moved on to mundane subjects until finally wrapping up in just over an hour's time. As everyone disconnected, Kristoff turned to Ansen. "What did you think of your first council meeting?"

With nerves still heightened, he ran a hand through his hair. "We had talked about the possibilities for retaliation against the reformers, but it was something else altogether to hear it discussed so nonchalantly. To hear open advocacy for killing one of their leaders was shocking."

"Interesting observation. This war has gone on so long with so many attacks and counter attacks that the level of violence no longer appalls us as much it should." He faced Ansen. "But we settled on the path that gives the reformers the choice to avoid bloodshed. If things escalate, it will be because of their decisions, not ours."

"I certainly liked that." His lips pursed. "You mentioned a plan in place for Bree. What's that about?"

With no hesitation, Kristoff replied. "There is a plan in place for every child of a society member, that's all I meant." His words were warm and seemed sincere. "The plan your father had brought you here, and her father's plan may yet yield the same result, but no matter what happens, she will be the one to ultimately decide."

Ansen couldn't sense deception, but in his gut, he felt there might be more to the story and that Kristoff wasn't in the mood to say more, so he moved on. "Alright." He changed the subject to another item of discussion on the call. "I know it's top secret, but can you share any more information on what you found out about the reformers?"

Kristoff chuckled. "I admire your curiosity, but it is best for all if that information remains hidden. I am guessing it will not stay secret for too long and the reformers may yet self-destruct, without the need for us to lift a finger."

CHAPTER THIRTY-THREE

Gwen and Ray waited in the green room just off stage of the Luke Rider show. They had chosen this late-night host as their first interview after the social media explosion that followed their baby announcement for two reasons. The first was because he had the highest rated show in this coveted time slot and would guarantee that they would have a wide audience. The second was more personal. Luke had been the first major host to book Gwen when her career was just taking off. She was a tough young woman from Fresno's wrong side of the track, and his public embrace of her music was an important boost to her meteoric career. Her flaws and psychic scars never seemed to bother him. He was a real fan and a good friend. She held Ray's hand. "Don't be nervous, you've met Luke. He's one of the good guys."

Ray rubbed his free hand slowly up and down his black jeans. "Hanging out with him at a Grammy after party is one thing, doing it on live TV is something else."

"Come on, pretend we're just talking to him on our patio." She laughed. "Loosen up and be yourself, everything will work out."

His worried look persisted. "That's easy for you to say. You've been on stage in front of millions of people, and done countless interviews. This is my first."

Thad, the spunky intern with a lock of electric blue hair, stuck his otherwise bleach blond head in the room. "Come on guys. Luke is finishing his monologue and you're the first guests. We'll wait in the wings."

She held Ray's hand and smiled as Luke introduced them while the band played the walk-in music. She looked up and spoke as they let the applause build. "I love you. You'll do great." They walked out and Gwen strutted in her thigh high black leather boots while rocking a matching Boho sweater dress. She waved to the raucous crowd which pushed the noise level through the roof. Happy in her element, she purposely gave an exaggerated rub of her stomach as she strode toward Luke. "I love my Blazers!"

He gave her a Hollywood kiss on the cheek before shaking Ray's trembling hand. "Great to see you two again."

They sat on the couch as the crowd continued to roar. Gwen stood and waved. "I love you all!"

Luke let her fans rain down their devotion as she again took her seat, until the applause finally subsided. He spoke in seeming jest. "Anything new with you guys?" Both Gwen and the host snickered as the audience laughed, while Ray sat frozen, like a stone gargoyle. Luke kept the banter going. "Seriously, congratulations on your fantastic news. A new baby on the way."

Gwen's face lit like a rising sun. "It fills my heart with joy. It's more than I ever could have imagined."

The positive energy from the crowd relaxed her, and when she glanced at Ray, even he seemed less tense. That expression didn't last long as Luke asked his first question. "Gwen, I've read your social media posts, and while you don't specifically say, it sounds an awful lot like you're carrying what might be called a 'Designer Baby.'"

The crowd that moments before had been as loud as a football stadium during the playoffs, was now quiet as a library. Gwen flicked her red hair. "Ray and I prefer to speak of Madeline as a Huntington Disease-free girl. As most of you probably read, Ray and I are both carriers who will almost certainly fall victims to this hideous disease. There was an extremely high probability that any child we had together would be born with the gene if we hadn't acted."

Luke's smile was as bright as the klieg lights onstage. "Oh, her name is going to be Madeline. That's so pretty. Is it a family name?"

Patting her husband's knee, her voice warmed. "We're naming her after Ray's mother. Huntington's took her when she was only thirty-seven years old."

The host touched his tie. "Wow. So young. You two have had it rough."

"That's the cloud that we've lived under for as long as we both can remember. What we did was new and radical, but would anyone here not do the same for their unborn child, if they could?"

Luke continued in amazement. "That's some crazy stuff. I heard a talking head on another network say that was both illegal and immoral. What do you have to say to that?"

Ray's frozen expression never changed as Gwen laughed. "You mean that blowhard, Larry Knewell?"

Smirking, Luke nodded. "The very same."

Feeling snarky, Gwen looked straight into the camera. "Larry Knewell can kiss my ass because he doesn't know what he's talking about!"

The crowd roared, seeming firmly on her side again as Luke interjected. "He says it's clearly illegal to implant genetically altered humans in this country, and immoral because it's playing God. Changing a human's genome, in this case Madeline's, without her consent."

As quickly as the crowd had roared moments ago, it was again as quiet as a cemetery. Gwen returned fire. "First of all, it's illegal to *hire* someone to do the procedure. We all have the right to do what we want with our bodies, right? And I happen to be married to someone with the brains and skill to do this himself. That's right. We built our own lab and Ray did it all. I married a winner didn't I, girls!"

The women in the audience responded wildly as Gwen waved her hands, egging them on. Luke seemed to revel in the energy of this segment, letting them go until they calmed on their own. "Ray, my man. You're setting the bar really high for the rest of us guys. I'm lucky if I can change the refrigerator light bulb. What am I supposed to do if my wife wants a baby girl with green eyes?"

Ray turned stiffly but seemed to surprise himself with a funny answer. "Luke, it's never too late to get started on your doctorate in genetic engineering." Laughter rained down on him, eliciting what looked like his first genuine smile of the evening.

Chuckling, Luke continued. "Okay, so much for the illegal part, Ray. What about the moral part? You're making choices that will impact the life of another human forever, and they have no say in the matter. What if you get something wrong?"

Nodding, Ray now appeared much more comfortable. "Let's take the easy part first. Every child has a chance of having something go quote 'wrong'. It could be either a physical impairment like Sickle Cell Anemia or a mental impairment like Downs Syndrome. People still make the choice to have children and love them regardless. I'm confident in my skills and really believe that Madeline will not be born with a genetic disorder, but even if that were to happen, we would love her just the same. We felt we had to take this chance, seeing so many members of our family fall prey to a disease that some describe as having Alzheimer's, Parkinson's and ALS, all at the same time."

Luke grimaced as clapping audience member's hands registered approval. "Sounds horrible. I'm beginning to understand. What about the other complaint? That you're making those, and other changes to Madeline without her consent?"

Ray's shoulders relaxed. "Let's be real for a moment, Luke. We're always trying to balance the scales in favor of our children. Women take folic acid prenatal supplements to prevent spina bifida. That's trying to give them a head start, isn't it? And we've all heard about exclusive preschools who accept children onto their waiting lists the day they're born. Again, parents doing what they think is best. We all know parents, or have been the children of parents who push their children into every activity. They want to give them enrichment experiences to perhaps help them get a college scholarship, or maybe in some cases, into the NBA. Did those young kids have much, or any, say in those situations?"

"You're hitting a little close to home there, Ray. I've got to get to the gym first thing in the morning to watch my six-year-old son's basketball team." Luke laughed. "He's the leading scorer, you know."

Now Ray laughed. "You see what I mean. Gwen and I decided on a few advantages we wanted for Madeline and are giving them to her in a new way."

"I'm starting to see where you're coming from. Say, who taught you how to do all this?"

Ray looked totally relaxed. "Dr. Cielo Chavez..." Only too late did he realize his slip. "I mean, I had lots of brilliant professors and I learned from all of them."

The banter continued for several more minutes, but Gwen handled all of the remaining questions. After coming off stage, Ray could barely stand. "I fucked up so bad out there."

Gwen was confused. "No, Ray. You rocked. Didn't you hear the crowd? They loved you."

"Gwen, I said her name on national television." His face was ashen. "Don't you understand? How could I do that to her?"

Flipping her hair, Gwen responded callously. "That's her problem. Besides, you said she drove everyone in the lab like Alaskan sled dogs. Why worry about her?"

He grabbed Gwen's shoulders. "All that's true. But she's also brilliant, and I learned more from her than the next ten professors combined. More importantly, she hung out with some really dangerous people, and with all that's going on, we don't need any more trouble."

Thad, the intern, interrupted. "You two were simply amazing. Follow me and I'll get you to your limo... unless you'd rather hang around and chat with Luke after the show."

She pointed in an exaggerated gesture, ready to move on with the evening. "To the limo!"

After getting into the back of the black car, Ray resumed. "I don't know what made me say that. What was I thinking?"

Gwen heard his complaint, but she was happy with the interview and that was all that mattered. "You were doing what I suggested, talking to Luke like you would at a party. Like I said, the crowd loved you, that's all that matters."

Looking through the tinted glass window on his side, Ray mumbled. "This is going to be bad."

She sighed loudly, frustrated that he wasn't focusing on her needs. "That might be true in the morning, but right now your problem is that I'm starved, so you need to get me to a restaurant. How about Umeda, on Melrose? I'm in the mood for Japanese tonight."

CHAPTER THIRTY-FOUR

Zadie chose a simple black blazer and skirt with a white blouse for her first time speaking in front of the board. She usually considered herself a confident presenter, but with the topic of her presentation today, she felt physically ill and considered calling in sick. With her run to the bathroom to throw up after the last meeting, she felt no one would question her absence. She wrestled with which path would give her the best chance at hiding her betrayal, and decided keeping appearances as normal as possible was her best course... if she could pull it off.

In her day job as an executive for a major PR firm, she had given countless ad campaign pitches for all kinds of products. The corners of her mouth tipped upward as she remembered pitching an ad for a home space-heater with the image of snowballs melting in hell. It was just weird enough to win the account. Her smile disappeared as she looked around the table at the powerful members of the Reformed Tree of Life board. Liza took a seat signaling it was time to begin. Zadie clicked a button on the hand-held remote revealing a photo of Gwen Blaze in concert before tens of thousands of adoring fans. She caught her breath, then began. "This is our target."

There was no side talk as they stared at the image of one of the most famous people in the world. Even those members who hadn't listened to pop music in years knew her face from countless magazine covers and TV appearances. She advanced to the next slide showing a shot of Gwen, and her husband Ray's, appearance on the *Luke Rider Show*. "As you all saw or heard, earlier this week they appeared on this late-night show and confirmed that they are indeed expecting a quote 'Designer Baby."

Jim Campbell interrupted before the next PowerPoint slide appeared. "The husband said he learned it from that Frankenstein, Dr. Chavez. If more people know how to do this procedure, the battle is already over."

"Thanks for the lead in to my next point, Jim." An image of a sterile looking lab filled the screen. "As many of you might recall, the skills and knowledge to do this are already available around the world. What's keeping it contained are strong laws and public unease at tinkering with what it means to be human. These are the very same sentiments that have been forcefully expressed in this room. This performance by Ms. Blaze and her husband gives us a golden opportunity to work behind the scenes to make their lives a living hell. After we're finished, no other woman would dare to follow in their footsteps."

Zadie looked around the table and knew she had them in the palm of her hand, the thrill of doing what she did best propelling her. She caught a glimpse of Liza, seeming pleased, and proceeded in confidence, her silky black hair swishing as she turned back to the screen. "Our campaign will have three main prongs." She clicked again and a bullet point was added. *Religious Groups*. "The Right to Life movement is deeply embedded into American culture and can amass an immediate response, the likes of which perhaps only the NRA can match. The Catholic Church has a long-established stance against genetic engineering of humans based in part on the fact that some embryos are used while others are destroyed. I've worked with Liza to develop a set of talking points for distribution to all flavors and stripes of the movement. We can help frame this as a procedure that is immoral and the equivalent of man playing God."

Liza spoke supportively. "These groups have a lot of clout and are already up and running. Our efforts will cost us almost nothing, keep our fingerprints hidden and prove highly effective in throwing at least a scare into any other woman who might consider this path. What's next, Zadie?"

The next slide appeared with the caption, *Inequality*. "In our country and around the world, groups focus on different kinds of inequality." Sub points loaded as she continued. "There's economic inequality, social inequality, racial inequality, etc. Human gene editing plays right into these kinds of discrimination. Let's talk about economic inequality. For a long time, only the rich would be able to afford this technology if it were to become generally available. Do you think these groups are going to stand quietly by and let that happen? It will make Operation Wall Street look like a children's play date. We'll anonymously arm these organizations with ideas and talking points, suggesting Gwen Blaze be the first target of their rage. Can you imagine how protests outside her home... or her concerts will be covered?"

Positive murmurs and nods began, fueling her as she clicked again. *Politicians* appeared on the following slide. "Our society has donated generously to legislators on both sides of the aisle in this country, and around the world. It's time we quietly call in favors. We will ask they call the Blaze woman out by name when introducing new 'Designer Baby' regulations. Imagine the 'Gwen Blaze Genome Ethics Law.' Penalties must include lengthy prison terms as well as debilitating fines. What company executive or university leader would want to subject themselves or their organizations to these kinds of consequences? None that I can think of." She sat the clicker down and opened the floor. "What questions or concerns might you have?"

Jim spoke up again. "That's quite an impressive presentation, and I admit I feel better about the Blaze woman. But what about Bree Battle? How do we fight that?"

Zadie's face warmed, the thrill of winning the moment was intoxicating. "Jim, you and I think a lot alike, and Liza and I had almost the exact same conversation earlier. The Blaze woman actually helps us in that campaign as well. No one besides us has ever heard of her, but the heat and noise of the Gwen Blaze operation will consume Bree Battle when we choose to make her case known. This is also where we can tar and feather Dr. Cielo Chavez." She spoke with the fervor of the true believer she had been just a few weeks ago. "If done correctly, we can burn all of them to the ground in the court of public opinion. We hold almost all of the PR cards." A satisfied expression seemed to return from Jim, so Zadie wrapped up her comments. "I'm very confident that this campaign will achieve our results. I'll keep everyone abreast of actions and any adjustments we might make as the plan's execution progresses. I'll now turn it over to our chairwoman."

Liza rose as Zadie headed to her seat. Her sophisticated gray jacket with black lapels and pocket flaps over a shimmering silk blouse complemented her firm speech. "This is why I stand here today instead of Benjamin Brown. This approach doesn't end in botched assassination attempts and dead operatives. This approach keeps us hidden while others do the dirty work. This approach means we won't be killing members of the other branch of our society, leaving open the chance for a future return to fellowship." She paused, her voice taking a more serious tone. "It's also the way we need to proceed if we want to avoid a war with the originals."

Ezra Slaughter spoke for the first time since Ben's departure. "Sounds like you have news."

Liza's shoulders squared. "I received a call from Kristoff Svoboda this morning."

Grumbling bubbled around the table as Ezra replied. "What is the bully promising now? Whose company is he threatening to bankrupt?"

"No one's. It's a blackmail threat." Red fingernails drummed on the table for a moment. "He says he has information on one of our members... information that if exposed would completely destroy the reformed movement from the inside."

Zadie's eyes widened but she remained as still as a statue, thankful that all looks turned toward Ezra's snarling rebuttal. "Those cowards. I think most of the time they are bluffing. Did he give you any hints about this so-called explosive information? If not, I suggest we call their bluff."

Jim Campbell tilted his head. "Don't be so sure, Ezra. It was their meddling that held up my son's admission to Harvard a few years back. And that was just a disagreement over some mineral rights in Borneo. And remember Brenda Collins? They bankrupted her accounting firm after she brought a law suit against one of their members. We've fired real bullets at their members and thanks to Ben's foolishness, accidentally killed Master Li. Anymore slip ups like that and I'm sure we'll pay a hefty price."

The chairwoman brought the conversation back to the subject at hand. "They only demand that we stay away from the Battle woman, so there will be no more talk of armed attacks against her. Not only have they failed, they've made things worse. Ben and his old ways have run their course. These modern ways worked for the originals when they destroyed eugenics, and they will work for us as well. Let's give a warm round of applause to Zadie for spearheading this initiative."

Her blush was complete. Not from humility, but because her mind was already racing. Wheels turning as she began trying to figure out how she was going to keep her secret and not become the third target of the plan she had just presented. She felt an overwhelming sense of shame swallowing her, like some prehistoric animal being pulled down into the La Brea Tar Pit. But she maintained a poker face, covering her lie with words she no longer meant. "I hope those women get what they deserve."

CHAPTER THIRTY-FIVE

Ben Brown sipped fine bourbon whiskey in the muted light of his library, the cherry paneling giving the room a faint reddish glow. His thoughts drifted as he waited on the arrival of Ezra Slaughter. *I wish everyone had a name that both identified and described them.*

There was a knock on the door as Mrs. Bartley, the housekeeper, introduced the visitor. "Mr. Slaughter to see you, sir."

Placing his whiskey on a soft stone coaster as he stood, Ben greeted his guest. "Thanks for coming, Ezra." He extended his ham hock of a hand. "I know it's a risk."

Steel blue-gray eyes warmed. "I was glad to hear from you. We have much to discuss."

"Care for a drink? It's fifteen-year-old Pappy Van Winkle."

An appreciative grin accompanied the reply. "That's special, don't mind if I do. Are we celebrating something?"

Ben carried the bottle back, then handed Ezra a tumbler. "Perhaps. It depends on how our conversation goes, but either way, only the best for my true friends. I appreciate your vote of dissent on my ouster." He ambled to his chair. "So, how is the board, now that I'm gone?"

"It's not the same. You were the patriarch for the last ten years and your absence has left a gaping hole, as far as I'm concerned."

Nodding at the kind words, Ben continued his slow interrogation. "And after the Blaze woman's revelations? Did that shake them up? Have others begun to see things as I do?"

Ezra glanced at his glass then took his first sip. "This is the best bourbon I've ever tasted." Firm resolve seemed to take the place of earlier warmth. "Unfortunately, no. Liza has them convinced that an underground PR campaign led by Zadie will win the day."

"I see. But you and I know better, don't we?"

A hardened gaze returned, and his words punched. "I understand why Zadie might feel that way could work. She's young, and in the PR business, I get it. But Liza? She infuriates me. By closing her eyes to the danger right in front of us, she's endangering everything our society stands for." He took another sip. "There's more news, Ben. The originals threatened us over the armed actions we've taken. They say they have information that will destroy us from the inside if we don't back off."

"Do you believe them?"

"Hell no. I remember the era when might made right and we fought them straight up. We won some and lost some, but it everything was out in the open. They've all gone soft, like over-ripe avocados. Our board, the originals, every single one of them. Why can't Liza see the immense risk she's taking by not immediately ending this threat... once and for all... even if the originals do try something. Our ancestors may have done some objectionable things, but at least they weren't afraid to make bold moves when they felt it was the right thing to do. This board has the backbone of an octopus."

The venom in Ezra's words hung in the air like a poisonous fog as Ben agreed. "My point exactly. As I see it, you and I have two choices. We can watch over six hundred years of planning and work wither on the vine of an incompetent board... or we can take matters into our own hands."

Ezra sat up straight. "I'm listening."

Huge fingers drummed on the oversized desk as he unveiled a plan. "I say we run a parallel operation... just you and me, and a few of our most trusted contractors. The Blaze woman is always out in the open, so I say we target her. That shouldn't concern the originals."

A knowing nod preceded Ezra's words. "It's risky for me as a current board member, but I like the way you're thinking. We'll lose everything that we've worked for if we don't do something." He finished his drink. "And if all goes the way we plan, you'll be hailed as the true visionary that you are. Power hungry Liza will be out, and you'll be back as patriarch."

"I like the way you're thinking, my friend. It's time for true patriots to lead the society back to our roots." He refilled their tumblers, then raised his in a robust toast. "To the greater good."

CHAPTER THIRTY-SIX

Morning light streamed through the windows of Bree's suite at Kristoff's estate. She rolled away and pulled the sheet over her head, wishing she had closed the curtains tighter. A knock on the door added aggravation. "Go away. Pregnant woman sleeping!"

Instead of stopping, the knocking grew louder, followed by Ansen's familiar voice. "Bree, it's me. Kristoff needs to talk to us. Something about Gwen Blaze and another baby. He says it's serious."

"What?" The sheets were reluctantly pushed back. "Say that again."

"There's news of another designer baby. It's Gwen Blaze, and Kristoff says he needs to talk to us. Can you be ready for breakfast in fifteen minutes?"

She rubbed her eyes, removing the crust of accumulated sleep. 'Yeah... sure. Better make it twenty. I don't think I'll be moving very fast this morning."

"Alright. I'll be back in twenty minutes and we'll walk down together."

Stumbling, she made her way to the bathroom, startling herself in the mirror. She turned sideways to get the full effect. "Jeez. I really am full on prego." The sharpest kick she had yet felt confirmed her diagnosis. "Whoa there, little man. How about waiting until I'm all the way awake." Her eyes caught her reflection again. Hair a mess, frumpy PJ's and a protruding stomach. "You're sure a sight." After a full fifteen seconds of staring at her changing body, Bree let out an uncertain breath. "I guess it's time to also talk to Svoboda about his plans for me and my baby. I need to make some kind of deal to have a bit of freedom without getting assassinated, if that's even possible. And what's Gwen Blaze gone and done?"

Splashes of water on her face, dabs of makeup, and a brush through her hair satisfied her that she was at least presentable. A dig through the closet delivered a pair of stylish distressed maternity jeans and a striped button-up blouse. "I really have to give props to whoever went shopping. They have a great eye, except for those old lady PJ's."

The knock came right on time. Exiting the room, her eyes lit seeing her ex looking better than ever, triggering a smile that pushed her grumpiness far away. "Good morning, Ansen. Any idea what's up with that singer?"

As they began the long walk to breakfast, he pulled out his phone and turned up the volume as he prepared to replay the Luke Rider late night interview from a couple days ago. "While we were high tailing it out of China, she was making news." He hit play and held the device out as they continued along. When it finished, he slid the phone in his pocket. "What do you make of that?"

Before she could answer they rounded the last corner and saw Kristoff. "Good morning," he said. "I hope you both found your accommodations adequate."

"That is the most comfortable bed I've ever slept on," Bree gushed. "Made it really hard to get up this morning."

Their host nodded. "We do our best. And sorry about the early start, but unexpected news has arrived."

The smile on Bree's face disappeared. "Ansen showed me the video from the television interview. That was some kind of crazy."

Ansen's eyes drew together. "My only thoughts are about what this means for Bree. Does it make her more, or less safe? Is it good or bad for us that Gwen Blaze is being so public about what she's doing? Is Bree still safe here?"

Kristoff's lip curled slightly. "This is why we need to talk. The actions those two have taken changes everything. Please, sit." He winked at Bree. "We will all think better on full stomachs."

In the morning light, his kindly face and advancing age made Bree think he must be someone's grandfather, and wishing she had known hers better. "I was never a girl to turn down a meal." She rubbed her stomach. "Even more so now." The smell of cheese and chives being folded into omelets competed with the scent of warm maple syrup being poured over waffles.

After breakfast, Kristoff deposited his napkin on the empty plate. Silent wait staff swooped in and removed the dirty dishes in hushed service. With small talk concluded about the food, meeting the Randall's and Schulz's last night and, the stunning view, they turned to the topic of the morning. "It would seem that you are not alone in carrying an enhanced child."

Hearing it phrased that way again caused Bree to cringe, a bitter taste in her mouth. "It sounds like she at least had a choice in the matter."

A tilt of the head preceded Kristoff's answer. "Perhaps. But as I understand, she, like you, felt there was no other option. As she describes it, she did what she believed she had to do to have a baby not condemned to death before it was even born."

"Still, it wasn't like she had a gun to her head, like I did." Unfocused tension coursed through her body. *I have to let go of this anger. It's not doing me... or my baby boy any good. It's not just about me anymore, so I have to focus on getting answers.* "Do you think this makes it better or worse for me?"

"Probably a little of both. We have another council member here, let us get his thoughts."

Ansen visually startled. "What? Are you talking to me?"

"Yes. I always listen to the wisdom of my peers. You are a council member, so I seek your understanding and advice."

His cheeks brightened and he spoke with a small quiver in his voice. "I'm still getting used to this council member thing." He smiled nervously. "My first thought is that this major scientific advancement... the ability and willingness to actually move forward with a genetically modified human can only draw worldwide focus to the process. If Bree's..." He paused, searching for the right word. "...*condition* becomes public, things would get worse in a matter of hours." He glanced at Kristoff, seeming to look for agreement. "Right?"

A single head nod accompanied his answer. "Agreed. And what positives may come of the Blaze woman's disclosure?"

Bree stepped in as Ansen appeared to ponder his answer. "For now, she will be the center of all debate on this controversial subject. From what I can tell, she is a master of social media and can call on legions of followers to immediately level the playing field in the area of public opinion. Should my... condition... become known, I wouldn't be alone. I would have an instant ally."

A gleam flashed in Kristoff's eyes. "You are as smart as advertised. I completely agree with your assessment." The pride in her seemed short lived as he voiced new concern. "And that brings us to the biggest danger for all of us."

Before he could finish, Bree interrupted. "The one and only Dr. Cielo Chavez."

Kristoff bowed. "Her name was said aloud on national television." His head rose slowly and his eyes turned toward the vineyard in the distance. "She is the nexus of everything. She connects to Gwen Blaze through the singer's husband. She connects directly to Bree and to the Tree of Life Society. And most importantly, she could be criminally liable."

As a practicing attorney, Bree filled in the blank. "And with the right legal pressure applied, she could flip on all of us. She might strike a deal with prosecutors to spare herself prison time if she tells all she knows and supports it up with documentation. I would be exposed, as well as the society. She and I don't have the friendliest relationship, but I don't want her put in the same kind of 'back against the wall' position I was in."

"She's always lived up to her vows, so I do not think she would ever tell a soul, but if she did, a secret kept for over six hundred years could be exposed in a matter of minutes." Kristoff's face looked pale as his far-away gaze continued. "I know this is relatively new to both of you, but we have members in governments and corporate boardrooms around the world." He sat silently for a moment as both Ansen and Bree left him with his thoughts. He turned to them. "And while Bree has her life tied to this project, thousands of others could be destroyed as well. Governments could fall, wars might start. There is no predicting the fallout. We cannot let that happen."

Bree relaxed, her hand laying easily on her baby bump. "I'm all for that. What do we need to do?"

Kristoff now leaned back as well. "Dr. Chavez is a society member and we will protect her at all costs. First, the lab in Peru must be destroyed. Too much physical evidence there, and since her name is now public, it becomes a high-profile target for both profiteers and our enemies." He stroked his chin. "And... we will have a fiery new breakfast companion by this time tomorrow."

Flinching, Bree shot a hard glance. "I'm assuming you still have a firing range. I want to get in a little practice before she gets here."

CHAPTER THIRTY-SEVEN

The limousine crept up Manhattan's Sixth Avenue in heavy evening traffic on the way to the headquarters of the twenty-four-hour cable news channel, CBN. As the car neared their destination the occupants caught their first look at a swarm of protesters. It was very similar to those that they had been dealing with anytime they dared go out in public. Tonight, an equally large group of Blazers were also on hand, in a shouting match with their ideological foes. Gwen Blaze rubbed the back of her neck as she stared out the tinted window. "Why can't the world just get along?" She spoke as much to herself as to Ray.

Ray held her other hand as his leg nervously tapped. "I'm afraid that's never going to happen, and after tonight, things may only get worse. Are you sure you want to do this interview after what you said about him on Luke's show?"

The hand that had been rubbing the tense muscles in the back of her neck now slid over her rapidly expanding bump. A lilt added energy and light to her words. "I called him a blowhard and said he could kiss my ass." She snorted. "Wonder if he'll bring it up tonight?"

His head shook. "Do you ever take anything seriously? Larry Knewell isn't just some late-night talk show host hoping to get laughs from the audience. He interviews presidents and senators. We can tell the driver to keep going and skip this whole mess. It would be better to have him bad mouth us as a no-show than to say something that just makes things worse."

That comment was like a match to a fuse, and in seconds the explosion occurred. "Fuck that, Ray! I'm proud of what you did. What *we* are doing." She yanked her hand away from his, mad he still didn't see the situation the same way as her. "I'm going to go in there and defend Madeline, even before she's born. That's what a mother does. What kind of life can she have if we act afraid or show shame?"

Ray lowered his head. "I'm not ashamed... you know that. There's just a case to be made for laying low. Everything in our life doesn't have to play out on center stage."

Before she could answer, the car came to a complete stop and the driver's voice spoke through the intercom. "We've arrived at your destination."

Thick glass muffled the shouts and screams from the assembled mass of humanity on the other side. When the valet opened the door, the cascade of voices rushed into the luxurious cabin, like invisible energy, recharging the singer. A hand reached inside to assist her exit, ushering her into a cordoned walkway, with Blazers on one side and protesters on the other. Ray followed close behind, but Gwen was already at the rope signing autographs and taking selfies with adoring fans, seemingly oblivious to the nasty chants from the other side. He dutifully trailed behind her, mumbling, "That's my wife alright." He glanced around as cameras and cellphones snapped pictures from every angle. "And this is our life."

At that moment, an object whizzed in front of him, hitting Gwen's hip. She screamed as security guards simultaneously rushed them inside as others tackled the assailant. Once in the lobby, she examined her cheetah print gown and was pissed. Language from her tough upbringing spewed. "Shit, Ray. Look at my fucking dress! Those dickheads have no class."

He picked bits of tomato from the silky material. "It's not that bad, really. I'll bet they have something in the dressing room to make this disappear."

A shimmering golden stiletto heel extended, opening the thigh high slit in the evening gown. She stepped determinedly toward the bank of elevators. "Remind me to send the dry-cleaning bill to CBN. Now, get me upstairs."

As promised, a magic spray was applied to the fabric and the remaining stain disappeared. The wait in the green room was short, and in no time, they were seated on a couch beside Larry Knewell during a commercial break. He smiled. It was the same smile Gwen had seen on TV whether he was interviewing a politician, celebrity or serial killer. She felt he was a real pro because she could never tell when he was sincere, or when he was full of bullshit.

There were several more seconds showing on the clock before they would go live as he unofficially welcomed her. "It's a pleasure to meet you, and welcome to *Rare Air*. I'm a big fan."

It seemed an appropriate name for the show as Gwen felt herself in a rare mood tonight. "Really? Then it's about damned time you had me on. Stella McGuinn has been here twice."

The line of his lips turned upward on the ends as he rubbed his hands. "We're going to make history tonight."

Jared counted down the return from the commercial break. "In five-four-three-two-one."

The camera seemed to love Larry, and he appeared equally in love with himself. "Welcome back to *Rare Air*. It's a real pleasure to welcome my first guests. Gwen Blaze has just concluded her two-year *Why Me?* world tour. The show set records for highest overall gross as well as most costume changes per show while the hit song of the same name has spent thirty-eight weeks, and counting, at the top of the pop charts. Welcome, Gwen."

With no admiring studio audience, Gwen turned her charm toward the camera, blowing kisses. "I love you, Blazers! You're the best in the world!"

The camera now turned to Ray. "Joining Gwen this evening is her apparent rockstar of a scientist husband, Ray Manza. Welcome, Ray."

A stiff half-wave returned to the host with an equally stiff reply. "Glad to be here, Larry."

Leaning in, Larry wasted no time. "Gwen, while the tour was a huge success, you've managed to pull off an even bigger feat. You and Ray are simultaneously on the covers of *Time, Cosmo,* and *Scientific American.* That trifecta has never been achieved. Does all of this publicity surprise you?"

Her hand conspicuously rubbed her enlarged stomach. "I love it, Larry. Ray and I have done something special and I think the world needs to know and understand our decision. I'm honored to grace those covers."

A light caught the host's eye in a twinkle. "Just to be clear, Gwen. What you've done is create a genetically modified embryo that you are now carrying. I reported on this last week and you called me... let me get this right." He glanced down at a note. "Here it is... 'a blowhard' and said I could quote 'kiss your ass.' Virtually every scientist on the planet agrees with me when I say that the procedure is both illegal and immoral."

A bold swipe with her hand signaled her disagreement, and her energy level ramped up. "We've addressed all this before, Larry. We feel it would be immoral to bring a child, and her name is Madeline by the way, into this world doomed to develop a fatal disease if we have the ability to prevent it. Ray did everything himself, so there's no reason for law enforcement to be involved."

"But you're playing God. You're pushing technology to its limits without understanding all of the possible unintended consequences."

Gwen was about to answer when Ray interrupted, his voice defiant. "That's the way science works, Larry. Three hundred years ago surgery was considered by most to be playing God. Cutting open a human body and tinkering with organs to save the patient, rather than letting God's will prevail. Now there are over forty-eight million life-saving surgeries per year in the US. What we're doing only seems radical because it's new."

A head tilt by Larry met that comment as Gwen sat back smiling admiringly, watching Ray at his best, defending her and their baby. She considered herself a street fighter and saw in him as an equal, although different, kind of fighter. He was the partner she had searched for her entire life.

Larry continued his grilling. "I get the Huntington's Disease edit that you made, I really do. But you didn't stop there. It's rumored that you've engineered her to have a singing voice like Gwen... and let me put this as delicately as possible. It's been reported that she will have very impressive physical measurements. How can you defend that?"

Her relaxed pose didn't last long, and her words were as sharp as daggers as she jumped back into the clash. "You're a man, so you probably wouldn't understand. There were over 300,000 breast augmentation surgeries in the US last year, so it's not exactly weird for a woman to want big boobs. We just took care of that ahead of time."

Larry appeared riled up. "If this kind of thing is allowed, where will it end? Glow in the dark skin? Three eyes? There would be no end to what people would imagine. What you're doing is changing what it means to be human!"

A fire seemed to burn inside Ray. "You think all this is new? With DNA sequencing technology, science has discovered that modern humans contain an average of two percent Neanderthal DNA. How do you think that happened? Over in Australia, three to five percent of Aboriginal DNA is from another extinct hominid branch called the Denisovans. Think about that for a moment. One way or another, we've been changing what it means to be human for a very long time."

Nostrils flaring, Larry switched tacks. "Even if all of that is true, it's still wrong. Only the very rich, or someone like Ray with extremely advanced skills, could give those kinds of advantages to their offspring. It's classism at its worst."

"Come on, Larry. That's not how scientific advancement spreads, and you know it. Today you can buy a CRISPR gene editing kit online for personal use. Self-experimentation is already happening! There's a guy out there using CRISPR trying to cure himself of AIDS. This technology is here and no one will be able to stop it from reaching every corner of the globe."

Larry picked up his small stack of notes, straightening them. "While you make compelling arguments, millions disagree with you. The Catholic church has taken a strong stand, as well as other Right to Life groups, and most governments. Your views are clearly in the minority."

Throwing his hands up, Ray replied. "The Church? The same one who banned human autopsies for almost eight hundred years as defiling a human body? They significantly slowed scientific discovery in medicine, only to later change their minds? That Church? They should stick to matters of faith and leave science to the scientists."

"And governments? They regulate all manners of different sciences and medical devices. They clearly have a say in this."

Ray fell back with a heavy sigh. "Maybe for now. I'm not here to advocate for a world consensus on this issue. I'm here to advocate for Madeline, our soon-to-be-born, Huntington's Disease-free baby girl. I just want the world to leave us alone."

Larry turned to a new subject, toning down his hostility. "I understand there was an incident outside our building this evening."

Gwen reengaged, still angry over the incident. "Someone hit me with a rotten tomato! After all we've been through it scared me to death."

An understanding nod preceded Larry's words. "I hear you've been dealing with some serious threats."

The usually flamboyant singer slumped, suddenly feeling the weight of the recent weeks on her shoulders. "It's been vicious, Larry. My life has been threatened by gunfire, stabbing and explosives, just to name a few more common ways of killing a pregnant woman." Gwen looked directly into the camera, pleading. "Please, whoever's out there and against what we've done, see me as a human. Please see me as a woman who wants to have a healthy baby. Please see my child, Madeline, as an innocent. We mean you no harm, and ask the same from you." Tears welled and began gently falling.

Larry seemed to recognize the moment as a ratings bonanza and let the pause linger. After a long silence he reached for her hand before turning to the camera. "To my millions of viewers, I ask that you hear this woman's pleas. I'm here to ask the hard questions, but not to judge. It is clear to me that anyone who advocates for protecting human life can't at the same time advocate for harming a woman and her unborn child."

Gwen sensed Ray move closer, placing his arm securely around her shoulders. "Thanks, Larry. Maybe you're not such a blowhard after all."

CHAPTER THIRTY-EIGHT

The lighting in Ben's library had been dimmed. He and Ezra stared intently into a monitor receiving video from California. Having conducted numerous operations as a younger man, the start of a mission always got his blood pumping. He glanced at Ezra with a gleam in his eye. "I wish I were there with them."

Callan McDougal spoke low, his voice transmitted to a team of four other commandos as well as back to Ben and Ezra. "The subjects were observed entering the home at twenty-one hundred hours. Surveillance has established there is a protection detail of four armed guards, as expected." He turned his head side to side, providing a video view for his benefactors in Atlanta. "We are a go on your orders."

A quick look was exchanged, then Ezra confirmed. "You have a green light. Repeat, green light."

The video jostled as Callan took his final position prior to the assault. Ben raised his whiskey glass. "Finally. We begin ridding the world of this disease before the infection spreads."

In a coordinated blitz the attack began with ruthless efficiency. Two of the attackers came around a hedge and four quick shots later, the guard at the end of the driveway fell. They then charged toward the house before taking cover behind a short retaining wall on the terraced lawn. Shots rained down on them from another guard on higher ground. "Team leader, Echo One and Two drawing fire at site two."

"Keep their attention as we secure the location."

"Affirmative." Echo One and Two took turns holding their guns inches above the wall, firing potshots as a diversion as the return fire chipped away at the brick atop the low berm.

A burst of automatic weapon fire ended the threat and Callan relayed the update. "Site two secured. Guard two neutralized. Proceed to site three."

Echo One and Echo Two resumed their ascent of the sloped driveway. "Front door in sight. Floodlights now on and movement observed inside." A bullet ricocheted off the concrete driveway, a chip hitting Echo One in the leg. A second round found a home in Echo Two's arm. They scrambled to find cover, lying flat behind a car parked in the driveway. "Echo Two injured. Repeat, Echo Two injured."

Another spray of bullets crackled in the dry night air as Callan announced the update. "Guard three neutralized. Echo Two, can you self-evacuate to the rendezvous zone?"

"Affirmative. I'll be waiting."

The news reached Atlanta milliseconds later. Ben rubbed his thumb over the side of his bent index finger repeatedly. "I was hoping for no casualties this time."

The assault continued in California as Callan's feed streamed. "Charges set on the front door." A small explosion obliterated it and the remaining four members of the squad entered the mansion.

A spray of bullets slowed them down momentarily as female screams from deep within the home joined the chaotic noise. Ben yelled at the screen. "That's her! Go!"

An RPG fired by Echo One exploded in the general vicinity of the last guard on the property, ending the armed resistance and filling the huge domed entrance with dust and the haze of charred wood mixed with gunpowder. Callan's voice carried over the wireless network. "Split up. Find the woman and terminate on sight. Repeat, terminate on sight." Climbing over the rubble, the team spread through the house like a swarm of angry bees seeking their target.

They heard the female voice again. "Go, Ray! Go!"

Callan adjusted his course mid-stride. "Target confirmed." Just as he entered the master bedroom, he caught a glimpse of … what?

A shrill female voice screamed. "Hit the button!"

"Fuckkkkk!" Callan's curse echoed as the wall seemed to pivot and seal shut. He raised his weapon and held the trigger for ten seconds, firing over a hundred rounds into the facing wall.

Ben's voice filled the team's ears as they all entered the room with Callan. "What the hell's going on?"

Lowering his weapon, a dejected reply beamed back to Georgia. "Panic room. They have a damned panic room."

"Jeez! Why can't we catch a break in killing these women! Fire another RPG."

"If their room is even halfway up to snuff, all we'll do is give them a headache." His words drifted back to Atlanta with a faint whiff of defeat. "Here goes nothing."

The team took cover on the other side of the door as Callan launched a round. The deafening explosion resulted in concrete chips, dust and smoke billowing out of the confined space. Callan peeked in through the smoke, seeing what he seemed to expect. "It would take all night to break through, and we don't have time on our side."

Echo Two chimed in from the rendezvous location. "Flashing lights headed up the canyon."

Callan hung his head, his voice clothed in dejection. "Echo team heading toward ex-fill. Mission aborted."

The monitor went dark in Ben's library as the two men sat quietly, each taking a long swig of fine bourbon. Ben set his empty tumbler down softly on the coaster. "Is it just me, or did it seem a lot easier to kill our enemies in the old days?"

CHAPTER THIRTY-NINE

The Reformed Tree of Life emergency board meeting had been called to order with the attack on Gwen Blaze as the primary topic. Zadie always thought Jim Campbell could have been the model on which all other Credit Union Directors should look and sound like. He always wore a conservative nondescript suit, and his diagonal striped ties were always backed by starched white cotton button downs. The always polished leather shoes grounded his center lane style. Today, he had the task of reporting what was known and what had yet to be understood about the attempt on the singer's life.

Standing, he spoke in a low, raspy voice. "Last night at nine-thirty pacific time, a coordinated attack was launched at the Malibu estate of Gwen Blaze and her husband. Four of their security personnel were killed, and reports are that automatic weapons and grenade launchers were used by the assailants. Nothing was taken from the home, so it is presumed this was an assassination attempt. Had they not secretly installed a state-of-the-art panic room, they would surely be dead."

From the head of the table, Liza questioned. "Do the police have any ideas on who perpetrated the attack?"

"Not yet. We have a source in the department who says that blood was found on the scene, presumably from one of the attackers. They're running DNA analysis, but so far no matches."

Removing her glasses, Liza's tone sounded conspiratorial. "And do *we* have any idea as to the identity of the assailants?"

Jim nodded. "We have some suspects. As you know, we normally employ our own teams for sensitive operations. But there are times when using independent contractors is in our best interest. Word on the dark web is that an independent operator, with whom we've worked in the past, is involved."

"I see. And any ideas who contracted him for this job?"

His head lowered. "No concrete proof, but we have a suspect in mind." He exhaled a shaky breath. "I'm saddened, but not surprised to report that Ben Brown's name has surfaced in connection with this operation. If so, then he's gone rogue."

Zadie scanned the other members faces, trying to gauge their reaction to the news. Most looked sad, two seemed shocked, but one member wore a curious smirk that she could only interpret as pleased. Hearing her name called by Liza, Zadie stood, ready to give her update. "It goes without saying the events of last night complicate our PR campaign against Ms. Blaze."

Glancing at her audience she saw hard stares turn toward her significantly expanded pregnancy. *They know... or will soon.* She swallowed hard, trying to contain growing panic, then continued as calmly as she could. "Our goal was to build a wave of public disgust at what she's doing, and as we hoped, it's been working. The big turnout of protesters at CBN headquarters the other night was only one example of the anger that, until now, had been growing against her. The last thing we needed was to give her a platform to garner sympathy."

Liza quizzed. "How's it playing so far? Is that what's happening?"

Thank God. All about business... not about me. "Unfortunately, yes. She looked shaken and terrified in the video of police and firefighters escorting her and her husband from their bullet ridden and bombed-out home. That image alone undid much of what we had accomplished. A large segment of the public may be against what she did, but almost no one wants to see that level of carnage directed at an expectant mother, who also happens to be someone they feel like they know through her music."

Jim's brow wrinkled. "Then what's our next step? She still needs to be stopped, or at least demonized so that others won't want to follow her path."

"Agreed. Having said that I would suggest temporarily pulling back on our agitation of groups directly opposed to her. Social justice and pro-life groups still have campaigns in place, so we can focus on other, less visible avenues. What happened to her can help us in behind the scenes lobbying to get state and federal laws fortified, both here and around the world. Stricter laws will be a key part of preventing any future attempts to create designer babies." Zadie hated what she was about to say, but she was good at her job and needed all the cover she could get to keep her secret. "Then, after a few weeks of relative calm, we can crank the heat back on her personally, making her life a living nightmare."

Heads nodded as Jim again spoke. "And what of Ben? What if he makes another attempt on the woman's life?"

Zadie's eyes locked with Liza as she took her seat. "That's above my pay grade, so I defer to our chairwoman."

The only sound in the room was the whoosh of the air-conditioning, running almost constantly in the annual summer battle against the hot Georgia sun. "Ben is a society member, who until a few weeks ago, was chairman of this very board. I'll reach out and see if a truce can be arranged. If not..." Her words hung heavy as a dense fog, as all waited for the other shoe to drop. "If not, then he will be dealt with like any other threat."

Everyone seemed to accept her analysis and soon assignments were doled out to board members in regards to state and federal officials to target. A few other miscellaneous items were then handled, and soon members were milling around in small talk before heading back to their public lives outside of the society. Liza pulled Zadie aside. "Looks like your pregnancy is progressing nicely."

An edge was detected in the comment and she swallowed hard as she told her pre-planned lie to cover what was really happening. "Yes. Now I understand the saying, 'eating for two.'"

An unexpected hand reaching for her bulging center caught Zadie off guard. Liza smiled. "Ah, a first-time mother. Speaking from experience, every extra pound gained now is an extra pound to lose later. It gets mighty hard to find time to go to the gym after a new baby changes your life."

A blush came naturally, triggered by her disgust at herself for all the lies she had told, and would yet tell. "I've sworn off late night ice-cream and pickles. Well, at least the ice-cream part... mostly." She played to Liza's motherly instincts. "Any other words of advice for a first-timer?"

The glow was instant. "Take lots of pictures. Life becomes a blur when the little one arrives. You'll treasure those memories long after they grow up."

"I'll do that. And I hope you don't mind if I continue to ask questions, you know, woman to woman?"

"Not at all. Every woman's pregnancy is a little different, but most are remarkably similar."

Zadie smiled as innocently as she could. *Liza, you have no idea how wrong you are.*

CHAPTER FORTY

All test animals had been removed the day before and now kerosene was splashed on everything, starting on the top floor of the Peruvian lab all the way down to the baseboards in the basement. The building, whose leather furniture and scented rooms previously smelled of wealth and progress, now smelled of grimy petroleum and ruin. Dr. Cielo Chavez's eyes glistened, painting her in an unnatural light, which didn't last long. "Somehow I always knew it would come to this."

Miguel held a box of matches, looking pained. "Would you like me to start the fire?"

"I built this monument to the future, and now it must come down." She grabbed the matches forcefully. "I do not flinch when hard decisions must be made." Friction and the resulting chemical reaction lit the small wooden stick.

The flames spread fast, snaking up open stairwells like shadow serpents climbing ancient pyramids. The two stepped back as a wall of intense heat and light began consuming the building in a ruthless rage, destruction its only goal. Miguel spoke softly. "Shall I take you to the airport now?"

Standing defiantly, she slowly turned her back on the fully engulfed structure, roaring lithe tongues illuminating the darkness. Her thoughts now focused on the future, the building already an afterthought. "Have you reconsidered my offer?"

The orange and reds of the inferno lit the night as Miguel answered. "It is a very tempting proposition. To be your second in command would truly be an honor." He stammered. "But the world you live in is so... so foreign. I do not wish to embarrass myself, or you."

Their shadows danced as the flames leaped to their highest levels yet. "I can teach you the ways of the world, Miguel, and you will thrive. What I cannot teach is what you have in your heart, in your soul. That is why you are here with me tonight and not one of my other more worldly assistants. I can replace those other attributes and traits in short order, but trust... trust is the most valuable quality in my line of business, and takes years to build. You are one of the very few people on earth I truly trust."

His eyes seemed to want to say yes while his face appeared shaded toward no. "But my family? I could never leave them."

It was time to sweeten the offer. A hint of a grin graced her black lipstick as she pressed her case. "I agree. Family is the most important thing in the world." The grin broadened. "I remind you that without my help, you and Lucia would not have your two lovely children." She reached for his hand and spoke softly, almost kindly. "Perhaps someday you might want more?"

"Yes, I owe a debt that could never be repaid." He lowered his eyes for a moment, then raised them in a look of... hope? "Lucia and I have been talking about a third."

A full smile spread as she sought to close the deal. "Then we have arrived at our answer. Call her, tell her you have good news. However, we have to move quickly. We will all go together, but we must be at the airport in three hours."

"We don't have passports. What will we do with our home? Our dog?"

Her arm went around his shoulders as she guided him away from the blazing fire toward the van. "These are the things I can teach you. With a single call I can arrange passports and the sale of your home."

"Are you sure? You can do that?"

"Yes. And soon you will be in charge of making those kinds of arrangements for me and our future patients. You will be a man of importance."

His gaze seemed uncertain. "I see. And our dog?"

"He's part of the family, right? Bring him along. After all, we'll have an entire plane to ourselves."

CHAPTER FORTY-ONE

The Glock 17 pistol seemed as natural in Bree's hands as the steering wheel of a car to most people. The whiffs of gunpowder and metallic tings of spent 9mm shells hitting concrete felt familiar, yet removed in time, like looking at old high school yearbooks. After her third near perfect target grouping, she was feeling nostalgic. "How about getting the shotguns and having a little skeet shooting contest? Head-to-head, like we used to."

"Now you just want to rub it in." Seeing staff members walking toward them with a platter of dainty finger sandwiches and pitchers of tea and lemonade, Ansen made a suggestion. "How about a snack first?"

With no warning Bree's stomach growled at the offer. "Ugh! How did you know it was time for my two o'clock feeding?"

Kristoff strolled behind the servers. "Taking out a little aggression?"

Knowing looks met his quip as they took a seat in yet another outdoor dining area so nice that it could have been featured in an HGTV show. It overlooked fields of golden barley beginning where the green grass of the skeet shooting range ended. Sandwiches of cucumber paired with salmon, curried chicken with watercress lettuce, and roast beef and Swiss offered sumptuous variety. After eating their fill and exchanging good-natured banter about who was the better shot, Kristoff broached a serious subject. "There has been another incident with the Blaze woman, a very serious incident."

Relaxation evaporated like a droplet of water on a hot burner as Ansen spoke. "How bad?"

Handing his phone over to the two of them, they stared at the image on the screen. "This is the photo that ran on the cover of the *L.A. Times* showing Gwen and her husband being helped out of their bombed home. The article says the secretly installed panic room is the only reason they survived."

Taking it from Ansen, Bree enlarged the image, looking closely at Gwen's expression. "She looks confused...afraid. Who could blame her?"

Kristoff nodded as Bree handed the phone back. "Our source in the LAPD says that it was a coordinated military style assault. While the police are in the dark about who did this, other sources tell us it was probably carried out by a team affiliated with the reformed branch of the society. The same people who gunned down the Houston oncologist, and financed the attacks on Bree in Nevis and China."

"They won't stop until they kill us both, will they?" She averted her eyes in a downward glance of disgust.

A long pause hung in the air until Kristoff spoke. "They are very determined, but we cannot let that happen to you."

Bree's reticence of a moment ago was quickly displaced. "I'm in full agreement with that... and I'm tired of running. I say we fight back. Give them a taste of their own medicine."

"And when you say 'we', to whom are you referring?" Kristoff offered a questioning gaze. "Me, you and Ansen?"

"Come on, you know what I mean. Bring the full weight of the society against them. I don't know the capabilities of the group, but I've seen enough to know that it must be formidable."

"Ah, the Tree of Life Society. The society who spent tens of millions of dollars in research that resulted in saving your life from a terminal disease? The society to whom you have a direct hereditary link, back to its very beginning? The society which your father desperately wanted you to join? That society?"

A laughing snort from Bree seemed to surprise the old man. "Right... the same society that blackmailed me into carrying this science project." She patted her bulging bump. "Don't get me wrong, I'm very happy to be alive, and warming to the idea of motherhood, but don't wrap yourself and this society in a flag of purity. I know what you are, you're just like that reformed group. You would do just about anything to advance your cause, same as them. Gwen Blaze and I seem to be the ones stuck in the middle of your war. A shooting war where real people die."

His earlier smile had disappeared, making his blue eyes appear hard as gun metal. "It is said that the best way to get out of the middle is to pick a side. While it is true that you and your baby are very important to us, and I will do all I can to keep you safe, there are others in our midst that openly question why we are investing so much in a woman who is not officially part of our organization. A woman who might even be predisposed to revealing our secrets." Kristoff paused, his eyes locking on Bree. "If you wish to give the reformed movement a taste of their own medicine, join us, just as your ancestors have done for hundreds of years. The offer is on the table."

A gentle breeze ruffled the giant oaks behind them as all sat silently. She felt the weight of their expectations as her mind raced, recalling a dream from the previous night. In it, she was lost in the middle of a stormy sea with waves rising and crashing. As she struggled to keep her head above the frothing water, her father and mother approached in a small boat, calling to her. They extended their hands as they shouted above the wind. 'Join us. It's the only way to save yourself.'

A shiver ran up her spine, now realizing that might be the only way to survive in the very real, very dangerous world she now inhabited. But she was not ready to make that choice without more answers. "I don't even know exactly what becoming a member means. Like, I know the society is focused on providing a better life for their children, and there are clearly financial advantages. Just look at this place, or the comfy upbringing Ansen and I enjoyed. But is that it? Is there anything more?"

The smile that had gone missing moments ago from Kristoff returned, and with it a sparkle to his eyes. "The Tree of Life Society has always been focused on our children, trying to give them a leg up in life." His gaze seemed intentional toward her growing baby. "How we have done that continues to evolve, as you know."

"Yes, I certainly do."

His hands opened. "Over the centuries, the society has developed into a private organization with broader goals emphasizing human improvement, and social betterment. During the late 1700s we promoted the ideals of the Enlightenment in concrete, but discreet ways. Today we're involved in sustainability and climate change initiatives because we want our children to live in a better world. I know that is important to you, right?"

Bree leaned forward. "Are you serious, or just making that up?" Before the onset of her cancer, she had spent her life as an environmental crusader, from trying to save the whales as a teen to recently working on a project to protect the Australian barrier reef. If true, this was a big deal.

His chest puffed. "Remember when you were at Third Rock Sustainability, that anonymous two-million-dollar donation? Where do you think that came from?"

"That was the society. Really?"

"Yes. And we supported them long before you were brought onboard. The society is not perfect, but we have done a lot of good. Things that would make you proud."

She wasn't sure if that was true, or if he were saying that just to lure her in, but it made her think twice. "Okay, suppose I believe you when you say the society is more than just babies and money. What's the catch, the scary things hidden in the corners of the attic? What aren't you telling me?"

His hands came together, fingers interlaced. "You've seen that the reformed branch doesn't shy away from using violence to achieve their goals. Just know that while our side tries to avoid it, we won't hesitate either, if required."

"I get it, I just suggested as much." Saying those words, she surprised herself with her cavalier attitude, but after two attempts on her life and seeing what had happened to Gwen Blaze, she was more than fed up. "Those people really do need a dose of their own medicine."

"You also need to know that once you are in, you are in for life. You are sworn to secrecy and pledge unwavering support for the society's goals. In addition, all members promise to marry within the society and to raise their children in a manner that predisposes them to join when they reach maturity."

The muscles in her clinched jaw rippled at the mention of marriage and children. "And what happens if someone breaks their vows?"

Looking her dead center, his calm words carried the force of a sledgehammer. "To be clear, we take our vows seriously. Those who break their oaths become enemies. They are either sidelined or eliminated. No individual is more important than the whole."

"Oh…" Her fingers felt cold, even sitting outside on a sunny day, the word 'eliminated' echoing in her brain. "Then I need to be very sure, right?"

"I am glad we had this conversation. Ansen has recently been through initiation and should be able to answer any additional questions. Should you choose to accept the offer, we can hold the ceremony tonight, before the Randall's and Schultz's leave. We need at least five members present to form a quorum." He folded his napkin and placed it on his plate. "Now, if you will excuse me, I have important matters to attend. I look forward to your answer by dinner."

The plates were silently swept away by the staff, leaving Bree and Ansen alone and a dreamy quality coated her words. "Remember when we came here as kids? It seemed like some kind of ultimate summer camp. No worries, only fun. Riding horses, shooting guns, all under expert training and supervision." She closed her eyes and rubbed her temples. "We were oblivious to what was really going on, weren't we? We were being groomed, like kids in some kind of cult, like what's happening with Sage and Dieter now."

Reaching for her hand, he held it gently. "That's a little extreme, don't you think? Our parents gave us every advantage they could and I think we turned out to be responsible, sane adults. I also like to think that our attraction to each other was real, even if it was helped along without us knowing." He stroked her hand. "If you could guarantee that for your baby right now, would you take the deal?"

"Always the banker," she teased, "looking for a guaranteed return on investment."

He laughed lightly. "If you want to play that way, then you're the one always paralyzed by big decisions, getting lost in the details instead of seeing the big picture."

The comment hit close to home, but she didn't pull away. Her mind drifted back in time, to when she fled Nevis, unable to face Ansen with her decision to leave him, and she now realized that had been a huge mistake. Then her thoughts skipped to her discussion with Miguel in Peru, when she couldn't decide whether to accept the terms of Dr. Chavez's offer. He helped her see that it was a simple choice, choose life or accept her own death. Long seconds ticked by as their hands remained together, her thoughts bouncing between the offer just presented, her future life as a single mother, and memories of her dream from last night. She knew a decision needed to be made, one way or another. "You know me better than anyone. What are my blinders preventing me from seeing?"

He turned, looking her straight on with a smile she had seen a thousand times - sincere and kind. "Sure, the society has its problems, and the secrecy is more than a bit weird. But consider the upside you've been offered. You are going to have this baby whether you accept the offer or not. If you chose no, then you'll still get some help from them, but have a limited say in exactly what that help looks like. On top of that, you'll have no knowledge or influence over any of the other activities of the group, like the climate change initiatives Kristoff spoke about. Think of the influence and power you've been offered, the good that you could do. I'm just saying, when weighing the pros and cons of joining the society, look at the whole picture."

She pondered his words and a kernel of truth about herself crystallized. "I do often look at the downside risk first. Just cautious, I guess. As foreign as the society is to me, there are clearly upsides that I have enjoyed my whole life whether I realized it at the time or not, and I think I turned out fairly normal."

"Most people have things in their family story they keep hidden, this is ours. But with this secret identity comes real opportunities to do the things you've always wanted to do, the kind of things you wanted so badly that you left me to chase them. Now they are being handed to you on a silver platter, and this time they would actually bring us closer."

Considering the offer in this light, her mood warmed, filling her words with hope and possibilities. "I've been thinking about a new carbon reduction plan that could really have a big impact. Would they actually give me the control and resources to try to make the world a better place?"

"Bree, you have all the leverage right now. First, you are a descendant of an original and it's hard to explain how important that is to them. That alone put me on the council, and I won't be thirty until my birthday. On top of that, you're holding the ultimate trump card. You're carrying the most important child ever in their history, a child they believe could change the world. They would give you anything to bring you into the fold and keep you happy. They would absolutely give you the chance to become a major player in the environmental world. Think of the good you could do." He squeezed her hand. "All you have to do is say yes."

She could hear the plea in his voice and it tugged at her heart. Then the dream voices of her mother and father repeated their cries in her mind. 'Join us.' While she fought the idea, her resistance began to crumble. "I would be giving up so much control, but you make a good case. It's tempting."

"Yes, it should sound tempting. Granted, you will lose some personal autonomy, but think of how much you will gain by working from the inside. The opportunities are limitless."

"Would I just be taking the easy way out? Just doing what everyone else wanted me to do?" Her forehead wrinkled in uncertainty as a light breeze hinted of rain in the distance. "And what about that marriage clause?"

"Taking the easy way? Are you kidding? People are literally trying to kill you because of the baby you're carrying, and you've been offered protection. That's not taking the easy way out, that's being smart. And about that marriage thing, has anyone ever made you do something you really didn't want to do?" His gaze seemed to reach her soul. "Deep down, what's your gut telling you?"

Clouds of indecision reigned in her head as she sat still, trying to calm her mind and body as she had done under Master Li's tutelage. Her thoughts filled with a vision of an unbroken chain of her ancestors, hand to hand, reaching back in the haze of history to the founding of this order. Her mother and father next came to mind, their arms reaching toward her, their voices pleading. Slowly the clouds began to disperse and rays of sunshine pierced through. Her resistance crumbled further. "It is my heritage, I can't deny that, and it would make my life, and this child's life, so much safer. That's for sure."

"If your gut is telling you this is the right path, then this is what you should do. I know it, and most importantly, I think you do too."

Thoughts of marriage and children swirled in her mind. "Have I told you lately how smart you are?" Her thought was interrupted by a kick from the baby and she pulled Ansen's hand to the spot. "Hold your hand here, maybe he'll do it again."

Another swift kick followed and Ansen's eyes widened. "Wow. That's amazing! And Kristoff said it's a boy, right?"

"That's what he said." Dimples formed in her reddened cheeks. "The truth is, so much has happened so fast that I really haven't processed this whole experience." His hand felt good on her stomach and her emotions surged, her voice now trembling. "I'm really glad you're here."

"Me too." After a beat, he added another comment. "And if you join the society, we'll be able to share everything. No secrets between us."

A gentler kick brought giggles. "I think he likes that idea." Bree looked into Ansen's eyes, wide and unblinking. "I like it, too..." She leaned forward and her lips found their match in a long, tender kiss as all resistance fell away. "Let's go find Kristoff and tell him I'm in. All the way in."

CHAPTER FORTY-TWO

Tonight's limousine ride to the New York headquarters of CBN was in some ways similar, yet distinctly different than the one Gwen and Ray had taken just two weeks ago. Then, like now, crowds lined the street as they approached the building housing the *Rare Air* studio. That's where the similarities faded. While the crowd was larger than last time, it was no longer a fifty-fifty split of supporters and protesters. Tonight, Blazers far outnumbered the still raucous protesters. She mused breathlessly. "Look at them all."

"It never fails. When you call on your fans, they always rally around you."

Until she met Ray, her intensely loyal fans had been one of the few things in her life in which she truly trusted, and seeing them out in force tonight fed her soul. Her red lips parted, making her white teeth seem luminescent. "They love me... and I love them."

The driver's voice came through the intercom. "We've arrived at your destination."

On her previous visit Gwen had worn a cheetah print gown. Tonight, her fire-engine red choice indicated a different mood. "Those fuckers messed with the wrong woman. Let's do this."

The valet opened the door and Gwen stepped out, waving to fans showering her in rose petals and roars of adulation. The protesters were shoved to the periphery. "Thank you, Blazers!" She once thought the name her fans had chosen for themselves that played on her surname was a little corny, but tonight she reveled in saying it. The security forces were tripled for this visit and still barely kept the crowd behind the security cords as she continued acknowledging the throng of supporters. "I'll always love you!" The stroll to the front door was slow and leisurely as she basked in the affirmation and adoration. Her fist pumped triumphantly as she turned to face them before entering. "Blazers forever!" The adoring mass exploded in a frenzy not seen since the days when the Beatles first arrived in the US in the 1960's.

The glass doors closed behind them, dimming the volume of the screaming hoard. Ray ran his hand through his long black hair as they walked to the elevator. "That's the craziest I've ever seen them. Maybe you're right. The attack on us really could be the best thing that's happened."

Her cutting smirk spoke to how close the attack came to killing them, and her skill as an influencer using it to her advantage. "Social media 101 says never let a crisis go to waste. They took their shot and missed. Now it's our turn to make them pay."

The trip through make-up was quick and in no time, they were being mic'd up on the set. Larry's eyes sparkled. "Your second visit. That makes you even with Stella McGuinn."

A relaxed Gwen retorted. "Promise me that you'll have me back after the baby's born. I don't like ties when I can be winning."

Jared counted down the return from commercial break before Larry could answer. "In five-four-three-two-one."

Larry looked directly into camera one, his expression and delivery as serious as she had ever seen. "Two weeks ago, Gwen Blaze and her husband, Ray Manza, were here talking with me about their soon-to-be-born genetically modified daughter, Madeline. The deep conversation on the pros and cons of the procedure was very informative for you, our loyal viewers. At the close of that discussion, Gwen and I talked about an incident here in New York where a tomato was thrown at her, as well as some very violent death threats she had received."

Turning to camera two, he continued. "Two days ago, Gwen and Ray survived a massive attack in which four security guards were killed. Their lives were spared only because they had installed a protective panic room in their Malibu home." He moved to face the couple. "Thank God you two are all right."

Her shoulders pulled back defiantly. "I don't know what your viewers think about our choice, and I don't care. What I do know is that it takes a very big coward to come after a pregnant woman minding her own business in her home. I do care very much about that."

Larry nodded. "As I said then, anyone who advocates for protecting human life can't at the same time advocate harming a woman and her unborn child." He sounded genuinely concerned. "How has it been for you and Ray these last two days? You seem in remarkably good spirits."

A slight tremble nudged its way into her voice. "The hardest thing has been the loss of innocent lives. Four good men died protecting us. If not for their valiant efforts, we wouldn't have had time to reach the panic room. We've grieved with their families and are doing our best to make sure their loved ones are taken care of. It's the least we can do."

"And now? What's next for you and Ray?"

"We're determined to not let domestic terrorists win. We've just contracted an elite personal protection company run by a former Green Beret. All of our new guards are former Special Forces. It's costing us a pretty penny, but how do we put a price on protecting ourselves and baby Madeline?"

"And Ray, how do you feel about all of this?"

A heavy sigh forecast his reply. "It was either the extra protection, or go into hiding, and we didn't want to send that kind of message. In a few years, genetic engineering of our children will be as common as invitro is today, probably more so. Kids like Madeline will be so normal that there will be no need for these kinds of measures. It's a pain in the ass to be surrounded by guards all the time, but as pioneers, this is the price we pay."

"Gwen, speaking of Madeline, when are you due?"

The most normal question of the interview was at the same time the most loaded. Her eyes darted to Ray and he shrugged his shoulders. Slowly she turned back to Larry, eyes widening and glimmering. She loved nothing better than shocking the establishment, and Larry Knewell was about as establishment as they come. "I'm thrilled to tell you baby Madeline will be making her debut in just under four weeks."

Larry's head cocked to the side. "Uhm, did you say four weeks?"

The mischievous look of a child caught with a mouthful of cookies and hand in the jar matched her softly spoken words. "Yes. Just under four weeks."

"Uh, I'm no doctor... or math major... but something's off." His head tilted as he seemed to choose his words carefully. "Did you just tell us about another... uhm... enhancement?"

Nodding, she delighted in sharing the secret with the world. "Exciting, isn't it? Women can be empowered to decide how long they want to be pregnant. I'm almost finished writing songs for my next album and would like to be in the studio by October. When Ray told me he could make changes that resulted in a nine-week pregnancy, I jumped at the chance. I think a lot of other women will make the same choice when this technology becomes widely available."

Larry leaned back, his jaw slack. "What? You can do that? No wonder this whole subject is so controversial. What other changes have you engineered into this baby?"

Ray reached for Gwen's hand as she glanced at him and nodded solemnly. "Larry, I want to thank you again for your strong support of non-violence toward me and my family. It means the world to us. Because of what happened, this is where we draw the line. We're not going to comment on any other choices we've made until after she's born."

Looking like a hunter catching sight of big game, he pressed. "I understand your reticence, but you've just reignited the debate about the wisdom of editing the human genome. You can't just leave us in the dark."

She pulled her shoulders back farther, pushing her pregnancy enlarged breasts toward him. She crassly teased. "Oh Larry, those are secrets I have to keep, at least until she's born. How about I promise to do my first interview with baby Madeline on your show. We'll talk more then." She wiggled her torso seductively. "It will give us both something to look forward to. What do you say?"

He blushed through his make-up. "Well, since you put it that way, how can I refuse an exclusive interview with you and the world's first designer baby?"

CHAPTER FORTY-THREE

A light afternoon summer shower doused the exclusive Atlanta suburb as Liza's driver wheeled the black sedan into the driveway. He exited, bringing an umbrella to shield her from the welcomed damp reprieve of a string of hot days.

Her words were clipped. "Don't move the car. I won't be long."

Mrs. Bartley welcomed Liza into the massive foyer of the elegant home. "Please, follow me." When they reached the library, the guest was announced. "Ms. Liza Howard to see you, sir."

Ben stood and walked around the oversized desk, wrapping her petite hand lightly in his enormous grip. "It's so good to see you again, Liza. To what do I owe the pleasure?"

The cloudy day obscured the sun, giving the dark paneled room even more solemnity. "If you have as much respect for me as I have for you, then we can dispense with the subterfuge and get down to business. We know what you did." Her icy stare matched her words. "This is not a social call."

"Oh, I see." He seemed to feign surprise, then smirked as he waved toward a chair. "Please, sit." His fingers slid along the polished desktop as he ambled around to his well-cushioned executive chair, his huge frame slowly settled into place. Leaning forward with his elbows resting on the shiny wooden surface, he addressed her bluntly. "Say what you need to say."

The anger she had contained spilled and rushed toward him like a tipped over glass of water. "The Blaze woman and her cause are more popular than ever. You were warned that this could happen and because of your recklessness it's come to pass. Ben, I come as a friend, begging you to listen to the counsel of your peers. Don't keep going down this road."

A sneer added bite to his response. "Talk, talk, talk. That's all this board wants to do. Remember when we pulled our order out of the ashes, when we took action, bold action. You were there, working side by side with me. Our branch of the society was in shambles. The fallout from the eugenics debacle almost destroyed us and we were losing members by the dozens. Together, we instilled order in our ranks and eliminated outside threats with haste. I'll admit that sometimes it was messy, but we did what had to be done, and our order thrived. I think of those times as the good old days. All I see now is a bunch of comfortable egos afraid to rock the boat of their easy lives."

"But Ben, it's not the old days, good or otherwise. I understand your nostalgia, but the world has changed. Just look at what happened after your failed attempt on the Blaze woman's life. She was able to speak directly to millions of her followers through social media. They adore her and mobilized in support. That got her back on national television in two days to build more sympathy through traditional media. She's tilted the national conversation in her favor almost overnight. It's like you're fighting a digital enemy with a flip phone. Wake up and smell the internet."

His eyes tightened, face reddened and his voice boomed. "But I was so close to ending the threat. If not for that damned panic room we would be having an entirely different conversation. I would be welcomed back to the board with open arms. It's not a different world, Liza, just a different threat. Mark my words. If that woman is allowed to bear that child the flood gates will open and weightless arguments will be powerless. Enhanced humans will rule the rest of us in a generation... two at the most. You must understand that truth!"

Liza stood, then paced for a moment. When she turned to face him, her finger jabbed the air as she spoke. "We had her right where we wanted. She was closed away in her home, playing defense. Laws were working their way through government bodies everywhere. Public opinion was squarely on our side... and rising. Our campaign was working perfectly." She drew in a steadying breath. "Then you went rogue and screwed up everything. Your actions set the society back at least a year."

He flicked his wrist dismissively. "As we have both said before, let's agree to disagree. You see things one way and I see them another. History will decide which was correct."

Walking right up to the edge of the desk, she spoke flat and cold. "Listen, Ben. I didn't come here to negotiate. I came to give you a warning. Stop going behind the board's back with attempts on the Blaze woman's life."

A light snort came from his wide nostrils. "Or what, Liza? What are you and that lily-livered board going to do?"

Her hands landed on his desk as she leaned across, eyes locked. "As you said, Ben. I was there when we knew how to instill order in our ranks. Don't force me to do what you know I can." She stood straight, eyes still narrow and threatening. "I came here as a courtesy, because of your years of service to our cause. Don't mistake it as weakness." A couple of beats passed in silence. "I'll see myself out."

The door closed behind her and he slowly turned his chair to watch her car pull away. "She's not lost her spunk, that's for sure." He sat alone with his thoughts before spinning around and picking up the phone, dialing numbers from memory. "Ezra, we need to talk about our next move."

CHAPTER FORTY-FOUR

Golden late afternoon sun bathed the Czech mansion in warm hues as Bree and Ansen made their way to tell Kristoff of her decision. She gripped his hand for reassurance as they were shown to his office. "Sometimes I still can't believe this is all real."

"If you ever think it's not, just remember all the bullets you've dodged these past few weeks."

With that sobering thought, they walked into the huge office and she wasted no time sharing her decision. "I'm in."

Light flooding through the massive windows of Kristoff's stark white office seemed a perfect match for his ebullient response. "I am thrilled by your acceptance of our offer. This decision will simplify everything. You have made a very wise choice, for yourself and your baby."

Standing tall, but with the nervousness of a shotgun wedding still in her voice, she spoke. "I may have taken the long road, but I'm happy with my decision. It feels good to take charge of my life, to plan my own future."

"You will make a terrific Director of Sustainability for the society."

"I wasn't sure you would accept my terms."

His hand waved dismissively. "It makes perfect sense. I only wish I had thought of it first. Your credentials are outstanding and with a little one on the way, you have an even bigger stake in the health of our planet. This is a win for us all."

"I agree." The hopeful mood shifted as Bree broached a new subject. "I saw the latest Gwen Blaze interview. Sounds like she is facing the same threats to her life as I am, except she's doing it alone, and in public."

"That makes your decision to join the society look even better. Imagine where you would be if you were out there alone."

Looking down, Bree spoke softly. "I admire her. She's doing this for a noble reason, to have a child not carrying a dreaded disease. By doing it out in the open, she's advancing the cause for those that might someday choose to follow. I feel like a coward compared to her."

A beaming face generating the warmth of a proud grandfather appeared. "Bree, do not do that to yourself. Every person has their own path and it is not fair for you to compare yours to hers. Not fair to either of you. She has been in the public eye for a long time, and her years of managing social media now comes as easy as an Olympic runner taking a jog around their neighborhood. Look what you have done. You have been the lead subject on a treatment to conquer a terminal brain cancer. Think how that will help mankind when the results are released to the medical community?"

"But still, I'm here hiding while she's out in the open, loud and proud."

"And you are going to lead a global sustainability effort to save the planet. Think how important that will be. Do not worry, I am sure your story will be told soon enough, so until then, let us take things one step at a time. In just a couple of hours you will be inducted into the Tree of Life Society, following in the long procession of your ancestors. You will then take your rightful place in an organization devoted to improving life on this planet. It is a day to be happy and rejoice."

Her hands rested in her lap, consoled but still unsettled. "You're right of course, I am happy and ready for my initiation."

Kristoff stood, offering his hand. "The ceremony will not be for a couple of hours, so enjoy the afternoon, and afterwards we will have a celebration dinner to mark the occasion."

An immediate laugh preceded her reply. "I guess that means I'm heading to the kitchen for a snack. I don't want stomach growls interrupting the ritual."

True to her word she headed to the kitchen before taking a quick nap in her room. Upon rising, she examined the robes and undergarments that had been delivered earlier in the day. "Black over white. They sure take this seriously."

A knock on the door broke her train of thought. She found Ansen on the other side dressed in his all-white vestments with a red trimmed collar. She snickered. "You look like a priest right out of seminary."

A blush made his almost thirty years look younger. "Seems these robes haven't changed in over a century. I hear they were very stylish back in the day."

"At least you're not wearing a black one. It's kind of creepy, if you ask me."

Plopping down on the bed, he answered. "It's all about the symbolism. Just wait, it will all make sense."

Strolling over, she sank down beside him, resting her head on his shoulder. "Thanks again for all you've done for me these last few weeks. The shootout in Nevis, the rescue in China, being here with me now. You've been a lifesaver."

Seemingly on autopilot his arm wrapped around her. "I can't think of anywhere else I'd rather be."

She leaned up and kissed his cheek. "Nor I. Wait here, I might need some help getting the robe adjusted. I'll be right back."

With that, she went into the bathroom, returning in a few

minutes, her stomach now highlighted in the stark white stockings, under-robe and long-sleeved blouse. He beamed. "You look like an angel."

It was her turn to blush cherry red as she stroked her stomach. "I appreciate the thought, but I don't think angels can get pregnant. Now, help me get these robes on the right way. I want to make a good impression."

He held the liner and she slipped her arms through, then stood still as he zipped the velvet center panel. "It's all coming together."

She could see herself in the mirror as he draped the light-weight black outer shell, which accentuated the velvet of the inner garment. "I look like I should be handing out graduation diplomas."

"God, I love your sense of humor, but let's keep those kinds of thoughts just between us. The society takes initiation very seriously."

Twirling before the glass, she watched the robes swirl as she twisted back and forth. "They are pretty, and they do kind of make me feel important." She stood fixed, gazing at her reflection. "Obviously not something I would wear every day, but I like them. I think I'm ready."

They walked hand in hand down the hallways, following Frida to a set of double doors. "They are waiting for you."

The attendant turned and left, leaving the two alone for a moment. His hand brushed her cheek. "There's nothing to worry about. Just repeat after Kristoff and we'll be going to dinner before you know it."

"Should be a piece of cake... which sounds really good about now."

Smiling, he shook his head. "Serious, remember?"

"Got it. Let's do this."

Turning the knobs of the doors, both swung open and they stepped into a darkened room, lit only by candles. Polished silver candelabras lined the edges of the space while a massive pair framed Kristoff. He stood at the front of the rectangular room behind a kneeling bench, with a carpet runner extending toward the doors. Ansen positioned Bree at the opposite end of the narrow antique embroidered rug, then left her alone, taking his place up front beside the patriarch. Standing on each side of the carpet, near the padded kneeler were Daniel and Imani Randall, as well as Bernhard and Johanna Schultz, whom she had just met two days before. Like Ansen, all of them were dressed in white robes trimmed in red, shimmering like ghosts in the ethereal lighting, sandalwood incense wafting in the air.

From the front of the room, Kristoff began the ceremony. "The Tree of Life Society is dedicated to improving the human race and has adhered to our tenants for over six centuries. Tonight, a direct descendant of original members, Gustaf and Gisela Mann, seeks to join our ranks. We invite Ms. Bree Battle to come forward to receive the rite of initiation."

Like walking the aisle of an eclectic wedding, Bree slowly made her way forward, stopping when Kristoff nodded. "Bree Battle, are you here tonight of your own free will, with no hesitation, seeking to forever join our ranks?"

In a flash her mind traced the path from Dr. Cofferman, through Peru and China, to this gathering. While it sometimes still felt like a weird dream in which she was thrown about like a puppet, and despite so much about the society that she didn't know, she knew in her heart that no one was twisting her arm, she was doing this of her own accord. Her voice trembled ever so slightly. "Yes... of my own free will."

Kristoff's hand extended toward the leather upholstered kneeling bench where she knelt, awaiting his next instruction.

He spoke to the gathered members. "Tonight, a quorum has been assembled to witness and approve the initiation of Bree

Battle. These members will forever serve as model, mentor and friend. Witnesses, do you pledge your fellowship and support to Bree in all matters of the society, in good times and in bad, keeping all matters secret?"

Ansen's clear voice pierced through the quartet of Sage and Dieter's parents. "I do pledge fellowship and support, keeping all matters secret."

Kristoff looked down, the tiniest of uplift to the corners of his mouth. "And do you, Bree Battle, pledge your fellowship and support to these witnesses, and all other members in matters of the society, in good times and bad, keeping all matters secret?"

Her partially disguised smile matched his. "I do pledge fellowship and support to all society members, keeping all matters secret."

After a moment of silence, Kristoff continued. "Our founders started this society with one purpose, to achieve a better life for their children. Today, there are many facets of that pledge, but the core remains the same, marry within the society and raise the next generation in ways that predispose them to freely join upon reaching adulthood. Bree Battle, do you swear that you will marry within the Tree of Life Society and when you have children you will raise them in a manner that will incline them to join upon reaching adulthood?"

She bowed and reflexively her hand went to her waist as all looked on. She felt their eyes on her, sensing only warmth. When she lifted her head, she met each of their gazes, lingering on Ansen's longest. After a long moment of unspoken support, she turned to Kristoff. "I swear that I will marry within the society and raise this child, and any others I may have, in ways that will lead them toward joining when they reach adulthood."

The patriarch's smile broadened. "Please rise and shed the skin of your old life, taking a new coat of love, trust and protection." Sage and Dieter's mothers moved toward Bree, who now stood.

Her black outer robe was removed and placed in a cauldron beside Kristoff.

The patriarch turned to a stand holding a silver pitcher and poured sweet scented liquid atop the discarded vestment in the charred iron pot. After placing the vessel back on the stand, he removed the center candle from the candelabra adjacent to the container. "Your days of living in the darkness are forever being replaced by years to be spent living in light." Touching the oil and cloth the contents burned in a bright, floral scented blaze, as all stood in silent reverence.

Soon the fire dimmed, leaving only a fragrant aroma hanging in the air. Kristoff smiled. "Your new life begins now." With a nod, Sage and Dieter's mothers brought a new white robe with red trimmed collar, just like those of the other members, and placed it on her shoulders. Kristoff addressed the assembled group. "This robe represents your full membership into the Tree of Life Society for as long as you shall live. Welcome to your new family and may happiness and fertility bless your life."

CHAPTER FORTY-FIVE

Callan McDougal was taking no chances this time. After the surprise of learning that Gwen Blaze and her husband had a panic room, he was going back to the basics of killing - strike the target when they were at their most open and vulnerable. In Los Angeles that usually meant hitting them in their cars.

Echo One radioed an update. "Bomb in place. Falling back to secure location."

Three tours in the middle east had convinced Callan of the IED's utility, even as he despised its cowardice. "Copy Echo One. Eye's open, everyone, we finish this job today."

Twenty minutes of silence were interrupted with the first sighting. "Echo Three reporting subjects leaving the new residence and heading for the parking structure. Repeat, subjects leaving residence."

Ben sat alone in his darkened library, watching the operation unfold. Ezra agreed to proceed but chose to put physical distance between himself and Ben for this mission, keeping a layer of deniability should something go wrong again.

Callan knelt behind a scrub pine, holding binoculars with one hand and a cell phone with the other. "Echo Three, detail the convoy."

An anxious sounding voice replied. "There has been a change to the pattern, I repeat, a change to the pattern. *Three* limousines, not one, are between the SUV's. All have dark tinted windows. Positive ID's of subjects not confirmed. Repeat, ID's not confirmed."

A deep sigh registered on Callan's voice activated microphone. "Overwatch, they've stepped up their game. Seems real pros are running their show now. There is no guarantee on termination of subjects. Do you wish to proceed or abort? We await your orders."

A groan preceded Ben's words. "Time's not on our side." Callan waited in silence until Ben spoke again. "Take your best shot and do as much damage as possible. Maybe we'll get lucky."

"Message received." Callan addressed his team by radio. "I'll target the center car. Echo One and Two, target the lead limo with as many rounds as possible. Echo Four and Five do the same to the trailing one. We go on my count."

Seconds passed until the convoy rounded the bend and headed to a relatively isolated stretch of roadway. "Here they come." Callan kept one eye on the approaching caravan as his thumb hovered over the call button of the triggering cell phone. "In three-two-one." His thumb made contact with the phone screen and the roadside bomb exploded, lifting the center limo and tossing it into the oncoming traffic. An explosion of the gas tank a half second later signaled its complete destruction. Simultaneously, the two teams of shooters unloaded hundreds of rounds from their fully automatic weapons into the other two vehicles. This section of Malibu highway now resembled a faraway war zone, complete with the stench of smoke and the sound of screeching tires and roaring motors as drivers scrambled for their lives, or lay dead in their mangled vehicles.

Ben's words traveled almost instantly to the west coast. "Did we get her?"

From his concealed position, Callan hustled onto the roadway to inspect the completely destroyed car, his video feed jostling as he sprinted. Avoiding the tongues of fire, he finally got a good look inside the vehicle. His shoulders sagged. "Overwatch, I have bad news. This vehicle was completely empty, except for the driver."

A voice sounding full of despair responded. "Any news on the other two limos?"

A section of charred bumper caught the wrath of Callan's boot, sending it skidding across the road. Sirens could be heard approaching in the distance. "We're bugging out. I'll check in with my hospital sources and should have an update within the hour."

Ben's live feed disconnected and he sat motionless, barely even blinking. Finally, he walked to the shelf where he kept his best whiskey. He poured a double into a crystal tumbler etched with his family crest, then ambled back to his desk to wait for an uncertain sequence of events. He waited to hear from Callan the hoped-for news that Gwen Blaze was dead. If that happened, he believed that there was a strong probability that the board would cheer the result, even if it went against Liza's direct warning. He would be welcomed back as a hero, possibly being restored as chairman. There was also a slim chance that she held enough of a grudge to follow through on her threat. He reasoned that his actions would still have been worth it, even if it cost him his life.

The other outcome would be tragic. He would hear from Callan that Gwen Blaze had somehow survived. Liza would definitely retaliate and his death would be in vain. The Blaze woman's altered monstrosity would be born, signaling the beginning of the end for mankind. To him that would be a fate far worse than death.

After repeating his steps to the minibar two more times in the next hour, his phone finally rang, giving him a start. "What's the news?"

The long pause foretold Callan's reply. "She wasn't in any of the limos. They had her in the trailing SUV. The hospital reports only bumps and bruises from the evasive action taken by her driver. Like I said, the team she hired this time were real pros."

Swallowing the remains of this round, Ben set the heavy glass down softly, his voice now tired and scratchy. "We tried our best, my friend, I guess it wasn't meant to be. I suggest you lay low for a while, there's going to be heat for this."

Hanging up, he sat alone, waiting. He thought he saw the red dot of a laser on his desk, but in an instant it disappeared. *Was it really there or just my imagination?* When his phone rang again a few minutes later, he nearly jumped out of his skin. The caller ID showed Liza Howard on the other end. He answered cautiously. "Hello?"

"I told you to leave the Blaze woman alone or there would be consequences."

"Turns out she's the woman with nine lives. Barely a scratch from what I've heard."

Silence invaded the call for several seconds. "Ben, why didn't you listen? You were warned."

Staring straight ahead into the darkest corners of his library his words were heavy. "How much time do I have?"

"You were already in their sights. In fact, you would be dead if the call I just received had come two minutes later."

So, I wasn't imagining it. "What…" He swallowed hard, then started again. "What information stayed my execution?"

"I got a call from the team we sent to sift through the ashes of Chavez's burned-out lab."

"Oh? What did they find?"

Liza's voice hardened. "A name. A name was recovered from a damaged hard drive that makes me reconsider everything… including your approach."

A sliver of hope creased his lips. "Whose name?"

He heard Liza's cold words spilling out like an avalanche crashing down a mountain. "It seems we have a traitor in our midst. Zadie Springer's miraculous pregnancy isn't such a miracle after all, and that makes her even more dangerous than the Battle woman… or Gwen Blaze. She must be dealt with immediately."

Flashbacks of Zadie's seconding his ouster flooded his mind. "That bitch! She's betrayed us! For all we know she might even be working with them as a spy." He slammed his fist on the desktop. "This can't stand!"

"I think this is the information the originals knew about, and they are right, it could destroy us if it gets out. We could use a man with your skills. Would you reconsider our offer to remain on the board?"

There was no hesitation. "Only if you put me in charge of taking out these abominations once and for all."

CHAPTER FORTY-SIX

Zadie sat at her desk working on a PR campaign for a supermarket chain seeking to expand its market share in the growing plant-based meat substitute space. Hearing the ping of an incoming text she glanced at her phone which showed a sender marked only as PRIVATE. *Probably just spam.* The reminder ping a minute later pestered her thoughts like a phantom itch. Grabbing the phone, her stomach fell as she read the message in all caps. *THE BOARD IS HAVING AN EMERGENCY MEETING AND YOU HAVE NOT BEEN INVITED.*

Shaking, she tapped out a response. *WHO IS THIS?* Frantic minutes passed with no answer, her heart raced as multiple scenarios flooded her mind. Try as she might, she couldn't conjure a single good reason to be left out of a society board meeting. Her eyes darted around the open office, seeing only normal activity as desperation sank in. *They know.*

Her hands balled as she fought to regain control. *Maybe someone is just messing with me. I need to be sure. Think, think, think!* Scrolling through her contact list she found Liza's real-world office number and hit dial. She recognized the voice of Liza's secretary. "Howard Consulting. How may we help you?"

"Hi, Vickie, it's Zadie Springer. May I speak with Liza?"

"I'm sorry, she's out of the office."

"Do you know when she'll return?"

"No. She left unexpectedly. May I take a message?"

Struggling not to fall apart, she answered as calmly as she could, speaking words she knew to be absolutely true. "That's okay. I think I might know where she went." After hanging up she hit dial on another name, speaking in a panicked whisper when he answered. "Kade, they know!"

"Whoa. Slow down. What are you talking about? Are you okay?"

"No! Not at all! There's an emergency board meeting and I wasn't invited. They know!"

Silence filled the space between them until he answered in what sounded like panic. "This is bad. I just saw a report of another attack on Gwen Blaze. If they suspect us, then we'll be next. What do we do!?"

Zadie rubbed her forehead as desperation triggered an idea. "We call Chavez. She got us into this, maybe she can get us out. You go home and get a bug-out bag packed and I'll be right behind. I'll call her on the way."

"Right. I'm leaving now. Hurry, my love."

Zadie wheeled her Lexus sedan out of the parking lot and instructed the car to dial Dr. Chavez as she hit the on-ramp to the adjacent freeway.

A distinctive Spanish-accented voice answered the call. "How is my patient today?"

"Not well. Not well at all." The speedometer zoomed past the legal limit. "It seems our secret has been discovered by the board. You know what that means. This baby and me are now on their most wanted list. You may not care much about me, but I get the feeling you very much want this child to live. We're desperate, can you help?"

Hard-edged words came over the hands-free speakers. "I was afraid of this. Give me thirty minutes and I'll send coordinates for a safe house. You made the right decision to call."

"I hope so." Panic wrestled with anger in her mind. "Right now, I'm having second thoughts about ever contacting you in the first place."

The sharpness in the reply was unmistakable. "We'll talk about your decision-making process at the appropriate time. Right now, focus all of your energy on getting to safety."

A few minutes later, Zadie was pulling into her driveway at high speed, narrowly missing Kade's SUV. She rushed into the house, added a few more necessities to the bag that Kade had started while repeatedly glancing at the phone. Just as she pulled the zipper on her case, a text arrived. "It's Chavez. She sent an address for what she says is a safe place. Let's go!"

They tossed both carry-ons into the back of the SUV, then entered the address into the onboard GPS. Another text arrived and Zadie read it. "She said she would join us in the morning, bringing reinforcements. Until then, she suggests we shut off our phones completely to avoid being tracked."

Heading south on I-75, Kade looked over at her with an empty stare. "I thought we were smart enough to get away with it. We knew the risks, but I really didn't think this could happen." His gaze returned to the highway stretching into the distance, his voice sounding as if without hope. "Our old life is over, isn't it? It's gone. Our parents will disown us. We'll lose our jobs and half of our friends... all the perks of being society members." He swallowed hard. "We might even lose our lives." Seconds passed in silence until his hand struck the steering wheel. "What made us believe we could pull this off?"

She turned away without answering, a hand resting on her stomach, barely holding everything together. Her vacant eyes glazed as pine trees and mile markers zipped by. The only life they had ever known faded behind them like a permanent sunset, a dark night and uncertain sunrise waiting ahead.

CHAPTER FORTY-SEVEN

A pall hung like fog over the Reformed Order emergency board meeting. Adding to the unsettled mood was the reappearance of Ben Brown, now sitting in one of the twelve member chairs, not at the head as he had for ten prior years. Each of their eyes seemed drawn to him by some invisible unyielding gravity. Liza bitterly stated what had become obvious, venom in her words. "We have been betrayed by one of our own."

Jim Campbell reacted first. "Are we sure? I mean, could there be another explanation?"

The relaxing of her clinched jaw released angry words that sprung across the table. "We have intel that both Zadie and Kade left their offices today, without explanation, and neither are answering their phones. It appears they are on the run. That's *not* how innocents behave."

Mumbles were exchanged between several members until Liza corralled the conversation. "As you can see, Ben has accepted my invitation to take his rightful seat among us once again. I'm reopening our discussion on how to confront these bold-faced affronts to humanity. His arguments have taken on new weight based on what we suspect from our Judas, Zadie Springer." She nodded toward the big man. "Would you like to say a few words as we get started?"

Ben stood, buttoning his suit jacket. His arms extended broadly. "My friends, I rejoice at once again being in communion with you. Disagreements within families are common... and tempers do sometimes cloud our better judgment. I confess that my temper certainly got the best of me." His arms fell, hands clasped in front with head bowing slightly. "I'm not here to apologize for my views, but for the way I reacted to your well-founded questions. I was wrong to storm out and wrong to take matters into my own hands. It's possible that I may have made things worse, and for that I am truly sorry. I ask for your forgiveness."

Ezra Slaughter spoke spiritedly. "I think I speak for many of the joy I feel having you back in our circle. Your wisdom adds to our collective whole."

With the reintroduction complete, Liza directed the conversation. "As I mentioned, facts on the ground have changed, which means we need to reexamine our tactics. Our public relations approach seemed to be gaining traction, but the attacks on Gwen Blaze turned that around. She's more popular than ever and has embraced being the face of the human genetic engineering movement. Now we've learned that the architect of our PR campaign is carrying a genetically modified baby herself. Can we even trust that her plan was on the up and up, or instead somehow designed to blow up on us? The floor is open to any ideas on how to regain the initiative."

For several seconds no one spoke as eyes darted from person to person. Finally, Ben cleared his throat, drawing everyone's attention. "The bottom line is that there are now three of these abominations walking the earth. If we don't stop them, that number is going to spiral out of control and multiply like a pandemic, just as I predicted."

Waving his hand, Jim entered the conversation. "Wait just a minute, Ben. You've directed two attempts each on the Battle woman and Gwen Blaze. How has that worked out so far?"

Reddening cheeks didn't seem to match his smooth words. "I'll admit that these Gen Z'ers are harder to stop than I expected. But just because it's hard doesn't mean it's not the right thing to do. What happens when those cute little babies are born and Gwen Blaze floods social media with adorable pictures? What happens when she goes on every television talk show in the world with a cuddly bundle of joy in her arms? A tidal wave will begin, never to be stopped, just look at how mainstream invitro is today. The same thing will happen with designer babies. It's time to end this now, or the cause is lost."

Jim acted undeterred. "Harder to stop than you expected? And now that they know we're targeting them you think it's going to get easier? At this rate we'll expose the society to the outside world by the end of the month, or worse yet, trigger a response from the originals. Those seem to be bigger threats than these so-called designer babies. Is that what you want?"

Ben shook his head, appearing frustrated. "We're right back where we were. Afraid to make the hard decisions… afraid to do what's needed. It's past time to take action and everyone at this table knows it. Even you, Jim."

Leaning forward, Jim responded, his words agitated. "It's said that insanity is doing the same thing over and over and expecting different results. As far as I'm concerned, we've clearly reached that point." He took a sharp breath. "And on top of that, this time we'll now be going after one of our own. How many here were at Zadie's initiation?" He waited as seven hands slowly rose. "Ben said he made a mistake, and today he is back with us. Do we not afford Zadie and Kade the same courtesy of atoning for their errors?"

Ezra joined the debate. "Ben's mistake was one of temper and tactics, not a betrayal of core beliefs. Don't try and conflate the choices of Ben and Zadie, they are factors apart. And just to be clear, I think Ben's right. Our society will be as obsolete as a rotary phone if we don't stop this technological nightmare."

With dogged persistence, Jim continued. "Is the situation truly black and white? Can't we continue the PR campaign? It did show promise until Ben screwed it up." In his fiery speech a drop of spittle flew from his mouth. "Perhaps there is a third way?" He slammed his hand on the heavy table. "There has to be a solution where we're not intentionally killing descendants of our founders."

Folding his hands, Ben volleyed the ball back in Jim's court, raising his voice even louder than Jim's. "Speaking of getting screwed, that's what our PR champion did to us. And as far as a third way, I would be glad to hear such a proposal." Sarcasm seemed to drip from his words. "Come on Jim, let's hear it."

The blood drained from Jim's face as his eyes darted around the room and his voice lowered. "How about we just target the Blaze woman... and I guess Zadie as well. If we leave Bree Battle alone, we'll at least avoid retaliation from the originals."

Liza had heard enough. "You've both made valid points, which is how our board should work. The things on which we all agree is that time is not on our side, and that we can't let this divide our order. We must speak with one voice or the originals win by default. As Jim has suggested, I propose we target Gwen Blaze and our traitor, Zadie Springer. When they are eliminated, we make a decision on the Battle woman. Let's take a vote and see where we stand." She paused, allowing a moment for the members to gather their thoughts. "All those in favor, raise your hand."

Ben and Ezra immediately raised their hands and one by one, all others raised theirs as well. "The board has spoken and we leave united. Ben, you have whatever resources you need to eliminate these threats."

His face beamed, seeming glad to be back in control of targeting these women. "Thank you, Liza."

Her gaze hardened, sending a message as strong as her words. "And Ben, don't screw it up this time."

CHAPTER FORTY-EIGHT

For Bree, Ansen and Dr. Chavez, this was a business trip full of tension and unknown dynamics. These three sat up front in the jet as they crossed the Atlantic, removed from the family activities of the Randall's, so they could openly discuss the negotiations to come. Sage and her parents had joined them, taking advantage of the private flight to go back to the US. Bree mused. "What were those two thinking? Did they really believe they could get away with their plan right under the nose of the reformed board?"

Today, Dr. Chavez wore a tailored black pantsuit instead of her usual scrubs. "Desperation can lead one to do things they never dreamed... like swearing allegiance to a secret organization."

The dig hit close. "Touché. I deserved that." Bree sat in silence for a moment. "I bet they're scared to death. I can certainly relate."

"Mrs. Springer has seen the cold calculations of the reformed group up close. As a board member she was involved in the attempts on Gwen Blaze, and she also had a vote on the attacks that killed Dr. Cofferman and targeted you. She *should* be afraid."

The pilot announced their imminent arrival to the private airport just south of Atlanta Georgia, asking everyone to fasten seatbelts. In short order they taxied to a stop beside three black SUV's. Once on the ground Bree gave Sage a hug. "I'm sure I'll see you again soon. In the meantime, don't be in too big of a hurry to grow up."

Sage hugged harder. "Take care of yourself and that baby. I want to see pictures."

The family were loaded into one of the SUV's and driven away, leaving the two others for the rest of them, along with a security detail. One of the armed men opened a door for them. "Ladies and gentleman, it's a short drive from here."

As promised, they were soon turning from blacktop onto a gravel road which took them through a wooded area, finally arriving at a quaint, pale-yellow cottage situated on the banks of a small lake. It looked familiar to Bree. "I think I've been here before, as a child." She pointed to the small dock jutting into the water. "That's where my father taught me to fish."

Ansen chimed in. "Yeah, me too."

A nod from Dr. Chavez confirmed the likelihood. "From what Kristoff tells me, this place has been in society hands for generations. Free use of these kinds of facilities is one of the perks of membership." She shot a knowing glance at Bree. "You'll get accustomed to it again. Now, let's get out of the sun and introduce ourselves to Bonnie and Clyde."

Their security took positions around the bungalow as they knocked. Kade opened the door and seemed stunned as he pointed at Bree. "What's she doing here?"

Chavez led the group past him. "Get over it. We have business to discuss."

Zadie was waiting, standing in the center of the small living area, her pink designer maternity dress with tie riding above her baby bump was identical, except in color, to Bree's. Her eyes opened abnormally wide seeing the other pregnant woman. "I wasn't expecting to see *you*."

Sensing the jab, Bree rolled her shoulders back. "We have a lot in common." She forced a smile, trying to ease the tension. "I see we have similar tastes."

The surprised expression on Zadie's face softened. "I love the blue on you."

The ice was broken. "Pink. Does that mean you're having a girl?"

"Yes." All eyes darted toward Dr. Chavez as Zadie replied. "That was the choice that was made for us."

The awkwardness in the room was palpable as the doctor took control. "I love fashion as much as the next woman, but now it's time to talk about this situation."

Kade pulled out a kitchen chair for his wife. "Have a seat, everyone."

Taking her place next to her husband, Zadie spoke first. "I wasn't expecting to see you today, Ms. Battle, but since you are here, I want to explain my actions, and apologize."

"Please, call me Bree."

"Okay... Bree. Do you mind if I tell you a story? I think it will be helpful.

"Sure." Looking at Zadie suspiciously, Bree gave a nod. "Go ahead."

Lips drawn thin, Zadie began. "I was thirteen years old when my father took me to the Auschwitz concentration camp in Poland. If you haven't been, it's quite an experience. As we toured the death camp, I learned that approximately one million souls were killed there, mostly Jews. I sensed an overwhelming eeriness during the visit."

A tinge of doom coated Bree's response. "I felt the same when my parents took me at about the same age. I'll never forget it."

"Then you might understand how it hit me, when standing in front of one of the gas houses, my father explained that some of our distant relatives were among the perpetrators of these horrors. I couldn't believe it, but my father insisted. He said that our family must never again be on the side of that kind of savagery against humanity. It was only years later, when I was introduced to the society, that I fully understood what he was talking about."

"And you thought I was the embodiment of something as evil as the Nazis?"

Zadie blushed. "Well, not you as a person, but you as the vehicle ushering in an age where some humans, like your unborn child, could come to believe that they were superior to the rest of us."

Bree crossed her arms, now resting atop her expanded baby bump. "The truth is that I've had some doubts along the way about this pregnancy, but I've come to terms with my decision. I'm going to love, nurture and raise this child to the best of my ability. I want to instill in him the values of service to mankind my parents cultivated in me. Genetics alone don't determine a child's fate."

Matching Bree, Zadie folded her arms over her unborn daughter. "I have come to the same conclusion through my own journey."

Kade gently rested his arm over his wife's shoulder. "While our motives may not have been the purest in the beginning, this is where we are now. We appreciate the use of this safe house, but it's not a long-term solution."

Ansen leaned in. "As a council member for the Tree of Life Society, I'm here to explore a possible way forward, if you're interested."

With eyes that seemed to express both hope and suspicion, Kade replied cautiously. "We're interested."

In a steady, determined voice, Ansen began. "First of all, do you see any scenario where you could be accepted back into the reformed movement? Any way you could ask for forgiveness?"

Zadie shook her head. "I've been a board member for a short time, that's the same as a council member in your branch, and I've never seen or even heard of anyone accepted back who has been accused of being a traitor. What we've done strikes at the core of our beliefs." Her face fell and voice darkened in finality. "I can say with certainty that there is already a plan in place for our execution."

A nod confirmed Ansen's suspicion. "That's what I thought, though I wanted to be sure before we went any further. I understand both of you are descendants of originals, is that correct?"

They answered in unison. "Yes."

"Okay, good. That is very important in our branch of the society, and I believe the same for reformers, right?"

Again, they spoke in unison. "Yes."

"Based on the research I've done, our initiation process is exactly the same. The two sides are run very similarly in most respects. The division between us was caused almost exclusively by the fallout from the eugenics catastrophe. Your families vowed to return to the traditional ways, while the majority of families decided to continue exploring new ways to improve humanity."

Kade's voice grew louder. "We had good reason to take the traditional path. As we saw, it's all too easy to go astray."

Ansen put his hands up. "I'm not judging, just stating a fact, and the fact is far more binds us together than separates us. Agreed?"

The two reformers looked at each other, then Zadie answered for the pair. "We agree with that, we have a lot in common."

Reaching for Bree's hand, Ansen continued. "We're in almost the same spot as you two. What's different is, our branch views Bree and her baby as a good thing... a very good thing, perhaps even the path forward for mankind's ultimate improvement. The full resources of the Tree of Life Society are devoted to protecting her, not trying to kill her. Because of your decision and Dr. Chavez's expertise, we see you and your child exactly the same way. You're special and deserving of protection."

Shifting her pregnant body, Zadie leaned in. "What, exactly, are you proposing?"

"The society welcomes you to stay here as long as you like, but as Kade said, this isn't a long-term solution. What is a long-term solution is for you to switch allegiances, to join us in the larger community of Original Tree of Life Society members. After a brief swearing of loyalty ceremony, you would enjoy full rights and protection. What do you say?"

Staring at each other, Zadie and Kade seemed unsure of how to answer, and after a few seconds, she replied. "It's a generous offer, but you have to understand how hard that would be for us. We've been raised our entire lives to despise what your group stands for, and despite the fact that we've put ourselves in this position, it would be a big leap to make that change. We'll need some time to think about it."

Joining the conversation, Bree added insight. "I was in a similar place just a couple of months ago. My choice was to accept a bargain to save my life in exchange for carrying this baby. I see your choice as very similar. Live your life on the run, where you will probably die, or accept this generous offer that ties your stomach in knots. You think it's a difficult decision, not a simple one. When I was in your shoes a wise man gave me some good advice. He said, 'when the decision is between living or dying, it's always simple.' I believe that's where you are today."

Dr. Chavez had left negotiating to the young couples, but her sense of decorum seemed to never tolerate delays. "Come on you two, you don't need to be rocket scientists to see how few options you have. Accept this generous offer and let's get moving. Those reformers might be on their way here now for all we know."

Zadie shot Chavez a sharp glare. "This is our lives we're talking about and we'll take all the time we need. Come on, Kade, let's step out and talk about this in private."

The two stood and walked away, hand in hand through the back-door. The doctor chuckled. "I'll bet they are back in under five minutes." She opened her mouth to continue when her phone rang. Glancing at the screen her smug expression morphed into what looked like surprise. "I need to take this in private. I'll be out front."

Suddenly, only Bree and Ansen were left at the table. He gently took her hands as they sat alone. "What do you think of Kade and Zadie?"

A quick glance over her shoulder through the window showed them standing close together on the dock with intense looks on their faces. "In some ways I'm remind of what you and I could have become. Married, in love and trying to figure out how to live their lives."

"I was thinking the same." He paused a moment, his hands squeezing lightly. "Things are really complicated right now, but do you think there's a path for us to get back on that track?"

With no hesitation she moved closer, her lips meeting his in a long kiss. "I'm all for that."

Their kiss resumed with more passion until both the front and back doors opened simultaneously. Dr. Chavez displayed her usual tact. "I hope these life and death decisions aren't inter-rupting anything."

Bree let the comment slide, refusing to let the glow of the mo-ment dissipate too quickly. "Life goes on, Dr. Chavez."

Zadie and Kade now stood side by side just inside the doorway. Her words calm and seeming full of resolve. "Bree, thanks for your advice. While doing this would have been inconceivable two months ago, as you said, when it's life and death the deci-sion is easy. There are bound to be complications, but joining with you is clearly the best course for us, and our soon-to-be born daughter."

A wave of happiness overcame Bree. She rose, and in a few steps embraced Zadie. "We'll do this together. You're not alone."

Ansen now joined in offering a hand to Kade. "You've made a wise choice. Welcome."

True to form, Dr. Chavez abruptly changed the mood. "Enough of the kumbaya. Plans have changed. We need to get back on the plane for a new destination."

Bree's words cut. "What could be more important than getting both of us and our babies to safety?"

A crooked smile graced the doctor's face. "How about getting all three special mothers together?" Her twisted smile broadened. "Gwen Blaze wants to meet."

CHAPTER FORTY-NINE

The three-hour flight from Atlanta to Hollywood gave the passengers time to get to know each other, and more importantly, to get on the same page for their impromptu meeting with the megastar. Bree said what was probably on the mind of the younger people. "I hope I don't go all fan-girl when I meet her. I've loved her music forever."

Zadie added. "I can't seem to get *Why Me?* out of my head."

"I know, right! It's been the soundtrack of my life for the past couple of months."

Ansen nodded. "All that's true, but her status as a star is not what really sets her apart, it's the society." He motioned toward Dr. Chavez. "I'm having second thoughts about meeting her, even if she is carrying one of only three special children. Keeping the society out of public view is paramount."

Holding up her index finger, Zadie added another angle. "The reformed group viewed her as a major obstacle to stopping any more special children from being born. If we can find a way to work with her without revealing the society, this could really help us all. Her voice can change hearts and minds to our side."

A sigh from Ansen seemed to indicate his conflict. "I get that, but this meeting is dangerous for us in so many ways." He looked at the doctor. "What does her husband know about us?"

Chavez peered over her glasses. "I operate on a strict need to know basis. When Ray worked for me, he knew that mysterious rich and powerful people funded our research, but that's all. He's completely in the dark about the society."

Settling back in his seat, Ansen commented. "Then let's keep it that way. From what I can tell, Gwen believes in telling the world everything she knows. No secret is safe with her. We want to use her, but let's be careful not to get burned."

The pilot announced their imminent touchdown and soon they were again loading into large black SUV's, the favorite mode of land transportation for society business travel. As they drove through LA traffic, Dr. Chavez shared the logistics for the meeting that had been arranged by Gwen's security team. "I hope you like luxury with your security. We're headed to the Presidential Suite of the Beverly Hills Hilton."

Bree shook her head almost in disbelief. "Just weeks ago, I was a normal woman fighting a terminal disease, living my remaining days in a nice Houston apartment. Now I'm flying in private jets, meeting with Gwen Blaze in Beverly Hills, both of us carrying genetically modified babies. Don't get me wrong, I'm glad to be alive... and I'm excited about becoming a mother." She gazed out the window as palm trees stood sentry on famous Wilshire Boulevard. "But sometimes it feels like someone snatched me out of my old life and plugged me into some alternate reality."

Ansen held her hand as the SUV neared a private entrance, "This *is* your life now." He kissed her cheek. "I hope you like me in it as much as I like being with you."

She snuggled closer just as the vehicle came to a stop. "Looks like we're here. I hope I'm dressed okay to meet a star."

He beamed. "You look beautiful."

Between hotel security, Gwen's private armed guards and the team that accompanied the society members, there was enough firepower on the premises to hold off a small army. Gripping Ansen's hand as they walked, she whispered. "I like your presence, and I'm getting used to the idea of the society, but all these weapons of war still give me the heebie-jeebies."

Dr. Chavez knocked on the heavy wooden doors which were

opened by a large muscular man wearing a shoulder holstered pistol. "Ms. Blaze is expecting you."

One by one they filed in, spying a very pregnant Gwen Blaze, bare feet resting on a purple velvet stool. Sunshine streamed through one of the large windows, bathing her in a warm glow. Ray stood beside her, addressing Dr. Chavez. "Wow. You said you had a couple of surprise guests with you, but I wasn't expecting this."

The eyes of both couples landed on Gwen, and all seemed to try with varying degrees of success not to stare. Dr. Chavez appeared to be immune to the star power. "I think you'll be very pleased to meet these women. They have a lot in common with Ms. Blaze."

Gwen's casual but elegant gown flowed in a dark green wave as she stood. "Thank you for coming on such short notice. Ray has told me so much about you."

"I'm sure he has." The doctor seemed to have no concern about staring as she took a long look at the swollen mid-section of the singer. "I knew Ray had potential, but I must say that I'm impressed with his apparent skill."

Ray extended his hands toward the open seats in the very large living room. He addressed them as they all sat. "You know who we are, so how about some intros." He shot a questioning glance toward the two couples. "Who are you guys?"

Dr. Chavez gestured toward Gwen. "Ms. Blaze, I have watched from a distance as you introduced the world to the reality of genetically enhanced children, and I must say that you have done a masterful job."

"Thank you." She seemed pleased by the compliment.

"But you must have also felt alone as many hurled insults... and lately, much more dangerous attacks against you. I am here today to let you know that you are not alone." She motioned toward the two pregnant women in her group. "This is Bree and Zadie, and they are also joyfully expecting. And like your Madeline, their babies will be special in so many ways. Ray is not the only one who has the skill and will to take the next step for humanity."

The star's eyes widened, then a grin matching the warmth of the sunshine streaming into the room spread across her face. "Ladies, I am so glad to meet you!" She moved toward them, taking Zadie's hand first, pulling her up in an awkward baby bump to baby bump embrace. She then repeated the process with Bree. "We have so much to talk about!"

The corner of Ray's lips lifted ever so slightly as his face went pale. He turned toward Chavez. "I did it for love. Why did you do it? Money?"

His comment chilled the atmosphere and the doctor answered frostily. "Why I did it is none of your business. What should be all of our concern is how we work together to keep everyone safe, especially these exceptional new lives. That's why we're here, and I believe what you want to discuss as well."

Now together, the three pregnant women embraced until Gwen took a step back. "I can't believe this, but I guess we better figure out the security stuff before I get killed."

Bree held Gwen's hand a few seconds longer. "They've been after me too, it's just not been in the news."

The revelation seemed to catch Gwen off guard as she returned to her seat beside Ray. "Those people are horrible."

"And their attempts to kill us have only become more brazen." Ray concurred. "We've upped our security but I'm not sure it's enough." He motioned toward Chavez. "I contacted you because I remembered some of the scary people with big guns who used to come to the lab before you moved it to Peru. I was hoping that you might still have those contacts. I have a feeling Gwen and I are going to need *that* level of protection."

Ansen spoke for the first time. "I have connections to that kind of network. In fact, we're protecting Bree, and earlier today agreed to bring Zadie under our care. What kind of arrangements have you been thinking about?"

Ray stood, walking to the bar against the wall. "Anyone else want a drink?"

Only Chavez replied. "Bourbon, neat."

A small laugh came before his reply. "You haven't changed a bit." He laughed again. "With what we're discussing, I'll have the same." He poured the two drinks and sauntered back, handing her a tumbler filled three fingers high, then nodded to Gwen. "Tell them what you want."

Gwen rubbed her large belly. "I'm getting close to my due date and I'm really beginning to think about where I want to have this baby. The hospitals here in LA leak like a sieve when celebrities check in. Can you imagine the security and paparazzi nightmare that would be?"

Zadie had been quiet. "I'm really sorry about all that's happened to you. I can't imagine."

The words were spoken with such sincerity that Bree imagined Zadie was feeling profound guilt over her role in the attacks on both Gwen and herself. "We've all been under a lot of stress since these aren't normal pregnancies. Have you come up with any ideas?"

She nodded. "On top of needing a lot more security, it also needs to be well equipped. Ray assures me that the delivery should be normal, but even regular births can go sideways, and I don't want to take any chances. We haven't come up with anyplace that fills the bill, so that's why he thought of calling you. Ray says you rub elbows with the type of people who might have such a place."

Dr. Chavez laughed heartily. "Perhaps I underestimated you,

Ray. In addition to your skills, it seems you were very observant. Maybe we collaborate after all of this is over?"

His goateed chin pulled back. "Uh, possibly? First things first, though. Do you know of any place like Gwen described?"

Before she answered, Ansen stepped in. "I know a place in Europe."

Gwen shook her head. "Absolutely not. Some radical in congress is proposing a ban on citizenship for any genetically enhanced person not born in the United States. Says he wants to keep out undesirables. We have to do it here... and I guess that applies to all three of us, right?"

The comment caught them all off guard, then Ansen took out his phone and motioned toward the bedroom. "I'll make a call. I'm sure we can figure something out."

As soon as he closed the bedroom door Gwen, Bree and Zadie drew together like magnets, leaving Dr. Chavez and Ray alone. She raised her glass to him. "I'm proud of you, Ray. Surprised, to be sure, but proud."

A loud laugh came from the women and Gwen turned toward the two scientists. "We're ordering appetizers. You guys want anything special?"

"I'm guessing you're going to order the menu." Seeming amused, his thin cheeks plumped in a smile. "I won't go hungry."

Again, Chavez complimented him. "You've made her a very happy woman."

"That's why I did this." His expression morphed into a hard stare. "So really, why did you go all the way? Is it just for the money?"

She took a sip, appearing deep in thought, then took another before facing him. "The money is very good, I can't deny that. It's funded my research for years." She took another sip. "But there's more to it."

"Care to share?"

"Let me ask you a question. You worked for me for five years. Did you like me?"

He recoiled slightly. "We weren't friends or anything, you were my boss."

"But did you like me?"

He sighed. "I learned more from you than anyone I have ever known. Without you, Gwen would not be about to give birth to our disease-free baby girl." He paused. "But honestly. No, I didn't like you very much."

Not a nerve twitched. "This is who I am, how I was born. From a very young age my intellect was recognized, as were other traits that were not as socially acceptable. I often exhibited a lack of empathy, and had a low regard for moral boundaries. When combined with my low fear levels, toleration of danger, high self-confidence and social assertiveness it didn't take a genius to make a psychological diagnosis." They sat in silence for a few moments. "Go ahead, say it, it won't hurt feelings I don't have."

Ray's eyebrows arched. "Sounds a lot like the traits of a psychopath."

The expression on her face finally changed to a knowing smirk. "I like men... occasionally... but I see absolutely no need for the baggage of marriage... and certainly not children." She sighed. "I do get a level of satisfaction from proving myself the best in the world, and I rather like the idea of tinkering with what it means to be human. The wider the definition, the more it includes people like me. The world *will* see my achievement and I'll do whatever it takes to protect these mothers until they are born."

Just as Ray seemed set to ask a question, Ansen stepped back into the room. "Hey everyone, I've found a place."

A knock on the door was answered and platters of appetizers were placed on the dining table. Bree loaded up on hummus, pita chips and veggies while Zadie and Gwen's plates looked more like sampler platters. A cheery Bree signaled their attention. "My sisters and I are set, what's the news?"

Seeing the three women, all with plates loaded to the edge, Ansen snickered. "Looks like you all have identified some common ground. The question I have is, how does everyone feel about the beach?"

Gwen held a buffalo chicken wing as a pointer. "Tell me about security."

"We're talking about a private island in the Caribbean where we should be able to spot trouble heading our way. Plus, there won't be any nosy paparazzi."

The wing now had a bite removed. "I like that. Is it American soil?"

"Yes. It's part of the US Virgin Islands. One-hundred percent American."

The wing was now pointed toward Ray. "What do you think? Do you trust these people?"

Ray's fingers interlaced. "I have a much better understanding of where Dr. Chavez is coming from. She'll do everything she can to protect Bree and Zadie... and you as well. There is always risk, but I think it's a good plan."

Talking with her mouth full she gave her conditional approval. "Alright. I'm in. The three amigas until the end."

CHAPTER FIFTY

A week after arriving on the sun-soaked island, a semblance of normalcy lowered the combined anxiety levels of the three couples. While the apprehension level had dropped, it certainly hadn't disappeared as armed guards were everywhere. Bree had taken to trying to figure out exactly how many different security personnel were on the island, and by the end of the first week her count exceeded thirty. She made an interesting observation to Ansen. "It's a weird life when it takes this many gunmen around to help me relax."

On a typical day, the girls hung out together most mornings while the guys played golf on the small par three course, or fished from the pier. Lunch was usually poolside followed by plenty of naps throughout languid afternoons. Dinner was served late, also usually poolside. Afterwards, the couples either had a fun get together or went their own way for walks. When they hung out, the guys usually drank a few beers while they all took turns sharing their favorite playlists over the outdoor speakers, security shadowing every activity.

Tonight, Bree clasped Ansen's hand. "Care to find a spot to gaze at the moon?"

His arm draped around her back and ever-expanding waist. "Best offer I've had all day."

They walked on the sand at the edge of the lapping waves, careful to keep her long white cotton cover out of the water. They soon came to a small rocky outcrop where they sat close on the still warm stone, gazing at the moon and cuddling close, knowing a soldier stood guard less than twenty yards away. She rubbed his strong arms and leaned into his embrace. "I wish we could freeze this moment. Just you and me here together on this little slice of paradise. No gunmen chasing us, no frantic escapes...."

A soft hug answered. "It's been a great week, that's for sure. I'll stay here as long as you like."

A sharp kick redirected Bree's attention. She took his hand and placed it on her stomach. "Here, feel. I bet he does it again."

About ten seconds passed until her prediction became reality. "Wow. He sure seems strong." Ansen left his hand there and felt a rolling sensation. "I can't believe you're going to be a mother."

Bree put her hand atop his and spoke softly. "It won't be long."

"Are you ready for this?" Both of his arms now wrapped her.

"I wouldn't be ready even if this was happening in normal circumstances." She shook her head, releasing a tired giggle. "I'm sure not ready with all that's happened in this pregnancy." She was smiling. "The truth is, even though I'm not ready, I'm really looking forward to being a mother and raising this child."

She rested in his embrace, hearing relief in his words. "That's good." Quiet moments went by as he held her. "I've been worried about you. What's changed?"

The moonbeams bathed them in silvery light as she closed her eyes. "I was angry about having to make this choice to save my life, and it was scary as hell in the beginning. Then I felt blindsided when I found out the rapid timetable." Her voice quivered as she continued. "What I felt was that other people were making these huge decisions for me, like I was a puppet. I was yanked around the globe trying to figure things out as people tried to kill me."

"It must have been terrifying."

Opening her eyes, she continued. "It was, at least until we got to Prague. When I finally got some answers and safety, I started to get my head around the situation and regain control of my life. It's also when I began to feel the baby move. It's hard to explain, but I guess it's like what most women feel. No matter how this started, there is a new life inside me… growing… and we're connected. I can feel when he hiccups, and he seems to like it when I eat spicy food. I know when he is resting and when he's awake." She sat silently in thought. "Then there's the talk of him being special, and that's equal parts scary and exciting. Kind of beyond imagination."

"Sounds almost spiritual."

"It is, and that has surprised me."

His voice lowered and she detected a tremble. "I hope we'll stay close after he arrives."

The push of an arm or leg rolled her baby bump. "Whoa. Did you feel that?" Her smile grew. "I think he likes it when he hears your voice. It's probably a good idea for you to stick around."

The warmth of his kiss on the top of her head made her smile. "That's what I was hoping you would say."

Sitting still, a breeze ruffled her short hair. She tensed, then released a breath. "I know how much I want that future." She turned to face him. "I was so wrong when I left you before. I'll never leave you again."

The answering kiss was long and slow. When their lips finally parted his eyes glistened in the ethereal light. "I love you, Bree Battle. I always have and I always will."

Tears of joy filled her eyes. "I love you, too."

CHAPTER FIFTY-ONE

The late morning sun warmed the sand of the heavily guarded spit of land in the Caribbean Ocean. Gwen lounged between Bree and Zadie under a thatched roof cabana, calm waves hypnotically lapping a few steps away. Two weeks of safety had lulled Gwen into a sense of security and she held up her phone for a selfie. "Come close girls. I need to get us all in frame." She adjusted the camera. "Show your best side!" A few clicks later the photo was uploaded onto several of her social media platforms with the caption, *Girls in the sun having fun.*

Minutes later a tech in Atlanta picked up the phone. "Mr. Brown, we have a location."

Ben couldn't stop the grin. "Finally! Send me the info." The feeling was short lived as he looked at the photo and location information. "Damn it! What is it with these women!"

He paced, Liza's words ringing in his ears. *Don't screw it up this time.* He mumbled to himself. "How did they find each other?" He reached for the phone, then stopped. Seconds of indecision passed until he reached again and dialed. After a couple of rings, he heard her 'Hello', then blurted out his frustration. "Liza, we have a big opportunity and a big problem. We need to talk."

She listened to the information he had just received. "This decision is too important for us to make alone. We need the board's approval."

∞

A few hours later, everyone was seated around the conference table as Liza stood. "We have a tough decision to make, one that will set the trajectory of our order for years to come. It's probable that our action, or inaction, could even threaten our entire society's existence." She took a moment looking at each member. "It's a complicated situation and Ben will explain."

The lights dimmed and a PowerPoint presentation began with Gwen's post on screen. "Three hours ago, Gwen Blaze loaded this photo onto several of her social media platforms." Mumbles could be heard as the board studied the picture. "An image matching program identified the location as a small atoll in the Caribbean." The grumbling grew louder as he continued. "As you can see, somehow all of these women have found each other and taken shelter in the same location. The only good news is that since they are together, it makes targeting them easier. It gets a lot more complicated from here."

He advanced the presentation which centered Bree Battle's image in the photo. "With the Battle woman now teamed up with both Gwen Blaze and Zadie Springer, this definitely involves the originals. We've confirmed this with a title search of the island's ownership. We are all aware of their threats to us, and the level of security they could be providing these women." He advanced the slide again, showing the location of the island on a map. "In addition to the assumed level of security, the sheer logistics of attacking an island is daunting."

The final slide appeared displaying empty lounge chairs under the cabana. "The upside is that if we are successful, we would eliminate the genetic abominations in one swift strike. No more designer babies menacing humanity." He put the slide advance device down gently on the table. "This is the opportunity and the challenge."

Liza took the floor. "The threats are real, to the society as a whole, and to us and our families. The originals have promised retribution if we go after the Battle woman. While they rarely flex their muscle with physical violence these days, I would not rule it out this time. At the very least it's almost certain that we'll be hit with financial attacks, both to us personally, and our businesses. As we discuss our options, I want everyone to understand the costs."

Ezra spoke up. "But if we do nothing, what do we stand for? What would be our reason for even existing?"

Nodding, Liza commented. "That's a very good question. We've put a stake in the ground on genetically modified humans. It's not our entire reason for existing, but it is the single most important issue that separates us from the originals. As I see it, if these children are born then we have two choices. The first is that we abandon our principles and petition the originals for some form of cease fire or reunion."

The reaction from Ezra was immediate. "That would be a bitter pill to swallow. We've fought for so long it would be hard to capitulate. This issue is a threat to our entire species, and I know in my gut that we are on the right side of history this time."

Her hand went to her heart. "I agree, Ezra. However, if we don't end this now, we could continue our strategy of trying to ban, or inflame the masses to reject any additional human modifications. There are other movements who are going to continue that fight, with or without us. It is a viable second option."

That answer didn't seem to mollify Ezra. "I think we all know that once the horse is out of the barn, we'll never be able to stop it. Tell us about the chances of a successful strike on that island."

Liza's eyes shot toward Ben, who restarted the PowerPoint. An aerial view of the island filled the screen. "As challenging as the prior attempts on these women have been, this is many factors more difficult." He advanced the slide, showing a closer view of the structures. "There are ten large buildings in a secure compound, and even if we breach the outer perimeter, we don't know where they are housed. Using traditional methods, at best we can slip ten to twelve men onto the island under the cover of darkness, and even with the element of surprise, their chances of success would be low."

Narrowed blue-gray eyes stared back from Ezra. "Tell me there's another way."

The slide advanced with a fisheye view from above the isle. "Drones are a weapons system that have advanced rapidly. Several terrorist groups and outlaw states have deployed large unmanned crafts very successfully. In 2019 the Iranians avoided advanced radar to deliver a devastating blow to a major Saudi oil facility. As the technology has improved, the price has come down, and we can get our hands on one."

Ezra's voice brightened. "That sounds interesting."

Advancing the slide again, Ben continued. "In discussing this possible assault with Callan, we've developed a two-pronged battle plan that has the possibility to succeed. There will be a new moon in two weeks, providing a night with maximum darkness. Under that cover, a fishing boat repurposed as our operational base would deploy a dozen or so fighters in inflatable rafts in a fast approach. While they are on the way, we'll have the drone above firing missiles into the most likely structures to be housing the targets. If we get lucky, it will all be over before our forces hit the beach. If not, then the scene will be chaos as our troops arrive, giving them a better chance of finishing off any of the targets that survive the initial aerial assault. There are no guarantees, but this plan gives us a fighting chance."

Ezra nodded. "I like it. Well done, Ben. I'm all for moving ahead with the plan."

Across the table Jim Campbell shook a finger. "Not so fast, Ezra. Even if this attack is a total success, we're sure to become targets of the originals. Are you ready to lose your business? Have your reputation destroyed by their PR team?"

His face reddening, Ezra's voice rose. "This is a fight for the future of humanity. Are you afraid of a little inconvenience?"

Veins in Jim's neck bulged. "And what if they go all biblical on us? An eye for an eye, a tooth for a tooth? Are you ready to pay the ultimate price?"

Ezra's hand slammed down. "Yes! I'm prepared to sacrifice my very life for this cause!"

Jim took a sharp breath. "That's not the ultimate price, Ezra. We are talking about killing their children and I bet they come after ours if we succeed. Are you willing to sacrifice Thomas, Kelley, Sidney and Phoebe?"

The mention of his children's names seemed to stun Ezra. "They wouldn't dare."

"Are you so sure that you're ready to bet their lives?"

Liza had let the discussion go on long enough to get to these kinds of heart wrenching possibilities on the table. "This is why Ben and myself didn't make the decision on our own. If we do this there will be consequences for us, and if we don't there will be consequences for the world. Either way, we need to make a decision. Are there any other questions or comments before we vote?"

Jim leaned back, his hands face up on the table. "Let's say we do this mission and kill all three of those women and their Frankenstein babies. Good for us and all of humanity. After the originals retaliate, and they will retaliate, we have no assurances they won't just restart the program with new women. Are we willing to sacrifice our businesses, our lives, our children's lives just to slow them down for a year or so? Is that what we're talking about? Is this war already lost and we're the only ones who don't know it?"

Ezra flicked his hand in the air toward Jim. "If you're no longer committed to the cause, why don't you leave?"

Body language and voice seemed out of sync as Jim remained leaned back, while his words cut like an obsidian knife. "This board is where we examine the pros and cons of our major decisions. In this case, I'm making sure that everyone understands both, but don't mistake that for disloyalty. I've given my life to the society and will be here until the end. Maybe it's you who should reconsider your position if this plan can't stand up to inspection."

Liza again brought order. "I think we all understand the risks and rewards of moving forward. Going around and around isn't going to solve anything. It's time to vote." She stood and leaned against the table, her red fingernails aimed like guns firing at the attendees. "Those in favor of going ahead with Ben's plan, raise your hand."

Ben and Ezra raised their hands first, slowly followed by four more in the affirmative. Liza pronounced judgment. "With six in favor and five opposed, the board has spoken."

Jim protested. "Liza, as the chairwoman you can vote in any decision. If you vote against, it will be a tie, and all ties end as failure of the motion. Under rule seven, section three, I demand to know where you stand. What is your vote?"

Standing tall, she looked at Ben and then Jim as almost a full minute of silence built a palpable tension in the room. "Everything our forefathers stood for rests on stopping these births." Her gaze touched each member as she readied herself to cast the final vote. "There will be consequences, but without reservation, I vote to proceed with the plan. We move forward for humanity, regardless of the personal costs."

CHAPTER FIFTY-TWO

The three couples sat together on the terrace watching the sun go down on their island sanctuary. The guys were working on their third or fourth beers as the women sipped virgin daiquiris poolside. Ray had Bluetooth connected to the outdoor speakers, his 'Good Vibes' list playing softly in the background. Bree and Zadie joined Gwen when *Why Me?* began playing. Miguel came running and the fun atmosphere dissolved. "Everyone inside! It's an emergency!"

Now on alert, Bree grabbed Ansen's hand. "Let's go." As the group headed for the doorway Bree stopped, reaching between her legs, her voice quivering. "I think my water just broke!"

Ansen swept her off her feet in one swift motion. "Miguel, get Dr. Chavez! We're heading to the infirmary."

As they reached the inside hallway, Miguel went right and they turned left. Ansen kept a fast pace as he looked into Bree's eyes. "You okay? Tell me you're okay."

Both of her hands locked behind his neck as they made another turn. She glanced behind them and saw the other two couples following close. Her words vibrated to his pace as guards with guns passed them, running in the opposite direction. "This isn't the way I imagined this moment."

He laughed softly as he pushed the door open with his foot. "You were always one for drama and I'm guessing you'll pass that trait along to your son."

Dr. Chavez entered like a commanding general as sirens sounded inside the compound. "Go behind that screen and get her into this gown." She tossed a surgical gown to Ansen, then turned to the other two couples, pointing to a yellow line on the white tile floor. "If you wish to stay and observe the delivery, you must remain there. Is that understood?"

Bree let out a cry and winced as she stopped in her tracks while walking from behind the screen. "That smarts! I think I just felt my first contraction."

Ray put his arm around Gwen's shoulder as she announced their decision. "We're staying."

Zadie nodded. "Us too."

A nurse entered the room and before the door could close, Miguel stuck his head inside. "We could use anyone who can handle a gun. Things are about to get dicey."

Another contraction hit Bree as her face grimaced and she shouted. "Son of a bitch. These hurt!"

The nurse began attaching adhesive monitors to various parts of Bree's body. Ansen helped her onto the bed as medical equipment was moved closer. "I'm here, Bree. I'll be right here by your side."

Putting her hand on Ansen's shoulder, Chavez offered advice. "I have skills you don't, and you have skills I lack. Let's both do what we can to deliver this baby safely and protect us all from the invasion that's coming."

Furrowed brows flashed his confusion. "Invasion? What the hell is going on?"

Miguel spoke quickly. "Mr. Svoboda called and said that he received a text with a warning. If true, an attack is imminent and I understand that both you and Kade have weapons training. Is that correct?"

"Yes... but someone needs to be here for Bree."

Gwen stepped over the yellow line and marched bedside. "I'll be here for her, Ansen. You go. We'll need everybody available to fight if it's the same people who have already tried to kill me."

Following Gwen, Zadie went to the other side of the bed and took Bree's hand. "We'll both be here with her. Go fight for all of us."

Leaning down, Ansen gently kissed Bree. "Looks like you're in good hands here." He looked around at his new friends. "We'll fight to save all of your children."

A snort from Dr. Chavez caused them all to turn. "It's not just them, Ansen. You'll be fighting to save your baby as well."

His head tilted as his mind seemed scrambled. "What? What are you saying?"

Another pain struck Bree and she tensed before she could question the doctor. "Owww! This is a big one!"

Chavez responded as Bree's friends comforted her. "Now is the time to act, not explain. Just know that you will be fighting for Bree, as well as for *your* soon-to-be born son."

The sirens began a new, repeating pattern as Kade stepped closer and grabbed Ansen's arm. "We'll get to the bottom of this later. Right now, they need us. We have to go."

Ansen leaned down again for another kiss. "I have no idea what she's talking about, but I know I love you. Always have."

Kade tugged his sleeve. "Come on, buddy. Time to go."

Ray spoke as they stepped back. "Look, I don't know much about guns, but I'm not helping here. Maybe I can do something out there." Ray and Kade both gave a quick kiss to their wives and then the three headed out the door.

Another labor pain struck and Bree stated the obvious. "Arrrrgh!! They're getting closer."

Gwen now held Bree's right hand as Zadie took the left. "We're here for you, girl. We're all in this together."

CHAPTER FIFTY-THREE

With the men gone to fight, Bree looked at the women in the infirmary. "Thanks for being here with me."

Dr. Chavez sounded sincere as she spoke. "You're going to do great, Bree, and before the night is over you will be a mother."

Outside, the sun had completely set and the night was dark as pitch. Stars twinkled like diamonds against the black backdrop and the only sound was the lapping of the receding tide. Ansen positioned himself behind an outbuilding near the shoreline. Five other soldiers were spaced at regular intervals behind different structures between the beach and the main compound. A similar group of defenders were positioned on the far side of the compound. Ansen lay prone, an AK-47 at his shoulder, peering through the sights. Five spare magazines, each holding their forty-round capacity, were stacked beside him. His mind seemed to whipsaw between the bolt of lightning news that Dr. Chavez had just delivered and the imminent arrival of forces determined to kill them. "I've had it with this bullshit. Where are you, you sons of bitches?"

Miguel's voice broadcast into his earpiece. "The intel we received indicates a drone attack will precede the beach assault. It's all scheduled to go down in just a few minutes. Keep your ears open and eyes peeled."

Kade was positioned with Ray in a makeshift interior bunker, serving as a last line of defense, should attackers breach the compound. He asked over the radio. "Can we trust this intel?

Where did we get it?"

A voice from one of the soldiers broke up the conversation. "I've got radar contact with the drone. Here we go, everyone."

A fighter whom Ansen knew only as Joan stood in the open with infrared goggles. "Visual confirmation. I repeat, visual confirmation."

Sharp shooters, lined up their shots and a hail of bullets began as Joan relayed results. "We have made contact. The vehicle is on fire and losing altitude. Repeat, the vehicle is on fire and losing altitude."

Flames lit the night sky as the craft dove kamikaze-style toward the compound. A loud explosion shook the ground as one of the larger buildings was set ablaze. Miguel reported. "They hit the dormitory."

Ansen spoke into his headset. "Glad it wasn't the infirmary, but we've got trouble. Two inflatables coming ashore. They're here!" He fired his first burst and saw an attacker fall in the water.

Inside the action was just as intense. The fallen drone crashed close enough that collateral damage destroyed the hallway connecting to the infirmary, sending wooden splinters into the room. The three pregnant women screamed in unison as they were peppered by fragments. As if on instinct Dr. Chavez stood from her seat between Bree's bent knees, extending her body above the vulnerable woman, attempting to protect her from the flying debris. She took command. "Ignore the noise and focus on my instructions. On the next contraction it's time to push. Do you understand?"

She felt her friends trembling hands holding hers as she breathed hard. "I'm ready."

"Good. Save your strength until it's time."

In the control room, a camera captured movement on the other side of the enclosed main facility. A group of five commandos ran from the sea toward the buildings. Miguel relayed the information. "There is a third boat landing on the east beach! Who can intercept them?"

Ansen replied anxiously as he fired more rounds at the attackers trying to make their way from the beach into the compound. "We've got our hands full here. We'll be there as soon as we can."

Kade looked at a wide-eyed Ray. "Looks like it's up to us. Remember what I told you about that pistol. Point at the center of their chest and keep pulling the trigger, got it?"

His head bobbed. "Yeah, point at the bad guys."

No sooner had he answered, a black uniformed gunman came around the corner. Kade pulled the trigger on his rifle and a spray of bullets dropped the intruder. Kade glanced at a now ghostly white Ray. "Hang in there, buddy. This isn't over yet."

Ray's voice trembled. "Yeah, not over."

Back at the beach, Ansen took concerted return fire as bullets impacted his shielding wall. "Getting a little hot out here." He glimpsed Joan rise up and fire a volley in the direction of his attacker. The bullets directed at him ceased and he gave her a thumbs up. "I owe you one."

The reprieve proved momentary as gunfire erupted again. He saw her buckle, and yelled into his mic. "Joan's down! Repeat, soldier down!"

In the dark he saw movement. Joan's shaking voice called out. "I'm hit, but still breathing. Take care of these guys and get me a medic before I bleed out."

The sound of gunfire just outside the infirmary didn't help Bree relax. In fact, it seemed to speed things up. "I feel another contraction coming!"

Again, positioned between Bree's legs, Dr. Chavez gave orders. "Deep breaths until I say push. Not until then, understand?"

Sweat dripped from her forehead as she gasped for air. "Okay... okay."

As the baby's head began to crown, the doctor performed an episiotomy, then demanded action. "PUSH!" Her eyes now went to Gwen and Zadie. "Lean her forward!"

With one hand each being squeezed firmly by Bree, the two women joined their free hands behind her back and pulled her up from the bed, adding extra force to her push. Zadie offered encouraging words. "Hang in there, girl. You're doing great. It won't be long now!"

A primal scream filled the room. "Ahhhhhh!"

Dr. Chavez's shoulders lowered. "The baby's head is through. Relax until the next contraction."

Outside the door, more gunfire filled the air as additional black-clad gunmen arrived. Kade let loose spray after spray of bullets from his AK, momentarily keeping them at bay. He was swapping out his clip when another soldier rushed forward. "Shoot, Ray!"

Ray stood and pulled the trigger over and over until finally hitting the man. The intruder crumpled and Ray just kept squeezing the trigger, even after all the rounds in the clip had been fired.

"Good job. Now get down before you get hit." At that moment a shot rang out and Ray fell, now writhing on the floor. Kade aimed and dropped another combatant. "Hang in there, help is on the way."

Blood spilled in spurts as Ray grabbed his upper arm. "Damn it, that hurts like a son of a bitch!"

Kade's voice seemed to betray his concern as his words broadcast. "A lot of heat in here! We could use a little help!"

Hearing those words, desperation appeared to fuel Ansen's response. "I'll be there as soon as I can. Just hold on a little longer."

Miguel delivered new information. "Ansen, looks like only one target holding you down. You have to go now, or...." He didn't finish the sentence. "GO! NOW!"

There was no hesitation as Ansen stepped around the corner and delivered a steady stream of rounds toward the target's position, giving him a brief moment to make a run for the main compound. He covered the open ground quickly and as he stepped into the doorway a round blasted just above his head, sending wooden slivers onto his back. "I'm on my way!"

In the improvised delivery room, the action continued as Bree's breathing picked up. "Another contraction is starting!"

Chavez made the awaited announcement. "One more good push should do it. Are you ready?"

Her answer came between gasps. "Yes...yes."

Glancing at Zadie and Gwen, Dr. Chavez gave the order. "All together, on three. One, two, PUSH!"

The women moved in unison and Bree bore down. "Uhhhhh!"

Suddenly, they heard the doctor's excited voice. "He's here, Bree. Your son is born!" She cleared his airway, then held up the newborn who made his own gasp, then cried. "He looks perfect." The doctor laid the waxy-white-coated infant on the new mother's chest, umbilical cord still attached. "Hold him. We're not quite finished."

With her hands now free, Bree touched her baby for the first time and wept. "I can't believe it. Any of it."

The nurse who had monitored the birth stepped forward with two clamps. Dr. Chavez placed them on the still attached cord, then snipped between them, officially disconnecting child and mother. As chaos reigned just outside their door, she spoke in a voice as calm as a mill pond. "Everything is proceeding normally."

Just then, the full-fledged gun battle outside their door ramped up, with hundreds of rounds per minute filling the air. Kade radioed as he and Ray shielded below a concrete wall being blasted repeatedly. "Anytime now!!!!"

Joy and fear sent tears flowing down Bree's face, and both Gwen and Zadie joined her. Only Dr. Chavez remained stoic. She reached for a scalpel and moved between Bree and the door, seeming ready to make a last-ditch stand, if needed. "We'll not go down without a fight."

The noise outside the door rose even higher as Ansen arrived and fired on the enemy's flank. "The cavalry's here!"

In a final fury, which caught the enemy exposed, the battle ended. The stench of gunpowder filled the corridor outside the infirmary. Ansen's steps crunched as he walked on spent shell casings, checking the fallen bodies, making sure none remained a threat. "You guys okay?"

The relief in Kade's voice was palpable. "About time you got here."

With the sound of gunfire gone, Ray stood, blood dripping from his injured arm. "A little help here." Kade and Ansen advanced toward him to render aid.

They could hear Dr. Chavez in the next room. "Let's get this finished." The doctor had stepped back to Bree and spoke calmly. "Give me one final push to deliver the placenta."

A determined sound followed. "Grrrrrrrr."

With relief in her voice, Dr. Chavez summed up the experience. "You did good, Bree."

Kade put his hand over Ray's bleeding wound as he spoke to Ansen. "Get in there, man. Go see your son."

Ansen dropped his weapon and with a dazed look entered the room. "I'm here, Bree."

She answered in a weak but happy voice. "Come see him."

As he moved toward the bed Ray and Kade entered and Gwen caught sight of her wounded husband. "Ray! Ray needs help!"

Turning her head, Dr. Chavez saw the blood. "Get him over here immediately." She re-gloved quickly as he was brought to a chair. After an initial inspection she pronounced her prognosis. "This will leave a big scar, but he will recover." With that she began the process of cleaning and suturing the wound.

Gwen was by his side smoothing his hair as the doctor worked. "Thank God you're alright. I don't know what I would do without you."

He winced once as Chavez injected a numbing agent around the gash. His eyes looked glassy and he seemed stunned. "I killed a man."

Gwen responded forcefully. "You had to. He was going to kill us if you didn't."

Zadie and Kade stood between the other two couples, his arm over her shoulder. He whispered as they watched the drama unfolding around them. "Our own people were trying to kill us, kill our baby."

She leaned her head against his chest. "Look at Bree and Ansen with their new baby. I'm so happy for them, and that will be us in a couple of weeks. We made the right decision, the only decision we could make."

Miguel stepped into the room, seeming to take in the entire panorama. "The threat has been eliminated."

Ansen kissed Bree's sweat dampened head as she cuddled their newborn son, then turned to Miguel. "What now?"

"I've heard that a response to this attack is already underway. It's payback time for those that tried to kill you."

CHAPTER FIFTY-FOUR

Liza watched the video feed from the drone as it crashed, portending the unfolding failure of the mission. Callan radioed from the command ship as frantic calls from the landing parties signaled trouble. Hours later, his words still haunted her. *They knew we were coming!* Only Callan and two soldiers survived the doomed mission and when it was over, she called Ben. "How did they know?"

The sigh from Ben wasn't comforting. "I hate to say this, but my best guess is it was a leak from our side."

"Could it have been from Callan, or someone on his team?"

"Perhaps, but his team took massive casualties. Why would anyone in their right mind leak information and then walk into a slaughter? That doesn't make sense. Maybe the originals intercepted communications, but I doubt it. Callan is very good at hiding his tracks." She could hear his depression through the phone. "No, the most logical explanation is that someone from our board told them."

Her eyes scanned the comfortable home office she had curated like a museum exhibit. A French Provincial style desk and cadenza meshed perfectly with colorful fabric on the mid-century modern sofa. There was a dawning realization she might not see them again soon. "Who could have done this? Who would have turned on their own?"

A blunt reply startled her. "My guess is Jim Campbell. He's been hesitant to use force all along, plus he has a soft spot for Zadie."

A pit formed in her stomach as it began to make sense. "And he's seen originals retaliate first hand when they interfered in his son's college admission. Son of a bitch."

"It doesn't matter now. What's done is done."

Liza regained her composure as practical matters pressed. "We've been warned there would be retaliation if we attempted to harm the Battle woman. It's time to enact the Preservation Protocol. I'll send the emails and texts." As the last word left her lips, she heard gunfire on the phone. "Ben! What's going on?" More rapid-fire bursts were transmitted to her ear, then silence as the phone disconnected.

Panic set in as her heart raced. *Time to leave.* She shouted to her guard on the other side of her office door. "Walther, bring the car!" Shutting her laptop, she shoved it into her oversized bag, then took a forlorn last look at her office before heading to the door. Reaching for the knob, it swung open and an unfamiliar man dressed in black rushed in, knocking her to the ground.

A pistol was trained on her as he spoke from behind a mask. "One wrong move and you're dead."

"Who are you? What do you want?"

Two other men followed close behind, snatching her up and applying zip-tie bands around her wrists, now pulled behind her back. "You're coming with us."

On her way out the back door of her home she saw her guard, Walther, lying face down with arms spread, a rifle barrel resting between his shoulder blades. "I'm sorry Mrs. Howard."

The masked men lifted her by the arms into the back of a black SUV, shoving her toward the middle. They loaded, one on each side of her as they simultaneously closed the doors. The one who had addressed her earlier spoke again from the front passenger seat as the vehicle pulled away. "You have an incoming call."

With her arms firmly bound she leaned forward, bringing her

face closer to a video screen that had been flipped down from the interior roof of the SUV. It lit and flickered for a moment before Kristoff appeared. "Hello, Liza."

Her lips stretched thin in contained fear as she forced a reply. "Kristoff."

"I really hoped that we would not be speaking again after you were warned, yet here we are. You have left both of us with very few options."

She tried to formulate a coherent reply as she sensed that his voice sounded more sad than vindictive. "Was it Jim Campbell?"

A closed mouth smile met her question. "It is his decision that gives you the opportunity to live. We've known that Ben Brown and Ezra Slaughter have been the most militant against us and were surprised when you joined their side these last few weeks." He now spoke with firm finality. "They have been dealt with, never to trouble us again." After a beat, he spoke in lighter tones. "Which brings us to your fate."

Her stomach felt as if in freefall and her voice trembled. "My fate?"

The vehicle accelerated as it merged onto an interstate in the coal black night. "You are on your way to a very secluded location, and as a fellow Tree of Life Society leader, I respect you too much to play games. You have a choice to make in the next few minutes, in which *you* will decide your fate." He paused for a moment, seeming to let his words sink in. "You are being given the option to join us in a new world. A world where children are born, never to suffer disease. A world our society has dreamed of since its inception."

"And if I decide I don't wish to be part of your plan?"

His stare was as fixed on her as a laser. "Then you will see we have selected a very beautiful final resting place for you."

Her ribs hurt as she tensed, maintaining an outer calm while her entire body strained to fight, even against these odds. A dry swallow scratched her throat as she answered hoarsely. "I understand."

"Liza, for more than six centuries the society has sought to bring stronger, smarter people into this world to improve the entire planet. While lately we have been at odds on how to do that, I know that we both have the same goals. Right?"

Some moisture finally coated her tongue. "Yes. In that we are in agreement."

"Good, I am glad we still share the same ultimate vision." His face now beamed on the video screen. "Tonight, the society took a giant step forward. The first genetically enhanced human was born. Bree Battle delivered a perfect, health baby boy as your guns fired all around her. Joyously, the two other women will follow in the coming days. Designer babies are no longer science fiction, they are reality."

Feeling the blood drain from her face, she stammered. "It happened? She delivered?"

"Yes, despite your best efforts."

"And Zadie? How is she?"

"Both Zadie Springer and Gwen Blaze are well and will soon deliver on their own accelerated pregnancy schedule."

Her shoulders sagged as her mood deflated like a tire with a leak. "I see."

Kristoff sighed. "That brings us to your decision. The war between the two branches of the society is over. We have won, and as the opposing two leaders, it is now up to you and I to decide how this conflict ends."

She raised her chin, trying to remain dignified. "What are your terms?"

From his home around the world, he stretched his hands toward the camera. "I would like nothing more than to reunite our society. There has been too much bloodshed in this conflict. I'm asking that you begin the process of leading your followers back into union, healing our division in the common cause of advancing the human condition, just as our forefathers desired."

Knowing the answer, she raised an eyebrow and asked anyway. "And if I decline your offer?"

Kristoff spoke firmly and without emotion. "As at the end of the American Civil War, there can be an honorable surrender with all troops allowed to return to their families under one flag. If you choose not to surrender, we will bury you with proper rites, then do everything in our power to once and for all end the threat from the reformed branch. No quarter will be given and no prisoners taken. The end for your people will be quick and bloody, starting with the remaining members of your board."

She whispered her response. "I see."

The vehicle exited the interstate onto a small country road. Kristoff leaned forward, his arms on his desk. "Liza, your decisions have brought us to this place and I need to know how you choose to end this war. In unity or blood?"

She heard the vehicle's blinker, indicating a turn onto an even smaller road, or perhaps the final turn of the trip. She sat as tall as she could, summoning all of the inner strength she could muster. "When the choice is between the life or death of my people, the decision is simple." She pasted a smile over her fear. "I choose life."

CHAPTER FIFTY-FIVE

The green room at CBN was in a state of perpetual motion as the three young couples valiantly tried to keep their active babies corralled. Nashama the intern gave the warning call. "One minute!" The moms kissed the men, leaving them behind as they snatched up the squirming infants and headed for the set.

Bree heard Ansen address the guys as they marched out. "Better them than us."

Larry beamed as the women took their places on a sofa during the commercial break. "I'm a man of my word. You now have more appearances than Stella McGuinn."

Madeline almost escaped Gwen's grasp. "And I'm doing even better than my word. You get three designer babies for the price of one."

Jared spoke above the minor chaos on the set. "We're back in five-four-three-two-one."

The host appeared to radiate in the moment as he stared into camera one. "Tonight is one of the most important moments in broadcast history. We are introducing the first three genetically modified babies to the world. They look like perfectly normal children, and I'm told that for the most part they are. They have ten fingers and ten toes and their DNA has twenty-three chromosomes, just like you and me." He looked into camera two. "But as normal as they seem, they are also different... special. Some of their genes have been modified to give them unique qualities that are already becoming apparent." He paused, seeming to build drama. "Let's meet these special children and their mothers."

Turning, he addressed Gwen. "It's a pleasure to have you back under such happy circumstances. How about introducing the world to your baby and also to your new friends?"

The seasoned celebrity lifted Madeline, who now stood on her lap. "Say hello, Madeline."

The little girl mouthed the word on cue. "Hewwo." The crew on set oohed and awed.

Larry seemed amazed. "How old is she?"

Madeline patted her hands together in a patty-cake motion as Gwen answered. "She just turned three months. Pretty advanced for her age, isn't she?"

The amazed expression added a dropped jaw. "Fascinating! She's already talking and she's so big. Is this early development an intended result of the genetic manipulation? Is it the same for these other children as well?"

Madeline started jumping on Gwen's lap while simultaneously clapping her hands as her mother answered. "Absolutely, Larry. Remember, Ray and I will begin displaying the debilitating effects of Huntington's Disease in a few years and we wanted her to grow up fast, so she could remember us if we don't find a cure in time."

"She's amazing! Please, introduce us to your friends and their babies. The world wants to meet them all."

Looking to her left, Gwen began. "This is Bree Battle and her son Adam. He's the oldest of the three." Bree nodded, with Adam sitting calmly in her lap as the camera now panned left. "Next to her is Zadie Springer and her daughter, Ensley. She's the youngest by a few days."

Larry's smile seemed sincere. "It's a pleasure to have you ladies join Gwen on the show. Tell me a little about yourselves."

They had decided backstage that Bree would go first. "My name is Bree Battle and I'm the proud mother of Adam."

"Ms. Battle, we've all followed Gwen's journey to motherhood on two prior visits to the show. How did you come to be the first mother of a genetically modified baby?"

This was the moment of truth. Once all three mothers had survived the attack in the Caribbean, they felt a bond to each other that none had ever experienced with another woman. A pact was made to go forward together with their babies... in public... being as transparent as they could. This didn't sit well with the society, but Bree stood her ground and got her way, finally feeling in control of her life again. This was their coming out party and Bree gave a sanitized, revisionist version with as much truth as possible, with no mention of the Tree of Life Society. "I was dealing with a serious disease and during the course of my treatment I met a doctor who could cure me with an experimental treatment. Little did I realize she was the mentor of Gwen's husband. After I survived the medical procedure, she offered me the chance to have a special child. I jumped at the opportunity, knowing I would probably have trouble getting pregnant on my own later due to the powerful drugs that had been used to save my life. It was the best decision I have ever made." With only a hint of mischief in her voice, she spoke truthfully. "Having Adam has been the culmination of so many hopes and dreams."

"Fascinating! And you Mrs. Springer? What's your story?"

Zadie smiled, her story having a much easier relationship with the truth than Bree. "I'm like so many women in America who have difficulty conceiving. My husband and I tried multiple rounds of invitro without success and we were about to give up when we met Dr. Chavez. She's a miracle worker, and before long I was pregnant. Like Bree, we feel so lucky to have baby Ensley in our world."

Adam squirmed and nearly escaped until Bree caught his hand just before he fell. Larry flinched at the close call. "They sure are active. I guess that means they are all healthy?"

As the de facto spokesperson, Gwen fielded the question. "All tests indicate that they are healthy normal children. They're just maturing at an accelerated pace."

That answer seemed to trigger the next question. "Does that mean all genetically edited children will mature quicker?"

Baby Madeline was now reaching for the coffee cup on Larry's desk. Gwen redirected her with the shake of a rattle. "Not at all. Parents can control all sorts of variables. As I understand, if you want the full nine-month pregnancy and standard maturation length that will be totally up to you. It's probably the right choice for most couples."

While Gwen was answering Larry, Bree recalled the shock she and Zadie felt at learning their children would also mature on that accelerated schedule. *Just another surprise from the one and only, Dr. Cielo Chavez.*

Larry responded to Gwen's answer with a slow nod. "You're right. It would be weird to send your child off to college just five or six years after they're born. You ladies have ushered in a completely new world."

Gwen glanced at her new friends. "We try not to think too much about that, we're just enjoying our lives… without anyone trying to kill us."

Larry's face creased. "I'm so sorry for all you went through. The home invasion, the attack on the highway, even the dust up here at our headquarters a few months ago. Has all that stopped?"

They all smiled as Gwen answered honestly, leaving out the even scarier attack on the island. "Yes, at least for now. We all still have a lot of security around us, but it seems the groups who wanted to do me harm gave up after Madeline was born."

Bree suspected that Gwen understood there was another layer to the story, one that explained hushed conversations and private soldiers at the ready, but for now had not pressed. Gwen stayed with the pledge they had made together to be as truthful as possible. "I'm loving my life spending time with Ray and Maddy, thankful for peace and a few weeks of privacy."

"I'm glad things are better for you and Ray. You seemed awfully alone a few months ago and now you have at least two other women who are going through the same thing. That must be comforting."

"Yes, it is, and soon we'll be joined by many more. Have you seen all the posts from women around the world who want to start the process? Our trailblazing has opened the floodgates. Scientists everywhere now feel emboldened to help families in all kinds of situations."

Larry cleared his throat, skepticism coating his words. "As I understand, Dr. Chavez has built a new lab in the Czech Republic and is in the process of screening potential couples for this procedure. But most of these other new labs are in countries with loose regulations. Does it worry you that their results may not come out as well as they seem to have for you three?"

Gwen batted her long eyelashes. "Of course. Pregnant women have worried about the health of their soon-to-be-born children forever, and sometimes things don't come out as planned. I'm sure the same will happen in this new era, so I can almost guarantee that there will be children with birth defects. But that doesn't mean this choice should be taken away or outlawed. It only means that with more experience and evolving techniques we will surely get better. I envision a day when modified children will be the norm, not the exception, and I'm proud of the part we've played in creating that future."

Shifting a bit in his chair, Larry turned to the immediate future. "What's next for the three of you? New albums, new tours... more children?"

The last remark brought laughs from the three women. Again, Gwen went first. "Believe me, Madeline keeps me plenty busy. I have finished writing new material for my next record and will be in the studio later this month while Ray's busy in the lab working on a cure for Huntington's Disease." She looked to her left. "Bree, tell them about your work."

Bree swiped at her tawny hair, now grown long enough to need the occasional push behind the ear. "After taking maternity leave, I'm back at Third Rock Sustainability, now serving as the director. Promoting efforts to save our planet has long been my passion and I look forward to exploring new ways to make this world a better place for us, and our children." She glanced at Ansen standing off stage and her eyes lit as she continued. "I'm also in the process of planning a wedding to Adam's father."

"Congratulations! That's wonderful."

Happy dimples graced her face. "Thank you."

Larry now glanced at Zadie. "And what's next for you?"

Zadie's cheeks reddened. She and Kade had the most uncertainty in their lives at this moment. Many reformed members had switched allegiances at the urging of Liza, who was now working hand in hand with Kristoff to merge the two branches of the Tree of Life Society. Unfortunately, the business where she worked was owned by a member who had not yet come on board. "I'm between jobs right now and just enjoying being a stay at home mom for a few months. I'll go back to my career in public relations as soon as I feel ready."

Madeline again lunged for Larry's coffee cup, this time snagging it and tipping it over. Larry laughed as he placed the cup upright. "Whoa there little one. You're lucky I finished this before you grabbed it." She clapped and laughed as he asked another question. "They all seem so happy. What can you tell us about their personalities?"

Blushing, Gwen went first. "Madeline's so much like me that Ray says it scares him. She follows me around trying to sing and she loves getting into my makeup drawer more than playing with her toys. We're already such good friends. I feel so blessed."

"And you, Bree? What's Adam like?"

Hearing his name, Adam looked at Larry and smiled. "He's plenty active as well, and I'm guessing a lot like most other children. His dad has already gotten him a beginner set of Legos and they are his current favorite toy. You should see some of the structures he's built. He keeps us so busy it's hard to remember what life was like before him."

"Zadie, the same question to you. What can you tell us about Ensley?"

The smile on her face radiated happiness. "She's already very social with other children and adults. In fact, she even talks to her baby dolls and pretends they talk back. You're never alone if she's awake!"

Camera one pushed in on Larry as he prepared to deliver his closing comments for this segment. "We've had the opportunity to meet these women and their children. Many look at them and feel worried, wondering where this new scientific breakthrough will lead. They say every child has the right to remain genetically unmodified. They say it just seems wrong to play God. They say this will create a world of haves and have nots where the rich can afford to give their children even more advantages. They say they will fight for laws to level the playing field. Perhaps all of these worries may come to pass."

He turned, now framed by camera two. "On the other hand, many look at these women and these children and feel hope, also wondering where this new scientific breakthrough will lead. They say every child has the right to be born free of preventable diseases. They say mankind's genome has evolved forever and this is simply the next logical step. They say that the cost of technology always comes down quickly, which will lead to an explosion of new options and diversity for most of the people on the planet. They say they will fight for equality for all.

Perhaps all of these hopes will come to pass."

Larry now glanced at Gwen, Bree and Zadie sitting with their three beautiful children. "What I do know with certainty is that we are about to find out what combination of worries and hopes will materialize. These women and their children are the pioneers of our new world and I can promise that we'll be following their stories closely, with more updates to come. Until next time this is Larry Knewell on *Rare Air*.

In Prague, Kristoff and Dr. Chavez watched the *Rare Air* interview, then raised their champagne glasses in a toast. His mood was jubilant. "You did it Cici. The dream of the founders is now a reality!"

"We did it together." The usually stern woman beamed as she took a sip. "A 2002 Dom Perignon. What a good choice for this special occasion."

Setting his glass down, Kristoff spoke with animated hands. "Only the best for this day. It took us six centuries to increase the average member life expectancy by fifteen years, and now look what we have done in just a few weeks. Adam and Ensley will have an almost limitless lifespan!"

The hard edge of Dr. Chavez's personality reasserted itself. "We must keep this a secret, just between you and I. The world will be a dangerous place for those two as it is, and this information would put an even bigger target on them from extremists."

Those words stole a bit of joy from Kristoff. "True, and if it was discovered, it could lead to the exposure of the society." He paused, picking up his glass and taking a sip, then switching subjects. "What about the other child, Madeline? Do you think she has the same gene programming for extended life?"

An uncertain look clouded the doctor's face. "I don't know. I felt it was too risky to ask Ray until all of the children were safely delivered, and I still don't think it's a good idea. No sense raising suspicion. If his publicity-craving wife were to find out, it would be disastrous."

Kristoff nodded. "Then it is up to you and I to keep the secret until the time is right." He refilled their glasses, then offered a new toast. "To the fulfillment of the ultimate Tree of Life Society dream- eternal life!"

The End

Thank you for reading *Designer Babies Volume One, The First Mothers*. If you liked the book and would like to continue reading the series, *Volume Two, Growing Pains*, is available now. Also, I would be grateful if you would consider putting up some stars on the Amazon store page. Even better, if you have time, I'd appreciate a review. They are the life blood of independent authors, and your review would have a huge impact on my book's visibility to other readers.

David Witt

Designer Babies FACTS

Volume One

FACT: The first test tube baby was born in 1978 to much consternation and debate, and now there are more than four million IVF births each year in the US alone.

FACT: Scientists first cloned a sheep in 1996. Today, there is an entire championship team of cloned polo ponies in Argentina, and anyone with a few thousand dollars to spare can get an exact genetic replica of their favorite pet.

FACT: Labs around the world are experimenting with new techniques to cure diseases. In fact, there is already a genetic engineered cure for a specific kind of blindness.

FACT: Eugenic groups believed the best way to improve the entire human race was to eliminate those deemed inferior. They used methods like forced sterilizations of those deemed deficient, or even more drastic measures including the Holocaust. Six million Jews died at the hands of the Nazis.

FACT: The eugenic laws that were promoted resulted in the forced sterilization of over 64,000 people here in the United States.

FACT: China sentenced two scientists to prison for experimenting on human embryos, producing two children they claim are immune from AIDS.

FACT: Three hundred years ago, surgery was considered by most to be playing God. Cutting open a human body and tinkering with organs to save the patient, rather than letting God's will prevail. Now there are over forty-eight million life-saving surgeries per year in the US.

FACT: With DNA sequencing technology, science has discovered that modern humans contain an average of two percent Neanderthal DNA. Over in Australia, three to five percent of Aboriginal DNA is from another extinct hominid branch call the Denisovans.

FACT: Self-experimentation is already happening! There really is a guy out there using CRISPR trying to cure himself of AIDS.

FACT: The Catholic Church banned human autopsies for almost eight hundred years as defiling a human body. This significantly slowed scientific discovery in medicine, only to later change their minds.